GAME of SECRETS

GAME of SECRETS

| A NOVEL |

DAWN TRIPP

RANDOM HOUSE / NEW YORK

Published in the United States by Random House, an imprint of The Random House Publishing Group, a division of Random House, Inc., New York.

RANDOM HOUSE and colophon are registered trademarks of Random House, Inc.

Library of Congress Cataloging-in-Publication Data
Tripp, Dawn.
Game of secrets: a novel / Dawn Tripp.
p. cm.
ISBN 978-1-4000-6188-4
eBook ISBN 978-0-6796-0495-2
I. Title.
PS3620.R57G36 2011
813'.6—dc22   2010026781

Printed in the United States of America on acid-free paper

www.atrandom.com

2 4 6 8 9 7 5 3 1

First Edition

Book design by Susan Turner

For Karen Lustig,
and for my boys

GAME of SECRETS

TINDER

LUCE
October 1957

—Tell me, she says.
He glances toward the wall, the grimed pane of the
window, a cracked sky.

He can smell her breath, can smell wet leather from
the collar of his coat spread down on the floor underneath her, he can feel her eyes on his face, waiting.

—Day's getting on, he remarks.
—Tell me, she says again.

And he thinks of the fish he saw that morning in the
creek running down off Drift Road, the long pale
body of that fish, below the overhang of the bank,
slow like shadow itself, slipping home.

He felt a kick of recognition. Even with his hand on
the baited line, he did not drop it down. Something
in the movement of that fish, the boneless slow of it,

reminded him of her. He could tell her this. Or some other tin-can story.

—You got that polecat look, she says, a taunt in her voice—Is there some new tattooed bird you've got your eye on to pinch?

He scowls, and she laughs.
—Good enough for you, Luce Weld.
—Good enough for you, Ada.

She is stretched beside him, one arm flung over her head; he can see the fluted lines of her ribs through the pale of her skin, the black spill of her hair.
A pause, then she says,
—Silas is wise to it. Said the other night, if he ever caught up with us, he'd blow your brains out, hang me by my ankles, cut me open throat-to-clit, gut me like a deer.

Her eyes swing toward him as she says this, her voice level. She watches for the flinch. It gives her a thrill.
—Getting soft on me, are you, old man? She laughs.

Again he glances toward the window. The sun, lower now, scrapes his eyes, but the sky out there, the blue is still and clean and pure, like some hand has wrung the color from it.

He replays her words in his head—her husband, the threat, her tone of voice. He could tell her that this dinge of a room where they meet, this brief occasional time, an hour or two at most, this stolen time, is where he lives. With perhaps the exception of the Saturday-afternoon drives he takes with his daughter, Jane, every other minute, hour, day, of the week is just time spent.

He rolls a cigarette, lights it. She holds out her hand, he passes it to her, clouds of smoke drift, collide. She flicks the ashes to the floor.

Not long and she will leave. Stand up, put herself together, rake a hand through her hair, go off. But he will stay. Long after she has left, and his body is empty, everything missing, except that vague scent of her still on him, the glittering residual, he will sit with his back against the wall in the corner, smoke one cigarette after another, as the sky darks up and the night comes down. He will feel the night come as it drops like a creature through the window and moves toward where he sits on the floor. It will lap at his boots and rise, over his feet, his knees, his hands, he will close his eyes and feel it smooth and cool on his skull. His thoughts of her go wild in that night.

She is studying him now, her elbow bent, her head propped on the length of her hand, a smudge of light on her body. It feels vulgar to him, marred, like her body is a globe and that light's been painted on. He can see the scant dark stubble in the hollow of her armpit, the curve of it pressed near his coat, and her eyes are still on him, that certain look he has never seen in anyone but her.

Earlier, he had leaned toward her. Took a pearled button on her blouse between his teeth and bit it off. It was a cheap thing, flimsy. But she was furious and snapped it away.

He touches her face now, the flared bone near her eye, runs his finger slowly over it.

—Tell me, she says again now, her voice impatient, that faint edge not altogether kind.

His hand drops. She's past angry. Too late. It's a thing he'll never say.

—I want to get out of here, she says. Let's take a drive.

She grinds the cigarette he gave her out into the floor. When, days later, as he hunts in the woods and thinks back on this moment, watching her long beautiful fingers twisting that cigarette out, he will wonder how it might have gone if he had told her. He will walk the loop he always takes to hunt, up from the river on the Drift Road side. The trees begin to thin. He hears a sound, a snap in the brush. He stops, listens. The sound again—

PART I

KINDLING

RAY

MARNE
June 3, 2004

Back in January, I got the phone call from Alex that brought me home from California. The next week, I took my mother grocery shopping up at Lees. She got stuck only once, in the produce section, picking through the pears, unable to decide which ones she should buy. "So many choices these days," she murmured to me, apologetic and with a touch of sadness, like she could feel the glitch in her but was unable to correct it, so I decided for her. In the checkout line, I had that feeling you get sometimes when someone's eyes are on you, and I turned and saw Ray three aisles away and, for a moment, I couldn't place him, then all at once I did. His face looked thin, much thinner than it should have—a look in his eyes like they'd been scraped. Then the girl at the register was asking whether I wanted plastic or paper, and Ray was still looking at me, that look in his eyes replaced by something different that gave me a little jump, electric-like, and I stared back. Just stared.

"There's Ray," my mother said. I snapped out of it and gave him a wave like I should have in the first place, he smiled and waved back, and everything was natural, normal, like it should be. And after he'd made it through checkout, he stopped to say hello, and asked when I'd gotten back from California. By then, our groceries were bagged and loaded into the cart, and he walked outside with us, and the winter sunlight hit me hard as we stepped through the automatic door, un-tenable and bright, everything caught up short in the unexpected.

He was getting a divorce, my brother Alex told me. Of course, over the next couple of months, I'd run into him here and there. Or he'd drop by the house, looking for Alex. But whenever Ray's around, I can't seem to find two words to rub together, a tense kind of rustle moves through me—the wrong kind of feeling, I know, for someone so off-limits.

Two strikes up front: He's my brother's best friend, and Ada Var-ick's son. Ada's wreaked her share of havoc in our family. She was the irresistibly beautiful reason my grandfather Luce Weld was killed, back in 1957—murdered, so it's said, for loving her too much. Not that Ada's hold has been any lighter on the rest of us—look at my mother, still trekking over to the Council on Aging every Friday, still in thrall to her Ada and their games.

It's hard to imagine sometimes—it's a thing I've never quite gotten my mind around—how my mother, Luce Weld's only daughter, came to be friends with Ada Varick in the first place. Ada was twenty years older, a different ilk. I asked my mother once how it started, how she came to be invited into that knot of four or five women who met every Friday for Scrabble.

"Vivi Butler called me up one day out of the blue and asked me," she answered, simply.

"And you went?"

"Why wouldn't I?"

She seemed surprised that I would wonder, even shy.

I never knew my grandfather Luce. I wouldn't know if I tripped on his shade in the street. But I've heard the story:

Luce Weld—rakish no-good—bootlegger turned poultry thief. Ran booze back in the twenties, made money to beat hell, but wore trouble, couldn't keep that shit off his shoe. He did time for man-slaughter and, when he got out, managed to land a smart, pretty girl, my grandmother Emily. They had only one child, my mother, Jane. But Luce was no stay-at-home. He set his sight on Ada Varick, and it got stuck there. Ada, from what I have heard, was quite a stunner back then.

Luce went missing the fall of '57. His skiff was found staked to the marsh near the creek below the gravel pit off Drift Road. Talk was someone caught him stealing one too many times and dealt him what for. Ran him out of town or flung him off the flat edge of the world for good. Maybe. However it happened, it was all just talk until the state came down, took land, and started laying in the new highway. Early sixties, they dug fill for the new bridge from the gravel pit upriver on the Drift Road side. As one load of gravel got dumped, a skull rolled out, a bullet hole in it, neat as neat. Anyone putting two and two to-gether wagered that skull was the last scant trace of Luce Weld.

* * *

It's early June, and I am not looking where I'm going as I step out the storm door, or rather, I am looking down at the book in my hand, and I trip over the foot of a ladder, not realizing exactly what I have done until I hear the smash of metal on wood and a shout from above, the book has flown out of my hand, and the ladder is falling away from the house. I look up and see the flash of a boot disappear just in time over the edge of the roof, a bucket of paint set on a rung above knocked off—

Shit.

A splash of whiteness, vaguely coherent, spills past my face, patterning my shirt; it lands with an echoing clang as the ladder strikes the ground.

"You alright down there?" I hear Ray's voice call down from the roof. I glance up and his face appears. "Oh hey, Marne"—looking down from his gorgeous benevolent heaven at the idiocy that is me. My brother comes around the side of the house and takes it all in.

"How'd you manage that?" he growls. Yeah, Alex—like breaking Ray's neck was at the top of my to-do list. Picking up the ladder, he sets it back against the gutter above the door, and Ray climbs down. "I am so sorry," I mumble, unable to look at him.

"Paint missed your book," he says lightly. The book's lying open on the steps below me, pages askew. Ray scoops it up and hands it to me. "It's no big deal." His voice with that gentle hook in it I've begun to hear lately when he talks to me.

There's a sizable white pool of paint on the ground. Alex has started kicking dirt onto it, to soak it up. He's ticked. "Give me a hand, Ray."

"Here, let me help," I say.

"You've done your part," Alex sighs. "Get out of here."

I feel my face flush, and slip back inside. My mother's just coming up from downcellar. At first she doesn't seem to see me, she's got that distracted look, I can tell by how she moves, like her body's in glass, and for once I am grateful. But then she notices me as I head toward the stairs. Her eyes focus.

"What happened?" she says.

"Nothing." I set the book down.

"Is everyone alright, Marne? I heard a crash. What happened?"

"Just fine."

"That shirt's ruined."

"It's really just fine."

"Use some warm water. Here, sweetheart, take it off. I'll do it."

"No, thanks, Mom. Really. I can do it."

She follows me into the kitchen anyway, and we get into a bit of a scrap at the sink, about water temperature, should it be hot or cold for latex, soap or vinegar. This is her province, I know, I should let her call the shots, but my composure has slid off the map, and I just want to be left alone. "It really makes no difference, Mom," I say sharply.

"The stain'll set."

"It's not like it's Kool-Aid or blood."

She's pulling out bottles from the lazy susan. "It'll set if you don't get it out."

"It's an old shirt."

"It's a nice shirt."

"Lay off, Mom."

"You should try to save it."

"I don't need to save it!"

She stops, looks at me. "Warmer water," she says, "that's a bit cold."

She twists the faucet, I resist the urge to push away her hand and twist it back. Pretty soon everything's soaked through, the wet shirt sticking to my skin, and she's telling me I should just take it off, she'll get that stain out, but I have no interest in being caught at the sink window in my bra. My mother is still standing beside me, she's got her bottle of vinegar out, uncapped, some salt, a kitchen rag, and that calm and awful patience she will get sometimes when she knows she is right and it is only a matter of time before I come around to see it her way. And it occurs to me Alex was wrong. This is not working out. I should have stayed in California.

I hear a truck pass by, someone leaning down hard on the horn, I glance up in time to see Ray's brother Huck in his cherry-red F150, his hand out the window, casting his signature flick-off wave to Ray and Alex who are still out front in the yard, kicking dirt over the mess I made. They wave back, laughing. As the truck veers away, I can just make out the two bumper stickers he's had on there for years. One that reads: FOR A SMALL TOWN THIS ONE SURE HAS A LOT OF ASSHOLES. The other: PROUD TO BE AMERICAN. If there is one person walking the earth I can't fucking stand, that person is Huck.

Redneck throwback. Verge of cretinoid. He went after my best friend, Elise, when he was thirty-something and we were in high school, robbed her cradle, then dumped her for some slutty girl. Pushing sixty now, Huck can't seem to understand why the world hasn't shit gold coins on his head. He's still got that dazed sort of juvenile swagger, like he just stepped out of a Bruce Springsteen song run amok.

Ray's older brother, I remind myself wryly. Strike three. You Are Out.

I strip my shirt off, thrust it at my mom, and go upstairs to get the paint off my face and hands.

When I come back down, it's just noon. Alex and Ray are sitting at the kitchen table, drinking lemonade. My mother has fixed them sandwiches, cut on the diagonal like she's forgotten they're not ten years old. Ray gives me a quick smile. I pour a cup of coffee. Alex is skimming the newspaper, the obituaries. That's all he'll read—he's like our father that way. What else is news?

As I sit down with my coffee, my mother asks, "Can I get you something, Marne?" The rote question.

I shake my head. "I'm good."

"Some toast?"

"Mom, can't you just—" I see my brother's mouth tighten. "Well, okay," I say. "Sure."

A beat of silence. Ray gets up, walks out into the hall. I hear the bathroom door close.

I pick up my book, an old library book of my mother's I found last night in the shelf at the top of the stairs on my way up to bed. Wrapped in taped plastic, the call number 1174c stamped cockeyed onto the white sticker at the base of the spine. Through the sheer of the plastic, the black boards, squared binding, the letters of the title in stylized gilt. It was the title that drew me. *The Secret of Light*. But then I opened it and saw it was all marked up, scribbled notes in the margins, my mother's—I could tell by the handwriting, though it's childish. It surprised me when I found it. So unlike her, not to return a book due, and this one so long overdue, the last date on the manila pocket: 1957. She would have been around twelve. The year her father, Luce, disappeared.

I glance at her. She has pulled out two slices of bread for my toast and put them in the toaster. She turns the knob halfway around. They will come out too light. She comes over to the table with the bag of Wavy Lays and dishes out another round of chips onto my brother's plate. Alex is, has always been, a quintessential momma's boy. Forty-two years old, he still lets her cut the seeds out of his tangerines.

"Your shirt's out on the line, Marne," my mother says.

"Great. Thanks."

"The salt did the trick."

"I bet."

My brother shoots me a look. "Just be a little bit nice," he says quietly. Ray walks back into the room. His eyes flick from Alex to me. The toast pops up. Way too fucking light. My mother slicks the butter on and sets the toast on the milk stool beside me. She doesn't seem to notice the book. She goes and sits down in her corner.

"No notice yet for Pard," Alex says, passing the newspaper across the table to Ray.

"His wake's on Saturday," Ray answers, "you'd have thought they'd run the obit today."

"Might not have had room to run all of it."

Ray laughs.

"Tell you the truth," Alex goes on, "I was surprised not to see Huckie's truck wrapped in black crepe. How's he taking it?"

Ray eats a potato chip. "Oh, you know. He's shot down. Pretends not to be, but they were close."

"Fused," Alex remarks.

Ray laughs again. He's got a nice laugh. His face is sunbaked, from work. He is sitting at the end of the table by the door, his legs stretched out, paint on his jeans. He's a salvager. Raises boats. Goes diving for other stuff on wrecks and takes odd jobs; this week, he's been working here with Alex, painting my parents' house. Ray is the youngest Varick boy. Ada and Silas had five altogether: Junie, Scott, Huck, Green, Ray. Ray was youngest by far, kind of an afterthought, I've always figured, some last-ditch shot before his parents split. Ray has the look of his oldest brother, Junie, dead now, and he's tall like Scott, who came home from Da Nang and worked as a cutter at the fishhouse near Coal Pocket Pier. Of the five Varick brothers, Green was the only one I never knew, but I've seen photos. They all have a similar look. With the exception of spit-and-vinegar Huck, who's got light light eyes, near the color of frost, the rest of them were dark. Ada's look.

Ray notices me watching him and gives me another smile. He sets his empty lemonade glass down on the table.

"Were you working down at the restaurant last night?" he asks me. I nod.

"How's it going?"

"It's work."

"Been busy?"

"Starting to be."

"I'll have to stop down there sometime."

"Are you nuts?" Alex says.

"Why not? The food's good."

"Sure it's good, you just got to take out a second mortgage to eat it."

My brother won't step foot in that place, the restaurant where I work. He says it's for the summer crowd. Not in a bitter way. To him, it's common sense, just air. He's at home here, in this town where we grew up, where nothing much changes except a few more invisible people move in every year. He likes those people well enough: paints the trim on their guest cottages; he wallpapers their bathrooms.

"I can't believe there's nothing yet for Pard," Alex is saying.

"Well, don't lose any sleep," Ray answers with a smile. "There will be."

The dead in question is Pard Islington, Huck Varick's twin soul, whose hourglass ran out this past Tuesday while he was watching the Red Sox game with some buddies. Pard knew it was happening. He'd started having pains in his chest from the third inning on, kept popping his nitro. It was a good game, tight score, he didn't want to miss a thing.

Yesterday, too, was a long-lunch tribute to Pard, my brother and Ray swapping stories like the light is still on him. From what I've heard, Huck and Pard together were quite an event back in the day— boosting crates of clams off the floating piers, lobbing M80s, racing their cars down Route 88. Then that legendary Halloween, Huck got into a fight over some girl up at Alhambras when that place was bulging, just going full-bore—he and Pard got thrown out, drove around town in a pickup, fuming, stealing pumpkins off every porch. They smashed so many down on the Head Bridge, the town had to bring in a front-end loader to clear the road. There were two other boys in that illustrious gang: One overdosed on some alcoholic concoction he'd invented that included Robitussin, the other was drafted to Vietnam, got snuffed out there.

Pard was always an odd duck, some dark streak in him that gave me the chills. I knew well enough to steer clear, even as a kid. Sometimes I'd see him looking at me funny, like I was tainted somehow: Luce Weld's granddaughter. All that.

My mother is looking at me from across the room, her eyes steady, level, like she can hear me thinking this.

My brother and Ray are talking now about those drag races suzerain Pard used to convene at the state beach parking lot, one o'clock Sunday afternoons in the off-season. The homemade Christmas tree he and Huck set up with three lights—red, yellow, green. The dollar-bill game they used to play on that curvy stretch of Reservation Road, and wasn't it a miracle no one died.

"Well, there was that one guy," Ray says, "after he got creamed, nobody—" Alex shoots a look to silence him, then glances at our mother in her corner by the window, her face just turning away toward the screen like she has noticed something through it.

Alex gets up, sets his dish in the sink, unwraps the plate of cookies on the counter, takes three, and sits back down.

They won't tell those darker bits. They don't talk casualty, at least not here in my mother's kitchen. The details are cleaned up, in a kind of deference to her. Alex is like our father in that way, he protects her, he is fierce in that. Patient, thoughtful, in ways that I can never be.

What has always been curious to me is how easily Ray can tell the story of some knucklehead who met a speeding hot rod, struck so hard his shoes were still in the road, his brains scrambled in the sand dunes—Ray can tell that kind of story like a joke, even though his brother Green, at thirteen, wrapped a car around a tree less than a mile from here and took flight of this life. You have to believe the fingerprints of that are on him somewhere.

I bite off a small piece of toast and glance at my mother again, in her corner at the hem of things, half listening, half in that somewhere else she gets off to.

"California'll do it to you," I hear my brother say, and I realize, too late, I've lost the thread. "Hell, just look at Marne," he goes on. "Been home, what? Almost six months now, still sulking around, sleeping on Mom's foldout couch."

Alex will do this. When he feels I've been harsh with her, he'll bide his time then take a swing at me out of nowhere.

"I like the couch," I say.

"Makes you think it's temporary, doesn't it?"

"What makes you think it isn't?"

My brother shakes his head. "Who are you fooling, Marne? If you don't come to, fifty years from now, you'll be eighty-something, that couch'll be at the landfill and you'll still be sleeping on it."

He says this, and something inside of me snaps. I open my mouth, I don't know exactly what's going to come out of it, but then Ray clears his throat and says he doesn't think they take couches at the landfill anymore.

He says it just like that, in the calm smooth way he has. I feel a smile touch my face. I glance at Alex. He just looks kind of shocked. I don't know what he hasn't been seeing all this week.

I pick up yesterday's newspaper from the basket next to me, turn it over, read nothing.

Alex's phone rings. By the time he's fished it out and flipped it open, the ringing has stopped, the call lost. Signal out of range, roaming, roaming. He jiggers with it, hits a few buttons. No luck. Swears.

"I'm going to run up to the Head, Ray," he says. "Call the wife back, get some cigarettes. You want to come?"

"I'll wait here. Get me a Gatorade, though, will you?"

Alex's brow furrows. A curt look at me. "Sure," he says to Ray, then leaves.

My mother goes downstairs to put the wash in the dryer. I walk outside with Ray, sit down on the porch steps.

There is paint on his hands, I notice, occasional places the soap has missed. White flecks strung through his skin like stars. He catches me looking at them and gives me that quick half smile that sometimes I know how to read and other times, don't.

"You didn't start in California, did you?" he says. "After high school?"

"It was New York first."

"That's right, I remember now."

"NYU."

I didn't last. Even with the scholarship. Midsemester, sophomore year, I took a break, a temporary leave that turned out to be the rest of my life. For a month or so, I lived on coffee, cigarettes, and *The Christian Science Monitor*. I kept my studio in Hell's Kitchen, read a collection of stories by Camus, a biography of Jean Cocteau. I discovered the indulgence of Kate's Paperie. I started making origami creatures, boxes, stars. I grew my nails long and perfected the craft. My apartment was festooned with colored paper beasts. I was nocturnal by nature. I liked the sense of being on my feet, a body in motion. I took a job waitressing.

"So New York, then California?" Ray asks.

"Via New Mexico. New Mexico to LA. I thought I'd like LA."

He nods, and I can tell he's mapping out those interim years since he knew me as a kid and I was his best friend's runt sister—tracing out my life like those arced flight lines you see in airline magazines that color-code the usual, and less frequent, routes of travel.

The air is dry today, slant of spring light. Ray stretches out one leg, his knee cracks, and the silence between us feels a little tipped over, that sense I get when I am near him, everything inside me hanging by a hinge.

He looks at his watch. "Where's that big galoot brother of yours? We need to get back to work."

"They must not have had his brand of cigarettes."

"Either that or he's parked in his truck, smoking through them."

I shake my head. "I keep telling him: If he doesn't quit those things, it's going to be his news I'm reading in the paper."

Ray laughs. "We'll have to work on him."

"We will." The *we* is out of my mouth before I hear it, just slipped out. He is looking down, elbows resting on his knees, but by his face, I can tell he heard it. That tiny nothing.

Who wrote that the soul is nothing more than an occasional outburst of the mind? A longing not unlike a cord of sunlight that passing through dust motes lends them the appearance of being something more than what they are.

"Heard anything on the weather?" I ask.

"They're talking rain next week."

"You'll be finished painting though by then, won't you?"

"We should have it wrapped up tomorrow."

I nod. I consider asking Ray if he knows that tomorrow, being Friday, is the day my mother still goes to sit with his mother at the picnic table under the shade of a tree outside the Council on Aging, to play that Scrabble game she loves.

"So are you working this weekend?" he asks.

"Tomorrow, Saturday, Sunday."

"That would be the weekend."

"Every weekend."

"And then?"

"Then I get to throw myself around the house for a few days."

"You still making those little paper things for Polly?"

I nod. Polly is the florist up at the Head. Now it's half florist, half gift shop. She sells lighthouse magnets, sea-glass jewelry, handmade greeting cards, and my little origami doo-dahs.

I'm working on a shorebird mobile for her, I tell Ray, but it's the little picture frames that have been the sleeper hit. Polly wasn't sure how they'd go over, but on the weekends, now that the summer people have started buzzing down, those paper frames are getting snapped up. They slide in cut snapshots of their pets, their kids with snow-coned lips and salt-stiff hair. I never pictured myself as someone who'd be making knickknacks for tourists, but I guess you could say it's working out so far.

The other day when I was dropping off some stuff, Polly said excitedly, "For Christmas, I want you to make me two hundred birds, gray and white seagulls to do up a huge tree in the center of the shop, like that one they have down at the Museum of Natural History."

I just nodded, yeah sure, Polly, thinking to myself: No fucking way I'm still going to be here come Christmas.

I do not mention this, of course, to Ray.

"Do you make any money at it?" he is asking me now.

"I made more in San Francisco. Had a pretty good gig—worked for a baker out there." Custom-ordered cakes with my red paper parrots, silver bunnies, Japanese cranes stuck into buttercream frosting. It was a chichi place—a boulangerie. Seventy bucks for a ten-inch cake. They paid me well, threw in free packages of chocolate-dunked biscotti. I gained eight pounds.

"I've heard Polly's cheap as hell," Ray remarks. I'm surprised by his vehemence, then I remember that Polly is a friend of Ray's almost-ex-wife. Took her own husband to the cleaners in her divorce.

"She's okay to work for," I say delicately. "I get to fold paper, I make some money—make more down at the restaurant. You know how it goes. You patch it all together, you come out okay."

"I've got Anna Mondays and Wednesdays," he says. Anna is his daughter, nine years old, the same age and grade as my niece. "Tuesday I've got a pickup game. What are you up to a week from today?"

"You aren't asking me out?"

He shakes his head and laughs. "Just asking what you're doing next Thursday."

"Next Thursday, more than likely, I'll be sitting right here, in this spot."

"Alright," he says. "Six on Thursday then, I'll come by—?"

Growing up, my brother had a few rules for me: Do what you like, whoever you like, but don't get knocked up, don't get caught, and never fuck my friends.

Right as I am thinking this, as if on cue, Alex pulls into the driveway, guns past us a little too fast. I start to stand up, but then don't. I just sit. Just stay. Just where I am. Ray's eyes follow Alex's truck, pulling in to park behind his. Alex throws his keys on the dash and hits the truck door closed. I can see the square outline of the cigarette pack through his shirt pocket. He starts walking toward us.

"Ran into your brother up at the Head," he calls out to Ray. "Man, he bent my ear about that old skiff of his. Half an hour later, I'm still there, and he's still talking."

Ray laughs. "Huckie never shuts up about that fucking boat. Hey, where's my Gatorade?"

Alex stops. "I got it." He turns on his heel and walks back toward the truck.

"So?" Ray says quietly.

"Thursday's good with me," I say.

I feel him smile.

And there we have it: Ada Varick's youngest son, sitting on Luce Weld's only daughter's front porch, making eyes at his granddaughter. Who, as fate flipping has it, is me.

PART II

GIRL ON THE BRIDGE

LILIES

JANE
July 23, 2004

There's a certain hope you feel at the beginning of a game.

When the board is empty, the painted number squares in their stripped and perfect symmetry. You can see the pattern of them, the bare underlying design, the logical grid of how they connect, extending outward from that central star. The frame you will build a game upon.

Ada's wearing lipstick. Red. That fire-engine color that matches the paint on her nails. She notices me looking at it.

"Have I got a smudge?"

"Just a touch."

She draws her handkerchief from the pocket in her skirt and wipes it over her teeth.

"Gone?" she asks.

"Gone."

Just moments ago, when Carl dropped me off, I looked across the yard
and she was there, sitting at this picnic table waiting for me. A woman
made of sunlight. The red scarf at her neck, loose. The bony outline
of her, rim-soaked, half shade. Wearing one of those dresses she always wears; this one pink, a faint print etched into the cotton. The
style of dress Rita Hayworth wore. With the collar and buttons down
the front, the tie belt, still tight around her waist. Her legs crossed
under the table, she leaned in on her elbows. Behind her runs the wall
that divides this yard from the cemetery next door, light splashed on
the stones like the wet is still on them. From that distance, where I
paused across the yard, she looked younger than she is. Still thin, a slip
of a thing, the starch and the beauty still in her, just a faint glimmer of
sorrow clinging to her face, a kind of wistfulness that I only see in Ada
when I come on her like this, before she has noticed I am there, when
she is just a woman sitting alone, waiting at an empty picnic table by
the stone wall, a small black purse on the bench beside her, lunch in a
brown paper bag just like always, the top edge of it folded over neatly.

She has started to turn the tiles over to the blank side. Her fingers are
long. She works from one corner of the box-lid. I start from the other.
She has her reading glasses pushed back on her head, her hair in its
slow pin curls falling. Silver. Some dark still in it. Every Friday when
we meet, it seems, I need to learn her face again, her eyes that uncer-
tain color, not quite green or brown, the left one blood-rimmed, a
thick water at the corner of it, the eye she has some trouble with.

"Just now, Janie," she says, still flipping the tiles, "while I was setting here, waiting on you, I looked over at that line of wild lilies there
by the roadside. There's a clump of them lilies out front of my old
house on Main Road. Above Dunham's brook on the hill. You know
the spot, don't you, where the old wall's sunken into the brush and the
road bends? Every time I drive by that spot this time of year, I see
them lilies blooming all of a day like they do, and I notice how the
fields look some the same as how they used to. Cows put to pasture in

one and in another, the corn just up. They aren't farmers—the ones that own the house now—some lawyer and his wife from somewhere upcountry, Boston maybe—they lease those fields to the Smith boys for the tax break, but it still looks some the same, with the old gate still there, and the stoned-in burying yard down below where my brothers and I used to go and eat our lunch under that big tree. We'd pick some of those lilies, stick them in a mason jar, and eat in the shade, sitting on the stones, our feet dangling over."

We are almost ready—our lake of blank tiles in the scarlet box, the delicate markings of wood-color etched into their backsides the only clues to the letters they are. We've played this game so many times I should know which is a D, which is an X by those discolorations. How strange to think this may be the last time we flip these tiles. I need to tell her. Her fingers are moving slowly now, some thought unspooling through her.

"Those lilies always remind me of that gray horse I had. Did I ever tell you the story of that gray horse?"

"Hmm," I murmur, noncommittal. I love this story.

"My pa brought that horse home from up north once when he went up to trade. He'd bring them back green, and sometimes he'd take my brothers with him, but never me. I always wanted to go. He promised someday, but it never did happen.

"I must have been just seven when my pa brought the gray horse home. I remember my head just come up as far as his shoulder when I was brushing him out. He was big, no beauty, but he was fine. Built for work and he worked hard. Smart, too. He come to learn where the stones were in the field, and year to year he wouldn't forget, would go to step around them, even before the plow turned. My pa would pair him with one of the younger horses, hitch them both up, and within a day that gray horse would have the younger one trained. It looked after me, that gray horse.

"I used to go fishing, sometimes with my brothers, but more often on my own, with a cherry stick I cut back in the woods, some string, and a can with worms. I'd go down the path below the fields through the swamp woods and over the little stone bridge to fish trout in the brook. There was a snake living under that stone bridge. A big black one. Near six foot long, and once when I was crossing over, that snake come out from behind a rock and come after me, fast, like it was going to bite, and I ran. Just barely got away from it. And the whole time that day I was fishing, all I could think about was how I had to cross back over that little bridge to get home, and I knew that snake would be waiting on me there. Finally, come eveningtime, I set off, headed home, and that snake, he was there, in the dirt on the other side of the stone bridge, just lying there, skin stamped flat, dead as dead, splattered blood and gore and hoofprints through the dirt around him. Sometimes now when I drive by my old house and see those wild lilies, I remember all of that."

They are daylilies, I could point out. Not technically wild. I don't bother. I have told Ada this before, and she has given me that look and shrugged, that way she has, that little turn in her mouth like she knows one better. They don't grow just where you put them, she would answer. They get off on their own. Grow where they like.

December will be her eightieth birthday. Twenty years older than I am, she was born in 1924, when it was still an event to watch a plane pass overhead.

This will strike me at times—the rift in years between us. By the time I was three, Ada was in her early twenties, already working her stuff on my father. Given that rift, and every consequence since, how unlikely it is that Ada and I should still be drawn here together, to this board laid out, this rite.

There used to be four of us. Besides me and Ada, there was Ada's best friend, Vivienne Butler, and Caroline Wilkes. We met every Friday. We used to go bowling up at Midway Lanes next to the drive-in; then Vivienne blew out her knee, and Ada hurt her hip. Around that same time, they closed those lanes, bulldozed the drive-in to put up a Wal-mart. So we started playing Scrabble instead.

Caroline didn't like Scrabble. She said the game went too slow but, in truth, she was just lousy at it, and competitive, which Ada remarked once was a mix that didn't bode well. Ada was right, and Caroline quit playing with us after a year. We'd run into her in the community room, when we met for our Friday games. In the winter, or if the weather was poor, we'd play inside and Caroline might be sitting at another table there, with Betsy Cornell or Peg Amaral, playing Yahtzee or some other game you tear through in a quarter of an hour and put all your trust in the dice.

Vivienne was the one who loved Scrabble, even more, I think, than Ada or I did. Vivi was that way. She loved things easily. And she was wickedly good at the game. She could have clocked us both handily any day of the week, but she was a noble player, Vivienne, artful and generous. She wasn't the kind who'd intentionally make a move to sabotage someone else's chance. She played with an eye to the sum of the total scores.

She used to do those round-robin Scrabble tournaments they held in Fall River back when the game was all the rage. It was Vivi's board we started playing on, and her set of letters in the purple velvet Crown Royal sack with the gold-fringed drawstring, until she lost the Q and one of the M's. Then we started using mine.

Vivienne had a knack for making boodles—the term Ada coined for those plays you make when you use all seven letters at once and nab the fifty-point bonus.

Vivi's sole flaw: She always played for the words. She'd cling to two S's and squander three turns, fish or pass if she had to, trying to place P-O-S-S-I-B-L-E. Or she'd lay down some beauty like C-Y-G-N-E-T for no extra points when she could have nailed Y-E-T on a triple-word score.

"It's not a game of words, Vivienne," Ada used to tell her.

Over and over, she'd tell her.

"In the end, it all comes down to numbers."

Vivienne was an Arsenault, born French Canadian, a good Catholic, went to Mass twice a week, married Lawrence Butler, had fourteen children: twelve girls and two boys. They lived up in North Westport near the old Indian reservation. For over a quarter of a century, Vivienne changed diapers, washed, soaked, bleached them, strung them up like prayer-flags on the line. I remember driving by her house once with Carl when we were just married, and I was pregnant with Alex, and seeing Vivienne out there in the yard. It was all green and sunlight and wind through the grass, babies crawling over one another on her lap, toddlers stumbling, and the older ones laughing, running with a kite, and the hose was out, one of the tall girls, blond and leggy, holding it and water was spraying, shot all through with the light, the wind taking that water, and those diapers, bleached and whitened, lifted by that same wind against a blue sky that seemed to go forever. Vivienne glanced up and saw us as we drove by, and waved. It was one of those moments between moments where life extends, grows endless, and I wanted to stop, to walk into that moment, that idyll of no past or future, only a present of everything possible in those children and that sky. Then the road curved and we sped on. But sometimes still, I think of that. Like now, when I see the blank tiles facedown, all turned over, floating in the box-lid beside the empty board.

STAR-SPLITTER

JANE
July 23, 2004

"You planning to keep score today, Janie?" Ada asks me.

"Sure."

She nods toward the pad of paper we keep in the box and the pen that reads EYE HEALTH, ROUTE 6, with a phone number. I reach for the paper and pen while she takes out two of the wooden racks.

I am the one who keeps score. Ada always asks though, just the same.

She flips over a tile. E.

I pull a K.

I write her name at the left top of the blank page, mine beside it, as she draws her first rack of letters. She draws them like she always has, one from each of the four corners of the box-lid and three from the center.

She sets all seven in her rack. "Crap," she murmurs. She moves a few of them around as I draw mine.

S. F. U. R. E. A. F.

Suffer. Fuse. Ruse. Sure. Fears.

It's an old set, the game we play with now. It was my mother's. Someone gave it to my grandfather Gid in the early sixties—and Gid having no inkling or interest, gave it to his booksmart daughter, Emily.
She taught me to play. After she was gone and I was going through her
house, I found that Scrabble set wrapped in a grain bag, in the crawl
space under the stairs. It's not plastic, the board, and there's no
turntable underneath. The box is the burgundy-colored, cardboard
kind. Where it has split along the seams, I've taped it back with mask-
ing tape, so the box-lid still fits tight. I've never told Ada it was my
mother's. Not that it should bother her any with the time gone by. It
does brush through me, though, on occasion. I wonder how my
mother would feel about my Friday games with Ada.

In the fat margin on the side of the board where the letters that
spell the word SCRABBLE run down, in the lower corner that today is by
Ada's left hand, my maiden name is written in cursive script. I don't remember writing it. Only imagine I must have in some long hour of a
childhood game.

"What time did you get here?" I ask Ada now, one of those questions I always seem to ask.

"Just before you did."

"Did Huck bring you?"

She makes a face. "I drove myself. He got into it with me this
morning about that damn boat. He just won't leave off. Trying to
pork-barrel me into glassing it in. Seems that boat is all we've got left
to fight over."

Huck is Ada's middle son. His given name was Elton, but he shed
that quick. He's the one she lives with now, in the old hurricane house
on the postage-stamp lot near the town beach, on one of those skinny

lanes that run behind the dunes. Ada had five boys altogether. Lost two: her oldest, Junie, when his scallop boat went down ten years ago in a storm off Georges Bank. And Green.

She keeps still about Green. Almost never talks about him, even now—more than three decades later. But she'll chatter on about Junie daylight-to-dark. She's always claimed Junie was her favorite. And it might be so. She was seventeen when she had him, so they more or less grew up together. She says that of all of her boys, Junie was the one she understood, the one who understood her. She and Vivienne used to scrap about it, Vivi telling Ada you can't love one more than another, and saying the only reason Ada thought she loved Junie best was because he was her first, so she had him alone for that spell. Four years, it was, before her next one came along. She would drag him with her everywhere: snowshoeing through the woods behind the farm, Junie swaddled in blankets in a laundry basket tied to a sled she pulled. Late June, when the fireflies were out and the swordfish came in, she'd drive with him down to the wharf to watch the boats bring in their catch at the end of the day. Or on a fine morning, she'd strap him into a little cork life-vest and they'd motor out together over the bluegreen surface to the bell because he loved to hear the sound of it. She has told me this before, told it many times, like the memory of those mornings, the lap of a calm sea against the hull is a living thing still in her—

Even now when Ada talks about those early days with Junie, both of us know how much more isn't getting said, but I just smile with her and listen. Because when she talks about Junie, her face glows, and it is a simple glow, incandescent, pure, no hardness in it, like thinking of Junie draws her back into that brief smooth time in her life when there was a sort of rustic peace to things, she and Silas newly married, still in love perhaps. She hadn't started messing around. He hadn't tried to carve her up.

"All I've got's a four-letter word," she says now. "You got something better, Janie?"

She hates to start the board off small.

I shake my head. Lie. I've never liked to be the one who makes the first move.

Ruse. Suffer. Surf.

Ada lays down R-O-V-E. The O on the star, to keep me from using a high-point consonant on the light blue double-letter squares that flank it. She thinks about the numbers. She is good at the game that way. But she won't play tight like I will. Ada hates a closed board.

"What'd you bring?" she asks.

I glance at the package wrapped in the Lees bag. "Just some old junk I came across."

"I meant for lunch."

"Cheese and tomato."

"You always bring cheese and tomato," she says lightly, casually, but her eyes flick to the other package, curious now.

A strand of her hair has come loose. She tucks it back in place. "Boar's Head Ham was on sale at Shaw's," she says. "Four ninety-nine a pound." She draws four new tiles and sets them into her rack. "Picked up two bottles of Planters Mixed Nuts as well. They had them on special, buy one, get one free. Ray came the other night for supper and couldn't budge the cap open on those mixed nuts, he knocked it so hard on the floor the glass broke. He was stomping around, been in such a funk over that girl of yours. Even with her hair all sawed off." A pause. "Marne's a tough little person, isn't she? Won't let herself get tied down like she thinks that'll keep her free."

I shake my head. "She's just afraid she'll end up like me."

Ada snorts. "How's that now? Happily-ever-after's not good enough for her?"

I don't need to tell Ada that's not how Marne sees it. That's not how she sees me. A wife, a mother, nothing else. Never left the town she was born in. Never learned to drive.

Ada's just about had it with my daughter. She's made up her mind about Marne, and once Ada's mind is set, there's no wiggle room. She won't back down. I can't say it hasn't been a sticking point between us.

"I don't know why such a pretty girl as your Marne would go and cut off all that pretty hair."

Marne did have pretty hair. So blond when she was small. Almost white. Not at all like Alex. Like the other one, Samuel, Marne was fair. It was lovely long. Her hair. I remember the flow of it down her small back.

Thirty-five now, Marne has always been her father's daughter, trotting around after Carl. He taught her dominoes, pitch, hearts. She didn't get seasick like Alex did, and Carl would take her out lobstering when they were potting close to shore. She'd stand on a wooden crate and bait the traps. She was never one for dolls or toys, and she didn't much like hanging around the house unless I was baking bread. She'd help me punch the dough down, shape the loaves, and while things baked, we'd read. Marne always loved to read, loved her picture books, and longer stories, too. I read her the Norse myths and Emily Dickinson's poems. I'd glance down at her little face, scrunched up in concentration, rapt. It was the one time she'd sit still with me, snug in, her little hand clutching one of mine.

When did it start? I have asked myself this. When did that coldness begin to gather in her eyes, the disdain in her voice as she'd correct how I talked: "You're mixing your tenses again."

It started before she had left us for the first time—those little barbed remarks. I remember thinking at one point it was just some notion, some late-teenage, mother–daughter muck she was trying to sort through. Give it time, I told myself. That coldness, it will drop from her. Won't it? She'll come around.

"Are you going to take your turn, Janie?" Ada says.

"I'm still thinking."

"So what sort of old junk?" She nods to the package wrapped in the Lees bag.

"There was a poem," I say. Her nose wrinkles. I smile. "I took that out."

"You know I'm too stupid for poems."

"You liked that one I brought about the daylilies."

"Fair to middling."

"You liked the Robert Frost one."

"Which one was that?"

"About the farmer who burned down his barn to buy a telescope."

"What was that one called?"

" 'Star-Splitter.' "

"Right," she says with a smile. "I did like that one."

Ada has always liked the stars. She likes sitting out in the night. She used to say that apart from her granddaughter, the only good thing that came out of Huck's marriage to that rich girl from the Point was a subscription to *Smithsonian* magazine they bought for her one Christmas along with a pair of special binoculars that were good for roaming the sky.

Ada never liked that girl. Called her the carpetbagger. Huck's whole marital experiment lasted barely a minute. Ada still has those binoculars, though. "They're quite fine," she'll say. "They give you a nice wide view. You can hold them right up to your eye, and they don't turn whatever you're looking at upside down."

She is talking about Marne again now. She is telling me that the mistake I make is letting it get to me.

I tell her I don't.

"Oh, but you do, Janie. How could you not, really? You're like a piece of tissue blowing around, picking up things. That whippety daughter of yours needs a good talking-to. Needs someone to come along and tell her to get the hell out of that bad mood. How long has she been in that mood anyhow? Fifteen years?"

I smile. Thereabouts.

She wants to go a step farther, I can feel it, stir things up. She doesn't, though, for now.

A Scrabble board, Ada said to me once, is like the dark space between stars. You look up into that space and think it's nothing, you think it's got no use, because there's nothing in it you can touch or see or smell. But it's wild, that space, not empty at all, it's full of dark stars, black holes, heat, and storms that bend and squeeze the light that you can see.

I remember when she told me this, there was a smile on her face, that funny sort of quiet smile, almost complicit, I have seen her get sometimes, like we share a secret.

"Think of all the games we've played out on this board, Janie," she said to me that day. "All the words that we've laid down."

And all those other words we haven't.

She did not say it, didn't have to. I knew.

Those other words, as yet unplayed but living still between us.

I used to wonder what would happen then, if we did play out those unsaids. If there would still be reason for us to meet here on a Friday.

Would I come? Would she still be waiting? I thought about it this morning driving here. Holding the box on my lap as Carl drove, knowing today could be the last game.

I save one of the F's. I lay the S on R-O-V-E, and spell F-A-R-E-S going up. I could have written F-E-A-R-S, but there was no reason to make that choice when I had another. I could have made S-U-F-F-E-R for eight more points, but that would have opened up the board a little more than I like to. Besides, an F can be a useful letter to hang on to for a turn. Like an H, an F is the kind of four-point letter you can set on a number square and make it work both ways. Like a secret, it can be a thing worth keeping.

GRAY HORSE

JANE
July 23, 2004

Ada has taken another turn, played W-E-L-K-I-N off
the E, running down, she landed the K on the dark
blue triple-letter square—twenty-eight points.

She is talking about Huck and the fight they
had over the skiff. I can feel the fire in her, sparks
kicked up.

"So stubborn," she says, "how that one gets, yip-
yapping on about that boat, giving me the bull, when
it's his own damn fault for not looking after it like he
should. Every year, Janie, it's the same. I have to get on
him, nagging, to be sure he gets the bottom scraped
and painted, and him giving me that hangdog look like
somebody's just stole his bicycle, saying, 'That skiff
don't warrant the work, Ma, that thing's just junk,'
dragging his sorry feet like always, because he thinks
the world will wait to turn until he's ready. Just this
morning, I was having a nice quiet morning, just me
and my coffee alone out on the porch, and he come
outside, busting up my good peace and quiet, launch-

ing in about how we should either get rid of that boat once and for all, or have Pete Savage glass it in. I turned on him then, told him he can just forget about glass, that skiff's near as old as he is, it's mine, and there's no way I'm going to let anyone glass over that wood because what would it be then?"

She stops a moment, looking down at her letters, then at the word I have just made. A little word. K-I-P.

Her fingers drum the table. She is seeing something there; in the letters. Some word. I can feel it.

"He gets all het up," she murmurs. "That one. Hidebound just like his father was." She glances at me. A pause, and then she says, "I remember one winter, Janie, it was good and winter and Silas got into the drink. He started chopping up chairs for firewood, then other stuff as well. He would have chopped up that boat if Junie and I hadn't hooked up the trailer and brought it over to my brother Swig's house. All the years I had it, Silas hated that boat, and that night I knew he was so stewed, he'd have gone at it with an ax if I'd given him the chance, chopped it to kindling and splinters just like he did that baby grand piano that had belonged to his grandmother, the piano his mother used to play even when she was old and the rheumatism got bad in her hands, still she'd play, wring such sweet music from those keys. But Silas, he didn't care none what that piano was to her, or maybe that's why he went and did it. I'll tell you, though, I wasn't going to let him get his hands on that boat. He hated that boat, he did, hated it like everything I loved that had to do with water—"

Her voice breaks off. She looks down again at her letters. She takes one from the end of her rack, knocks two others apart. She sets it in the gap, and I feel the silence open between us like a field, those fine light threads that have stitched her life to mine—my father, her husband, our sons—

I never minded that web between Ada and me—before this spring, it never seemed unfree, but when those sparks between Ray and Marne began to fly last month, it dawned on me—it wasn't only the dead that bound me to Ada and it wasn't only the dead who were bound.

She dumps down three letters: C-A-D. Which surprises me. It is unlike her, to play small, not to mention setting a C on an outer edge. C's and V's—no way to build off them—they stymie up the board.

"There's a word for you," I say.

She ignores me. She picks her new tiles.

"You must be fishing, Ada Varick, to make such a weensy word."

She shrugs. "That C was holding me back."

I have drawn the X. I could put it against the exposed A. But I don't have the vowels I need to make it work well. Ada has reached into her lunch bag and pulled out a bottle of ginger beer. She unscrews the cap and drinks, then sets it down, bits of dust or air falling through the amber liquid inside. She always brings a ginger beer. Around the bottleneck, a trace of color, lipstick, glistens. I glance at her rack. She has the letters divided. Five and two. If it were Vivienne, that would tell you she had a five-letter word she was setting up for. But not Ada. Five and two told you nothing about Ada.

"I saw Huck this morning," I tell her.

"That so?"

"While I was on my walk. He was upriver some, tonging quahogs, in the deeper water off the Point of Pines."

Ada glances up. "You walked the bridge?"

I nod.

"Haven't done that in a while, have you?"

"No."

"When was it last, sometime back in the winter?"

"Yes."

"Around Christmastime, wasn't it?"

"That day of Christmas Eve."

She nods slowly. "Yes, that's right," she says. "That day. I remember."

As if it was a day either of us was going to forget.

This morning, I had Carl drop me at the corner of Drift Road and 88, across from where they diverted the brook when the state made their takings and laid the highway, that corner where the Wilkes family used to live, running across the road to draw their water from that brook. I started from there, and as I walked up the highway toward the bridge, I could see the sky opening ahead of me, that slight darker slip of the ocean between the pine scrub and the dune that faded in and out of view.

As I was coming up to the bridge, I passed the Cambodian man. He's been fishing the bridge a few years now, the only one who still does, it seems. He comes out from Fall River, wears a big straw hat. It's always the same: He'll fish there for a while, then the Staties come around to kick him off, and he'll get gone for a few days, then come back to fish some more until they come around to kick him off again.

"You should have come by to see me," Ada says.

"I didn't know if you'd be home."

She smiles. "Now, where else are you thinking I'd be?"

I put the X by. And set the second F into the cleft between the two I's. Double word both ways. Twenty points. If. If. Then I draw.

Ada hasn't moved. That surprises me. I had expected her to set something down right away. I felt she had something, I felt that sort of humming you can feel at times with Ada. It's all you can really feel with her. It's when you know she is holding some good word, just waiting for her chance.

But she is strangely quiet. Turning something over in her head. Her fingers drumming again, light on the table. A catbird calls from the woods behind us. A car pulls into the COA parking lot and up to the front steps. A woman gets out of the passenger side with a cane. She looks over in our direction, at me and at the game, and frowns a little. She holds the rail tightly as she makes her way up the stairs. The door closes behind her. And still Ada is quiet.

This morning, as I was crossing the bridge, just as my foot landed on the draw, pigeons flushed out from underneath, a rush of wings, they startled me. Without meaning to, my eyes followed them, on the wing coasting down. I saw her there: the girl from the snapshot, the girl I was once, I saw the reflection of her face above the shadows of the piles and the rail, the dark geometry of the bridge in the river. The tide was falling, the river pulling fast-like through her hair. I didn't recognize her at first. Then I did.

I still have that photograph. A few years after we were married, Carl took it into the city—a shop there—and got it reframed. Now it hangs in the front room on the wall above the little table where I've set the orchid Marne gave me for my birthday in April.

That orchid was a gorgeous thing when I first unwrapped it from the newsprint, three blooms on it, deep purple, a shock of white in the throat of each. But the frost had touched it just in the short distance from Marne's car into the house, and those blooms went by soon after, so now that orchid is all skinny branch, no bud on it. I know Marne wants me to toss it out. So like Marne to want that. She thinks it's got no chance of coming back. I keep it on the little table for the warm light coming through the window there, under the photograph of the girl on the bridge. When Marne's in the room, I've noticed, she doesn't look at that orchid or, if she does, it's with the same little hardness in her eyes she turns at times on me.

They don't take well, I could tell her, exotic things in this sort of a climate.

"Do you remember that man?" I ask Ada now. "That city engineer who worked on the new bridge? He was very tall, he wore those funny blue-tinted glasses. Do you remember the summer he lived at the Point, 1962 it was, the summer before they took the old bridge down?"

"You mean the one with the ducktail hair, always strutting around?"

"Yes, him."

She nods. "I remember."

He wasn't Westport. You could tell that at a glance—how he talked, dressed. Back then, you could always tell. Back then, they didn't try to dress local, didn't try to patch in. And it wasn't only how they dressed, sunhats or whales on their belts or how their kids tore up and down Main Road on their bicycles in chino shorts and flip-flops. It was that certain sheen they had, every one of them who came from a somewhere else seemed to have it, that city gloss still on them when they started washing in those first few weeks of summer as the weather warmed, their eyes wide, full of the river and the salt wind, all the free and thoughtless beauty this place was to them. We didn't mix. They were shadows to us. They'd come for their few months, then leave, and the village would be ours again, back to its slow and still, everyone burrowed into their own like eels in the mud. Growing up, I was in and out of every one of those houses down the Point. Now Carl and I walk up Main Road. We pass people. Nobody knows who we are.

Yesterday, though, I got to thinking about that bridge engineer, about those little snapshots he took. He rented Gid's shucking house that summer, the summer they opened the highway. It was seeing Marne yesterday dragging my book around, that old library book I picked up off the floor of my father's car years ago. I'd noticed her flipping through it earlier this summer, in a desultory Marne sort of way. That was right around when Ray started coming by, more for her than for Alex. Then things between her and Ray kicked up, and that book disappeared. Yesterday, I saw she'd dug it out again. All day, it seemed, she moped around the house with her nose in that book.

"He was an odd man," I say to Ada now. "That city engineer. Different."

Ada shakes her head, looking down at the board. "They're all the same."

She looks past my shoulder toward the road, then her eyes shift back to me. Her fingers are touching one tile on her rack, gently, the smooth bare edge. "Something else," she says, "about that gray horse. This I don't think I've ever told you. When he got old, his leg got hurt, his knee all swelled up, some infection in it. He couldn't work, some days could hardly walk. Finally, one morning, I remember my pa, coming down the stairs to breakfast, pulling his suspenders over his shoulders, and telling us that when he got back from the auction in Acushnet, he was going to put that gray horse down. My brothers went with him that day to the auction—it was just me and my ma in the house. Around nooning time, when we were washing the down-stairs windows, we heard a sound. It was like a train sound. We felt the ground shuddering through the floor, and we went outside and saw the horses, all of them, somehow they'd gotten loose, broke down the fence or whatever. Somehow they'd slipped through, and that gray horse, he was herding the rest of them, running them one end of the field to the other. My ma and me, we went down with ropes and hal-ters, tried to get them back up into the pasture near the horse barn, and finally we did, but they were wild that day, those horses, rearing up and bucking, unruly-like. He had made them wild. At last we got them settled, gave them grain and water, and they were all there, all except the gray one. We looked everywhere for him, even down the lower fields and in the fields across the way. We couldn't find him nowhere. When my pa and brothers got home, they set out searching, combing the fields, and it was down in the lowest one, close by the river, my pa saw a little place where the brush was broken down, just barely. They hacked in there and found him, the gray horse. He'd worked himself down into a little hollow, right down by the river. I re-member my pa shaking his head. No moving him now, he said. He's chosen his spot. That's the spot it'll be. So Pa called on Albion Parks from up Cornell Road, and Albion, he come down with his bulldozer. Horse was dead by then, and they mounded the dirt right over him there where he lay."

Ada stops. She leans to the left some, gives a little stretch to her back. Cat-like. Then she smiles at me, her eyes green now, a true green. The sun in them is bright.

"Now, Janie. Isn't that the way it should happen?" she says.

I look up at her, startled, surprised almost she'd say a thing like that, but then I see the impish look in her eye.

And I know. I know what is coming. I know by how she took her time with that story. Like she had all the time in the world. I know what is coming even before she starts taking the letters off her rack, even before she lays all seven of them down.

BOODLES

JANE
July 23, 2004

T-I-N-C-T-U-R-E

She has built it off the C in C-A-D, using a blank for
the R. T-R-O-V-E-S running across.

"Such a funny thing isn't it, with those joker tiles?"
she remarks lightly, drawing her new letters. "Do you
remember how Vivi would come right apart every
time she drew one of those blanks like she just couldn't
cope with the freedom of it?"

I don't answer. I am tallying her score.

"Twenty for the words," she says. "Don't you forget my fifty for the boodle."

I should have known. She would never play a small
word unless she was using it as a foothold to fling the
board open. She's got no charity for my style of keeping things tight. The part of me that shies from risk
rankles her. It's as close to a doctrine as I've ever
known her to hold: Ada has always played for an open
board.

"Cad indeed," I say. "You were fishing."

She doesn't answer, but by the faintly smug expression on her face, I can tell.

"Shining me on."

"I'm not the one who plots out her dinks twelve moves ahead."

"You plotted this one."

She laughs. "A little serendipity never did hurt."

She made that word once. Serendipity. Got a boodle for it. Ran the end of the word off S-E-R-E.

She takes another sip of her ginger beer, sets the bottle back, flicks something off her hand.

You remember the boodles. Those plays made, all seven letters dropped at once, a rack emptied. Even after every other detail of a game has been bleached from your mind, you will remember those words. Not just because each is worth that extra fifty-point bonus, even before the word itself is tallied, but because that play is so often the one that changes the flow of a game.

I-N-G-E-S-T-S
S-H-A-T-T-E-R-E-D
S-T-U-P-E-F-Y
S-I-L-E-N-C-E
T-E-N-S-I-O-N
T-R-I-B-U-N-A-L
E-X-T-O-L-L-E-D
Q-U-I-X-O-T-I-C. That was Vivienne's. As was A-L-T-R-U-I-S-T. Appropriately so.
C-A-M-O-U-F-L-A-G-E-D. That was mine, built off F-L-A-G.

Once, and this topped all else, Ada made U-N-K-N-O-W-A-B-L-E.

N-O-W was already on the board. She dropped U-N-K at one end, A-B-L-E at the other.

I remember that play like it happened an hour ago, Vivi shaking her head in disbelief, looking from the word to Ada's empty rack, then at me. "Only you, Ada," she said as she wrote down the score. "I can wake up and die right, now that I've seen that one."

And she did. Just a short time later.

Unknowable. It was funny, that word. When Ada set it down, at first blush, looking at it, I almost challenged. That quick doubt, my mind tipped. It didn't feel like a true word. I remember going down a list in my head, even as Ada was filling her rack with new letters.

know
knowing
knowledge
known
knowable
unknown

I kept thinking it should have been unknown.

There was a story my father, Luce, told me once about the standing stones off S'cunnet Point. Part of that old Indian legend about the Giant who, weary of the world, took his children out to play on a spit of land. He drew a line in the sand with his toe. The tide rushed in, the water rose. He turned his children into fishes and they were swept away under the waves. When the Giant's wife came home and learned what he had done, she made such a storm with her crying and her grief, kept up such a racket that finally the Giant took her body up and threw her down hard, and where she struck became those standing stones.

T-I-N-C-T-U-R-E

It haunted me as a child—that story of the stone wife.

Ada is watching a car turn in to the parking lot. "There's Louise," she says, but makes no move to call to the woman getting out. "Good Lord. Is that Louise? What in hell has she done to her hair? She looks like a carnation."

Her face turned slightly now, I notice a cut on the bone above her eye. I don't remember that. A thin darker line woven through her brow, a slight reddened swelling around it.

"Did you fall?" I ask.

"Hmm?"

"Your eye."

"Oh that. Dropped a pill under the table while I was talking on the phone, bent down to pick it up and managed to coldcock myself with a chair. Figured with Silas not around anymore, I'd have a go at it my-self. Hurt like the dickens. For a few hours, I was hobbling around like a half-bred cow. I must have looked a sight. Huck got all in a state when he come home that afternoon and found me on the couch, watching Oprah with a black eye and an ice pack on my head. 'Not a word,' I said to him as he come through the door, 'not one word about that damn boat or I'll go and tell everyone you did this to me.' There's still a bit of a shine." She points. I see it then, a deeper blue half circle under that one eye, like salt-glisten, I hadn't noticed it before.

"Did the same stupid thing about a year ago," she says.

waken
    To the judge blown bedlam
Of the uncaged sea

She is beautiful. Even now. You cannot look at Ada Varick and say that she is not, her face filled with the elaborate and delicate crossing of lines a life has wrought. On occasion, she might say something, or throw a glance at me, a spark in her eye like tinder lit, and in that mo-ment, the architecture of her face will rearrange into how I might have

seen her once. Before I knew her name, the first time I saw her perhaps, if there was ever such a time, walking the old bridge, fishing the
slack tide, one of her boys trailing after her. I will see that lost moment
like a shiver, her face as it was then, the flow of black hair off her
shoulder. How the wind took it.

I see her so clearly it's hard sometimes to imagine there will be a
time when she is not here waiting for me.

I touch the X. I could play it, but something tells me, wait.

Wait.

From the street, the sound of a car going by. Fast. The rush of air
after.

It's my favorite letter. X. Master of those two- and three-letter words
I love that Ada calls "dinks." As a rule, she doesn't like small words.
She doesn't like how I know them all, have memorized them, even
ones I don't know the meaning of.

"How can you play a word and not know what it means?" she'll
ask me.

"Because in this game, all I need to know is that it exists."

And she will shake her head, but technically she knows I am right,
and it gets her all in a twit. She doesn't like how I work those dinks,
braiding them close to tighten the board.

wot, od, nix, xi, kae, em, avo, nu

"I know what's coming," she says. "You got that playing scrappy
look, that little scowly-crease. Here." She touches the spot between
her own brows. "You get that look, that polecat look, and it reminds
me of him. You know, Janie, it's the only time you remind me of him."

She says this, and I hear a slight bend in her voice, away.

For a moment I want to ask her.

A week or so before Vivienne died, there was a game we played and a moment in that game, when Vivi threw up her hands and cried out, "Girls, you just won't believe this—I've got P-A-S-S-I-O-N, and no place to put it." Then, like she'd do sometimes, she turned her rack toward us, so we could see the letters there before she went to break them down. Like we might not have believed her otherwise.

It was four years ago this coming August, Vivi was out feeding the birds, stooped to pull a weed, and went toes up to the sun. A ruptured vessel in the Circle of Willis at the base of her brain. The result of a congenital defect they discovered after the fact, as they so often do. A weakness in an arterial wall. Asymptomatic. One of those silent, hidden tics afloat in the body we're born into.

Unknowable.

FROST FISH

JANE, TWELVE
October 1957

Every Saturday her father, Luce, came for her. And she would wake early, every Saturday, go before dawn down the road to her grandparents' house for her chores: bring in the milk, water the hens. Then she'd run back up the road home to change into a decent dress and start her waiting.

She told herself that she remembered the time he lived with them, that perilous time held in the balance, if a balance at all, the three of them—her mother, him, her—adrift together through the small house. She did not really remember, only knew that his shadow used to fall across the knots in the wide-pine boards of the floor, that he shook out his tobacco onto paper, rolled his cigarettes, sat near the woodstove, his long legs stretched toward its burning, while her mother turned a sock or the pages of a book, the snap, snap as kindling burned, and the cradle rocking with the baby that once was her, and his voice, the smooth low edge of it, mixed in with cooking smells—bruised onions, bread fried up—the scrape of a spoon against a pan—his voice she thought she could still sometimes hear like it was held in the walls, their whitewash and lime.

And even after he left—every Saturday, he would still come for her. Would always come, would never not, it was a promise that he kept, and she would wait in the parlor of that fall-apart house where she still lived with her mother, his once-upon-a-wife. And he would come for her there, even on the rainy Saturdays when you could hear the water slushing down the gutters; and even in dead winter, her favorite season, that certain honesty of winter, all things stripped back to being only what they are; even then, on those Saturdays of the most unkind weather, when the northeast gales drove in off the sea, and the cold flooded under the walls of the house that had not settled well—the wind in a high-pitched sudden whistle swelling up the belly of the carpet by a gust.

She would wait in the parlor, touching winter through the window in the patterns of frost, two coats on, rubber boots, a woolen hat and mittens she wore even inside, it was so cold. Her mother would be in the kitchen, and Jane would wait alone, until she saw the big blue Buick winding its lackadaisical way down Main Road, pulling up out front, her father leaning across the seat to open the door to her slipping inside.

They always headed north. Winter, spring, summer, fall. He'd turn around in some driveway, go back the way he'd come. Never went through the village at the Point, never by the wharf or over the Point Bridge. He knew, and she did as well, he was less than welcome there. Too many hated him: Jane's grandfather Gid being one. Gid, who always said he was a con. Bootlegging swindling no-good. Swig and Jimmy Lyons also, two others he stole something from once—she'd heard talk—they were fishermen both who carpentered wintertimes, and the brothers of that woman Ada Varick, whom Jane's mother never referred to by name, only called her "that woman," and Jane even young had enough of a sense to guess why.

They drove slowly through other parts of town. They drove the roads her father knew, the roads his life had been laid down on. He took his time, driving slowly, always seemed to find some different route, and had a different story, it seemed, for every turn, every corner, every house they passed and who was living there, some little bit scraped out, that in the telling took on a glint of something more, and she sat there quiet, listening, until they pulled up out front of the Head store. He'd ask her what she wanted and she'd answer—penny candy or a coffee milk—never really cared much, but for the awe she felt when she was with him, that slight delirious fire. She would wait in the car while he went in, the engine humming, and they would set out again, whatever he had bought for her held tightly in her hand— how slowly he drove, like he was carving the air. He'd take the right turn at Sisson's corner, and they'd stop in at his mother, Cora's house, for a mug and a talk.

And every spring, after the earth had thawed and the plow had turned it under, he took her looking for arrowheads through the fields—she would keep behind him, trailing his shadow as he paced the furrows, carrying the late sun on his back, his head bent, eyes working over the ground until he found a piece—the shape that he was looking for—quartz, whole. He'd dust the dirt off with his fingers, wash it in his mouth so it came clean off his tongue like a language. He would hand it to her and go on.

"I'm sorry," he said once, the last Saturday, when he came late, so late. It was deep into autumn by then, the dahlias in her mother's garden had come up fast, blooming all of a moment as dahlias will do, and it had rained a touch the night before, a soft wet still soaked over everything, slick on the leaves of the maple tree, the white complicated residue of a spider's work slung between the forked lower branches. She had been waiting by her window in the parlor looking onto the road. Watched the light as she waited—how it started in the morning, just touching in that most intimate way the outer edges of things, touching like it swore, *I will not go farther*, yet by noon already breaking, driving deep toward the heart of the shade.

"I'm sorry," he said when he finally did at last arrive. Only that. It was after four, her mother almost not letting her go, but then she begged and threw a fit, and so they went, even knowing as she did that it was too late to embark on any grand adventure, too late to walk into some green wooded stillness and find themselves gone. It was too late to do anything much, go anywhere, except down to East Beach, past the houses before the road hooked back.

They parked there, she and her father, Luce, all the way at the end of the beach.

It was 1957, a day in October.

"I'm sorry." He had said that, more than once, I'm sorry. Too late to do anything but sit together in the Buick and watch the waves roll in through the dusk, under the moon. Like a round door in the sky, and near full, she thought. A hole boring right into the evening daylight of their world. He took a long drag, and the smoke circled his handsome craggy face, a patch of it like fog trapped in a corner of the windshield. She watched his hands, his fingertips tapping the top edge of the steering wheel, tapping his fingers quick without seeming to realize. He told her how he used to come down here, to this beach to go for frost fish with his father when he was just a boy, about her age. They'd drive down on the wagon, with spears, a lantern and a bucket, just after the first good frost, when the whiting came in to breed. They'd come on a good dark night, no moon to spook the fish, just him and his father, and wade through the shallows with a lantern, and the fish would come, drawn by the light, beating in around one another, that light making them wild. Then a sea would lift them, wash them up onto the beach, and they'd be stranded: white, tails thrashing, caked with sand. He and his father would spear them up, one after another, handling them off the prongs into the pail until it was full, and when they got home his mother would roll those fish in cornmeal, fry them up, the skins sticking some to the pan, the outer flesh just browned, and he and his younger sister would eat them with their fingers.

"They'll only come on a white frost," he said, "leave at the first sign of snow. Just a flurry is enough to send 'em off. Maybe the start of next month, though, when it gets real cold, I'll bring you down one night." As he talked, some lit tobacco fell off the edge of his cigarette where it wasn't rolled quite tight, leaving tiny holes burned into the dark shirt he wore, holes his skin glowed through like stars.

She could lie down in the stories he told. Whether they belonged to a world he had lived through or not, there was a comfort to each one, a sheen to his voice in the telling. She knew what he was. A thief. A rum-runner back when. He'd made some money at it, killed a man, went to jail for that. Learned card tricks there.

When the silence fell in the car, she didn't break it, didn't want to touch it for fear he'd pull out his watch and remark that it was time to be getting her home. In that silence, his cigarette burned down, he stubbed it out.

There was a library book on the floor by her feet. She'd noticed it earlier, facedown, just kind of thrown there, the gilt letters on the cover through the shine of the plastic, the white sticker with the call number stamped crooked at the base of the spine. It surprised her to see it—her father thought little of books, called them birdscratch—she kicked the book over now, read the title aloud. He glanced down.

"Take it," he said.

"You want me to return it for you?"

"Naw." He shrugged. "Someone left it there, it's yours now."

He rolled another cigarette, put his window a bit lower, and said something about how that moon, rising there and coming up on full, was a hunter's moon, but the Indians called it the middle-between-moon, and she knew he knew that kind of thing because at the end of the day, most days, he'd wind up at the Green Lantern up on Route 6, pouring it down with Victor Perry, who was the last of the Troy Indian Tribe from the reservation, that skinny knobbed land they got for fighting against their own in King Philip's War. Victor Perry was the last male of the last family, the son of a famous herbalist, and when the City of Fall River took the reservation by eminent domain back in 1916 for its water supply, in exchange for the two hundred and some acres, they gave Victor a new house just up the road and a job for life, set him up as a sort of resident caretaker of the land that had once be-longed to his people before the city took it.

Her father had told her that story about the Perrys before, many times, too many times. He told it like it had some bearing, like some other man's fate or the fate of a tribe might be reason enough to ex-plain why he wore trouble himself, to justify why he stole what he stole and always had, when all it really pointed to was how, for exam-ple, he had to go all the way up to the Green Lantern on Route 6 to drink, because he wouldn't dare step foot into Laura's down at the Point Wharf. Too many men there who might be tempted to give him what for. Or worse.

That day of *I'm sorry*, that day of too late, after a time of sitting in the car, her father asked, "You want to take a walk, sweetheart?" and so they did, down the trail along the cove, to the pond lying still, the water skinned back at the end of the day to its own bone-lit darkness, calm and smooth and round. And a great blue heron they came upon and did not see startled, lifting off, its huge thin papery wings—that strange prehistoric design. The wind searched over the surface of the pond, shuddering once. She felt it enter her, the wind, like it had found the hole inside her, and that hole pulled the wind through. Her father did not speak. He only stood there, like some bloodless shadow near her, staring down, and for a moment it felt to her, without reason, that something had changed, without knowing what she knew, she felt it, something was already gone—drawn through that hole inside her the wind flooded through. Her eyes were dry like stone, and every-where she looked, each thing seemed to belong only to itself. The trees were the trees. The pond, the pond. Each thing was simply what it was and that was all.

Come dark, they trudged back to the car. Said nothing. She tripped once on a rock. He reached for her, she caught herself, said nothing.

As he dropped her off out front of her house, she saw her mother's hand at the parlor window, the heavy curtain falling, some relief in the drape as it settled itself.

"You better get on inside," her father said, his voice gruff like it got sometimes with leaving, and she slid across the seat and kissed him on the cheek, the smell of the cigarette smoke still on him, always on him. She breathed it in, off his skin, quick and deep, like she could take that smell of who he was. She took the library book and slipped out of the car into the stark clear night. Then he was gone, and he did not come again the Saturday that followed. Did not come at all. She waited, and her mother broke a plate that evening. By mistake, she said, but really because she was angry that on top of everything else, he had done this. "The end of it," her mother muttered to no one in particular, still angry, those hard lines driven across her forehead, two lines that did not waver through her pretty, careworn face. There was a new pinch to her mouth, Jane noticed, a quiet resolution like she would give him a piece of her mind when he came around again. Only he didn't come. And a few days after, somebody found his skiff floating alone, staked to the shore upriver, in the shallows by the gravel pit on the Drift Road side, his hunting coat with the plaid flannel liner draped over the thwart. They brought the coat to her. She was still, after all, his wife. No one seemed to know a thing. Not even his mother, Cora, had heard word about where he might have gotten himself off to.

I'm sorry.

Still she waited, the girl, the Saturday after, in the parlor by the window, and as she waited, she began to read that book that he had given her. She kept reading, waiting patiently, this story of light like a promise, but still he did not come, not the next Saturday, or any other after. I'm sorry, sweetheart. And only when a month or two had passed, it became clear that he would not, no not, never come again. She took a pair of her mother's nailclippers from the shelf in the bathroom cabinet. She took them into her bedroom, turned the key in the lock, and sat in the middle of the floor. Out of reach of the dirty golden light passing through the window, she rolled up her sleeve and cut, very carefully, into that pale softer skin along the inside of her arm, cut the shape of an eye, and she could see there, deep in it, a small fish working, the flick of a tail, a tiny faint thrash in the cut. The blood came, not fast, it only pooled, slow-like, as shadows worked into the room and the lengthening afternoon moved over the sill across the floor toward the blood on the pale of her arm, drying slow now, growing darker as it dried.

PART III

TRIBES

NYKVIST

MARNE
June 10, 2004, 1:30 AM

Light,

Nykvist said,

> *can be gentle, dangerous, dreamlike, bare, living,*
> *dead, misty, clear, hot, dark, violet, springlike,*
> *falling, straight, sensual, limited, poisonous,*
> *calm, and soft.*

I had forgotten this.

He must have said it once, was quoted, or wrote it somewhere, and I must have read it in that same somewhere. I only remembered it tonight, late, when I got home from work, still jacked from the tussle that didn't happen with the party of four at table 25, the remark made by the man with the trimmed beard and green sports coat (who always requests that corner table because he's one of those who likes to eat looking out at the view)—and it was as I was setting down his plate that he asked if I knew Carleton Dyer, and I smiled and said, "Sure, I know him," and didn't think I needed to point out he's my father, but then the man started in about how he'd hired Carl for some carpenter work and wasn't he "the real deal, a true local, and what a mind, genius really, in—of course—that non-book-learning sort of way. The real salt of the earth." He said it just like that, and I felt my ears burn like they'd been pinched, some kind of shame, his oblivious oblivion. I almost tipped his plate as I was setting it down, Chilean sea bass with couscous, grilled pineapple on the verge of sliding off the china whiteness over the table's edge into his lap. I almost did it, knowing I could manage and manage it well, but in the split second deciding it would not be worth losing the good tip I knew I could expect (he always left a fat tip—a regular, twice a week in the high season) and shouldn't I know better anyhow just to swallow it, a kind of fool remark that was his luxury to make and not meant to be unkind—salt of the earth—four words to touch a world—shouldn't I know better than to let it get to me? Bussing tables since I was sixteen, haven't I heard worse? So I smiled—when in doubt, just smile—I set down the last dinner in front of the woman seated next to him, her hair gorgeous, straight, shocking blond, and asked if there was anything else they might need. Another glass of wine? In fact, yes, he did. I'll be right back with that, I said. I served, cleared the table, delivered coffee, dessert, and, after an appropriate pause, the check. I did what I was there to do.

It was just after one o'clock when I got home, the house quiet, even my mother asleep. She'd left the porch light on, but only that, and when the knob turned and the door swung open and I stepped into that thick dark stillness, it was like walking into a shopworn palace of the dead.

I made a bowl of cornflakes, found a spoon in the drying rack, and took the bowl into the den and popped in the film. It wasn't one of Nykvist's. It was the only great one Bergman did without him. But it was during that scene when Max von Sydow challenges Death to a game of chess that those words Nykvist said once slipped out of me all of a piece like words can do.

Light
    can be gentle, dangerous, dreamlike, bare . . .

Only words. But I remembered them, and thought about my mother lying upstairs in the bedroom above my head, I wondered if in her sleep she could hear the sound of the television drifting up through the floor. Then I knew, in that gut way you know certain things, that she was not asleep, but awake, lying there beside my father. She had been awake all this time, waiting up to know that I was home.

It should be a comfort, shouldn't it? Knowing she's been waiting up—not this other thing spiking through me—that she's rifling with my solitude.

Death has accepted von Sydow's challenge. They have just sat down to play when I decide I don't need to watch anymore. I know how it all falls out.

I flick the power button on the clicker—trees, plain, knight, hooded figure, chessboard—all of it into the vanishing, down to the bit of blue horizontal light, the echo of light, in the center of the TV screen. Zip. The snap of cornflakes in the bowl, hitting milk. I let it soak in.

To my right, against the wall on the small table, the dark skeletal shape of that orchid I bought for her, that thing she keeps, God knows why when it's so far gone. And it occurs to me that one conceivable redeeming aspect of the man in the green sports coat, one nudge of common ground between us, is that he would, more than likely, know the difference between a Bergman film and *Casablanca*. Above me, a floorboard creaks. Listen. Steps. The soft creak, creak. Listen. Silence. Nothing.

I am imagining things.

I was six when I found her in the room upstairs. I had come up the narrow steps from the kitchen, climbing carefully—I remember this—carefully, those steps are old and steep and I was small, my hands feeling for the cool whitewash damp of the walls—it's odd, isn't it? these inconsequent details you will remember—and when I reached the top, saw the light only, at the far end of the hall, pale lemon-colored light streaming from the open door of that room that was unused. I walked toward it, drawn, until its warmth striped my bare legs. I noticed then my mother sitting there, on the floor near the old wash-stand, the basin and pitcher with their blue-and-white designs.

She did not see me. She sat with her back to the door. Light on the rush through the window touched her shoulder like a hand. Her head was slightly bent, her shoulders curved toward something in her lap, and I stepped into the room to see, stepped closer, and then I did see. An old bureau drawer she had pulled out, and in her lap a child's clothes I had never seen, I did not know, but knew something was not right, by the way she was touching them, folding those small clothes, lining up sleeves, hems, smoothing edges with her hands, refolding each piece, piece by piece, again into that drawer, unfolding and re-folding—the intention—*you sweet little one*—she was so calm and un-aware—what I must have felt—how could I ever fix it, save her, undo, knowing already in that instant there was nothing.

It's where the hardness starts. In the knowing there is nothing you can do.

I remember. Standing in the doorway—she never did look up—and I stood there, feeling that small hardness form inside me. Less than the size of a fist, but with an edge that, like a quick blade, cut my breath.

Years later, I went back to that drawer, yanked it open, found tow-els, blankets, cedar blocks. On occasion, though, still, I consider it. Hold the thought at arm's length. Distilled. Sanitized even by the glare of the rational mind. In the silence of the house where I was alone with her. That room ablaze.

Is it real? How you remember it now? Is it more than real?

They come at night—thoughts of this ilk—they shoulder in when my body's exhausted, my mind wired—and a butterfly angst beating up against my ribs, trying not to feel, not to think about the fact that in roughly sixteen hours I've got a date with Ray Varick. Wanting, trying not to want, too much.

Yesterday lunchtime, my brother stopped in for coffee and a ham sandwich and, as he was leaving, threw a cool look at me, and said, "I hear you got plans for Thursday night." Like we were still teenagers, me horning in on his crowd.

I retorted something to that effect.

He just kind of glared. "Do me one great favor, and don't fuck everything up."

Light, Nykvist wrote . . .

. . . *hot, dark, violet, springlike, falling*

It can all come down on you like this. Can't it?

Zip.

DISCOVERY

MARNE
June 10, 2004, 3:30 AM

I still can't sleep. I'm more than halfway through this little library book, the one I found a week ago in the shelf on the landing at the top of the stairs, slipped in between Millay and my mother's Dylan Thomas collection. *Selected Writings. The World I Breathe. Adventures in the Skin Trade.*

My mother is, has always been, a Dylan Thomas freak.

It's by some unknown polymath, this book, *The Secret of Light.* Even under the library plastic, the cloth has frayed, a thready fringe with the board coming through and a water stain shading the top edge. I've tried to decipher her handwritten notes in the margins. There are sections of it I can make out, stanzas, fragments of poems—lifted, not hers. An Auden bit I recognized, lines about the crack in the teacup that opens a lane to the land of the dead. That one caught me up. Understandably so. And I read the other marginalia near it to see if, taken together, there would be a larger vision I could make sense of. But it was like trying to fill a su-doku grid without enough numbers to start, and I gave up. It's all too disparate. Some mental shorthand that must have had a cogent logic to her once. Just fragments now—jotted like cramped answers in very light pencil. Smoke.

The weird thing, though, is it's just this book. In all the years I've been tossing around, I have never seen my mother write in a book, never seen her underline a passage or dog-ear a page. I thought per-haps I might have missed something, but I searched the shelf and found only this one marked. And a library book. She must have known she'd never return it.

Four pages in, I have to admit, I almost ditched it. Not my mom's kind of book either. New Age before the term was coined, hock cos-mogony masquerading as physics.

But there is this one idea. It drew me in and won't quite let me go—about how the world we see, what we think we see, is only one side of the hemisphere.

> Light cannot be seen. It can only be known. That which the eyes "feel" and believe to be light is but wave motion simulating, the echo of light.

The first time I took a passage from a book, I was nine: *The Wizard of Oz*. I didn't cut it for the debate about choosing a heart or a brain. I cut it for Dorothy. Her puzzlement. Her caught in between. I did it crouched on the floor of the downstairs coat closet where my father kept his guns. I used a pair of sewing scissors. My mother winced when she saw the excised page, but said nothing. She didn't tell me it upset her, but I could read it in her face so when I did it again a few months later, another passage from a picture book about the life of Michelangelo, I made sure I did that cutting in front of her. I took my time. Left a slight, purposeful, perfect margin of white space around the paragraph, neat corners at the indents.

Looking back now, I know. I wanted to see what she would do. I wanted to wake her out of that distance I kept losing her to. I wanted her to stop me—her hand swift, ruthless, firm—to catch my fingers on the scissors, her grip tightening until mine released. I wanted to feel that strength in her, that line drawn, that edge, that ending point. I wanted to know there was a line. I wanted to know that if I fell into her, I would not just go on falling.

The cutting continued. Occasional, peripatetic takings. Even after my mother's reaction ceased to have bearing, or perhaps because I found other, less oblique ways of being unkind, still I did it. I kept the cuttings in a shoe box from the Star Store under my dresser.

Surprisingly enough, I never took from her. Never touched her "Do Not Go Gentle," her "Boys in Their Summer Ruin," her "Vision and Prayer." Never touched those precious ordered volumes, their swamp-colored spines tucked together in the little shelf on the landing at the top of the stairs.

There was no organizing theme or qualifying principle to the passages I chose. I cut what I revered, what struck me in a moment. It was an impulse, a habit, at times a need—food, breath, sleep—I was Ezekiel eating the scrolls—without understanding exactly what I did, or why. Until "Burnt Norton." Tenth-grade English. Mr. Mendelsohn's class. He was there for two years and then left, too good for us.

It was winter, that day, I remember, blue fists of snow kicked up and on the swirl outside the classroom window, as Mendelsohn read "Burnt Norton" aloud in class, he read the whole of it, and from the first line on, I was gone.

I skipped next period, Advanced American History, and went instead to the high school library, found "Four Quartets" in a collection, and read "Burnt Norton" through again, knowing I had to have it. Not all of it, but some piece, I needed those words against the skin, needed to feel that slight, secret rectangular fold of paper through the inside pocket of my jeans.

I was going to take that bit early on about the little bird:

go, go go . . . human kind cannot bear very much reality—

but instead, I opted for the seven lines at the close. I couldn't take both. At that time in my life, for reasons real and imaginary, I needed to be strict, to ration what I craved. But it was then, on that late morning in the second cubicle of the hushed school library, with a collection of T. S. Eliot's finest splayed open on a desk where someone had driven hard in black ink, **JOSIE P. SUCKS GOOD COCK,** as I set the blade point of my brother's pocketknife in tight against the binding, I realized: Grafting someone else's thoughts might just be the fastest way to cut yourself free of your own.

That's not worth nothing.

My best friend in middle school was Elise Daignault. We turned fifteen, and Elise turned suddenly beautiful, blond-trellised hair, the nubs of her breasts grown full. It came like a front—overnight—that shadow in her smile, in her eyes, the promise of sex that made men look at her in ways they never looked at me.

After we graduated, Elise started flying for American Airlines. I used to meet her for drinks in New York, when I lived there, then later, after I'd fled west, at the Four Seasons on Market Street when she was laid over in San Fran. News from home often caught up with me through her.

She would laugh. "You think you can burrow into some far-off scuddy pocket of the country. You think it won't nose you out."

"I don't necessarily think that."

"I know you, Marne—I've known you for twenty years." Then her exquisite face would grow serious, strained, I would smell the sweet stain of wine on her breath as she leaned toward me. "I know why you left," she would say, her voice a whispery rush.

"You don't," I countered. "Not if I can't nail it myself."

She shook her head, though, by then convinced. "I know, Marne. I'd be tripping on acid right now if I hadn't flown away."

These are the laws of the sunlit world: Elise needed to be right. And she was so beautiful, every sumptuous pulsing curve of her so beautiful, she deserved to be, I decided, not just partially right, but thoroughly, or at least in that moment to have the last word.

I let Elise wrap it up for me that night. It can be a kind of comfort, letting someone else draw out a plan for who you are. Besides, what would I have said? Some dry, mousy comment about small clothes in a drawer, my mother's distance, or worst of all the brutal little person I'd become in response. By age thirteen, it was conscious, tangible—the screwed-tight walls of the box I was twisting myself to fit into—a small town, my family's fraught history, the ghosts of all that bequeathed to me. I realized it one awful day as I sat by a patch of daisies, mindlessly plucking out petals, one by one: *Is she crazy? Is she not? Is she loco? Is she not?* When it was done, I looked and saw the whole patch worked through: torn petals, desecrated stems, no conclusive answer.

The distance, of course, doesn't hurt as much when you are actually gone.

Go, go, go, little bird.

Go.

CRUSH

MARNE

June 10, 2004, 6 PM

Waiting for him and he's late. Four minutes, five, eight past six, still waiting. I can't seem to sit still. The thought strikes me that he's forgotten, or is blowing me off. The thought itself—groundless and high school—never would have occurred to me waiting for a date to show up in San Francisco. I was a certified grown-up there. Now, though, being home, I've regressed.

It was laughingstock—how I futzed over what to wear. The stretchy twills felt too sexy, too tight in the thigh. And the cropped black slacks with the sheen, they were over the top—like I was trying too hard. I dug through my closet, pulled out an older pair of jeans, boot-cut, a rip coming at the knee. They were soft, though, eased in. A white buttondown shirt. Stalwart classic and saving grace for those of us who have no knack for style.

Seventeen minutes past six now. I walk out on the porch, then come back in, but my mother is in the kitchen, and the prospect of watching the big hand tick its way around the clock face while she chops onions feels harrowing, so I grab some green origami paper, go into the living room. Wait there. I start making a hopping frog.

On the end table by the couch, that damn orchid going downhill fast; above it on the wall, a black-and-white photograph of her, on the old Point Bridge.

She was around seventeen, 1962, I think—the year of El Cid. It was taken quickly. A snapshot. The composition is out of whack. It might have worked if she had been more at the periphery. As it is, she is too central, which throws the whole balance off.

As a child, naturally, I romanticized that photograph, assumed it was taken by my father—and when I learned it was the handiwork of some nameless outsider who worked for the state, I felt something inside overturn. It needled at me—who that man was, what role he had played in her life that warranted his failed shot hanging on our living room wall in its hokey frame.

Her hair is light in this picture, lighter than it is now, very straight. Already there's a wear to her features, that oddity about her. In her eyes. Not the color of them—a muted gray in his image—but the expression. You can see it. Something fugitive. Wind on the road.

It hits me suddenly—pieces, dates, falling together—clickety clack—wheels turning—that look in her eyes—disjoint—it hits me: That snapshot must have been taken right around the time her father's skull rolled out of a dump-load of fill. Neat sweet bullet hole—whose doing? (Silas Varick? Ray's father)—Let's not go there. No, no, no, not now.

Last crease in the paper. Fold Froggy's back legs down. Nice and flat. All done. I set him on the table, press his butt down. He slips out from under my finger, jerks forward, shoots up. Hop.

My bra itches. I should have known. What was I thinking? Anything more elaborate than cotton bugs me—rub of syntheticky lace on the skin—what was I thinking? I go upstairs, pull that calamity off—replace it with one that is sensible—then, I am grateful he is late—another example of destiny's logic in hindsight—what a waltz—the timing could not be more perfect: I am coming down the stairs, he drives in.

As we turn onto Pine Hill Road, he asks where I want to go to eat.

"Not where I work."

"That leaves a few options. You call it."

He's got that half smile on again, the smile that has begun to feel brutally unsafe. He is watching the road. Thin sheens in his hair I've just noticed, around his ears. Grays, I realize. It comes as a shock. My small-town icon. And it strikes me he might be nervous. He couldn't be nervous. But I suddenly wonder how many dates he's been on since he split with his wife, or would I be the first—a daunting thought. I try to recall the details: splinters of discontent, then some nasty indiscretion on her part, Ray is giving her the house for their daughter's sake, a noble gesture that makes my brother balk. He calls Ray's ex the "high priestess of cuntism," which he'll temper in my presence to "Hi-C."

Growing up, the truth is, I had such a crush on Ray, heart-thudding, and of course he barely noticed that my shadow struck earth. Except once, I remember, in winter. I must have been around eleven. I was out in the yard breaking icicles off the pine needles, sucking on them, when I saw Ray and Alex tearing up the rise toward the house. Ray was way ahead, his jacket flying. He gave a shout as he tagged the shed, then stopped to catch his breath. His skin was olive pale, cheeks flushed, his lips dark dark, his eyes shot around, then fell on me and stayed. There was a stump of icicle in my mouth, I remember the freezing wet melt, how it clicked against my teeth, the acrid taste of pine resin—and his eyes on my face filled with some kind of thing I had no language for.

"No thoughts yet?" he is asking me now.

That's hardly the issue, I think.

He keeps straight past the split, on the old road. We are heading south—away from most eateries.

"Let's go somewhere innocuous," I say.

"Does that translate: non-local?"

"The only local place I ever really loved was Manchester's."

"That's a moot point now. Besides, their food was lousy."

"Yeah, but who went for the food?"

He makes the right onto Hixbridge, down Potato Hill, then turns onto Drift. We pass the farm that used to belong to one of my great-grandfathers—that used to be a farm—is houses now.

You drive through town, and every road you turn down holds some littered vestige—the name of a brook, a glen, an old wall one of them built, or a house where some were born, lived, married, died, pulling rocks out of the same fields for two hundred years. You're wrapped in it.

When you first come home, you can't help but feel a certain nostalgia. You see the idyll of the place—you see it like a person from away might—that tranquil New-Englandy beauty, swathes of open land still left, the village at the Point, those cedar-shingled saltbox houses, the double-forked branch of the river, sea running into the land.

It's a particular point of earth—you come home, and the light here is like nowhere else. You think to yourself, I can do this. So you stay.

Where the trees break here and there, I can see the river. The sun is behind us, on its plunge.

I tell him I want to go to the Outback, up on Route 6.

He laughs. "Let me guess—for the atmosphere?"

"I like that fake Aussie stuff."

"So Outback it is."

We pass the brook where Susannah Howe was found, pregnant and drowned, in water that never would have seemed deep enough for drowning. This is the flip side, of course. It's like they smell you back—the more recently dead—they bide their time, give you some play with your rose-colored frames, then start swinging their feet. Gritty lovely warp of a world.

Ray is asking me about the new section of the restaurant they're pulling together—got all their permits in place, I tell him, they're slated to open mid-July—outdoor picnic style, modeled after that in-the-rough lobster place down in Connecticut. Red-and-white check-ered tablecloths. You get your ticket, take your food on a plastic tray. For the summer-people patrons who want to slum it for a night.

As the road straightens, Pard Islington's house comes into sight up ahead. I see him out front, not Pard of course, Pard died two weeks ago. Even with the welder's hood on, the flame bursting out the end of the torch, sparks flying, I know it is Huck. He is standing in the midst of disassembled tractor parts, welding some sort of bracket to an old chassis, hunks of scrap metal all over the yard.

No, I think. I think it hard even as the truck slows. Please don't stop. No. Please.

Ray pulls the truck onto the shoulder of lawn. Kills it. Leaves the key in the ignition. And me, no choice but to follow.

To the right of the house, a whitewashed flagpole, two flags strung up, worn by wind and rain; one the Stars and Stripes, the other with its Gadsden rattler. DON'T TREAD ON ME. Huck flips up his welder's hood as we walk over. It's been a while since I've seen him close up. He looks about the same as I remember, only old now, too.

There's a dog lying on a welcome mat set among the junk—Pard's mutt—half Lab, half something more menacing. It cocks its head, eyes trailing us, then lies back down.

"So this is it?" Ray says, surveying the tractor in its half-assembled state thus far.

"She'll be the ticket," Huck says, voice like dry bark. "Queen of the homemade class." With the torch, he points to the beer keg strapped to the chassis. "That there's my fuel tank."

Huck nods at me. "How you doing?" Gives me a queer look. Hasn't it always been a queer look from Huck?

There's a graphic on his T-shirt, a print that reads: CO-ED NAKED FOUR WHEELING. My girlish euphoria begins to deflate as it hits me in a less abstract way that the guy I've got this hot thing for is the younger brother of the knucklehead standing before me.

And if the shirt were not enough, or perhaps to test out where my loyalties fall, Huck launches into a full-blown invective—he's got XM in his truck now but he's still hooked on Fox News and is all steamed up—starts blasting on to Ray about the left-wing media conspiracy, how all them stations are on the smear against Bush, so busy pointing fingers and wringing their hands over the mess at Abu Ghraib, they neglect to mention the rising price of oil, how those sand sambos have us all by the balls.

Chatty for a Yankee. I'll give him that. Weevil-minded racist sputter stuck, ever so stuck, in the feudal, futile muck of this town.

I just stand there, trying not to listen, as the reasons why I left this place—why I keep leaving—stockpile.

Once or twice in the course of his harangue, Huck's eyes pull from Ray, clip onto me. Again that look, like it's just not registering for him, even though he's distilled and conquered the big-picture political concerns that face our nation today, he just cannot reconcile what *I* am doing here. Flapper-cropped fartsy bluestocking. Slip-slide-away-wannabe-city girl. Snob. Interpreting his look—no challenge—it does strike me that I may be pegged even a notch or two lower on his totem pole than he is on mine.

There's a stain on the leg of his jeans. Engine grease laundered-in. Set. The shape of Madagascar.

Here's the rub. I hate Huck almost exclusively on principle. I know this. I wish it were more. I wish he had slighted me, made some crass, offensive advance, done something nasty. I wish I had a concrete reason to legitimize my dislike.

Once I made some caustic remark to Alex about Huck and his convictions. Alex gave a little smile and nodded. "Yep. Huckie's just about as judgmental as you."

I remember this now, wishing I hadn't, and thankfully, Huck has moved on. A more neutral topic: the upcoming July Agricultural Fair. The main attraction of the year in these parts, even beating out Christmas. Huck's telling Ray the story about how he and Pard drained that beer keg and got the idea just about a week before Pard shit the bed.

The dog gives a short bark.

"What's your problem, Dutchess?" Huck says. For one terrible instant, I think he is talking to me.

"Is she yours now?" Ray asks.

"Yeah. She always liked me better anyhow."

There are flowers planted in short intentional rows along either side of the back steps. An NRA bumper sticker peeling with the green paint from the screen. The flowers, though—iris in bloom—and some other young bulby green things shooting up as well. I never would have taken Pard to be the sort who took to setting flowers.

Ray has noticed me looking at them. He cups his hand near one of the taller iris, holding it without holding it, not letting the bloom touch his skin. Knowing I can't, I swear I can see the shadow of the color in his palm. As if I'm nearer than I am. As if the air is a fluid that color steeps through. As if.

You feel it in the body—this kind of desire—a storm in the body.

"Alright then," Ray says, addressing me, "are you ready?"

I nod.

"Good luck with it, Huckie," he says. "See you, Dutchess." We walk back toward the truck. He opens the door for me, then climbs in on his side. We drive away.

I glance into the side mirror, see Huck in the yard by the dismembered metal hulk of the homemade, Huck there in his welder's hood, Madagascar jeans and CO-ED NAKED T-shirt, Huck holding his torch, his small-town petty smallness growing every second more minute. I watch until the road curves, and he and Pard's house drop from view.

* * *

At the Outback, Ray tries to talk me into splitting a Bloomin' Onion.

"No, thanks," I say.

"You've never tried it."

"I wouldn't like it."

"How do you know, Marne," he says with a smile, "if you've never tried?"

Kind of like being done up the back door. "Some things I know," I say.

It was true, what I told him before about this place. I've always noticed it. How everything here is arranged in such a way that you never wind up looking out the window. You've got the air-conditioning and the twitters coming at you—the "g'day matie" talk, the kangaroo boomerang décor—it's easy to forget the Route 6 strip outside—the mall and drone of evening traffic; the hot fetid smell of exhaust; the fainter stink of trash.

The waitress has come with our drinks. She flips out her pad. "Are you ready?" she asks.

I'll have to think about that.

Ray orders a steak. No surprise there. And one of those onions.

I opt for the Queensland Salad, with grilled chicken, double on the jack cheese, but no cheddar. And no diced egg. The waitress is scribbling, making her 86s.

I tell her I am in her boat. I hate people who order like me.

Her eyes lift, a blank look.

"Dressing on the side," I add.

"It's always on the side," she murmurs, collecting our menus. "Anything else?"

"She's all done," Ray says. The waitress walks away.

"You probably shouldn't make that assumption," I remark.

"You love to be difficult, don't you?"

"It's really no effort."

He smiles.

I study his face. Try to remember the first time I laid eyes on him. It's harder than I expect. He was underbrush in my world before I struck it. He is familiar to me that way.

He tells me he was late picking me up because he ran into his sister-in-law Claire, Junie's widow, up at Cumberland Farms when he stopped for gas.

"I told her I was on my way to pick you up, and she said she was at Polly's last month, bought two of those little paper vases you make, the ones with the violets."

"I never see Claire anymore," I say. "Haven't seen her since I've been home. She's not remarried, is she?"

"No. That won't happen."

Claire taught in the middle school. Fifth-grade math. She retired the year I graduated and, after Junie died, went on to spend the greater part of her days eating éclairs in the bedroom, tuned to the police scanner.

"Junie was the golden one," Ray is saying. "The hero. The peacemaker. He was the one my mother couldn't keep her eyes off of. We all looked up to him, even Huck. When my father was being a nut, Junie stepped in, watched out for us. He was so sure of himself, always seemed to know just what he was about."

It surprises me—not what he says, but the change in his expression, the shift in his voice. Some sad, darker kind of honesty, almost a weariness I am not used to seeing in him. Apart from Huck, Ray rarely talks about his family. Never mentions his father, certainly not to me. He didn't grow up under that roof—his mother left Silas the year he was born—still, from what I've heard, his father would come around, make trouble, rope the boys into it—Ray's brother Green an obvious casualty of that. Silas was a drunk, and violent, more than likely the one who planted that bullet in my grandfather's skull. That's the open secret anyway—but the one you talk around.

I didn't know Junie well. He was much older, the oldest of the Varick brothers. Pard's yard couldn't hold a candle to Junie's: a wall of lobster pots piled as high as the garage, bait barrels running the length of the stone wall, a seafoam-green Chevrolet and five or six old boats, one with a busted hull, goldenrod sprouting out of it. He kept sheep down back.

You did feel, though, that if the world went to hell in a handbasket, Junie was one you'd want to stick around. He was old school. Broke down deer tails to make his fishing flies. Survival-of-the-fittest type. All male. Food, water, shelter. Competent with guns.

I remark on this now to Ray, and he laughs. "He could get pretty testy about property lines. Spent the last two years before he died bucking some neighbor who wanted him to clear out that junk, plant some hydrangeas."

"And there was that letter—" I say.

"What letter?"

"Oh, I loved that letter." And I tell him how when I was in California, Alex sent me a copy of a Letter-to-the-Editor Junie wrote when the Concom issued a cease-and-desist against him for cleaning his brook without a permit.

Ray rolls his eyes. "Oh yeah. That letter."

"Quite erudite, I'd say."

He gives me a look. "Be careful what you warm up to, Marne—"

"No way, that letter was perfect. Elegant, arch tone—how did that last bit go? . . . wait, no don't tell me, I remember . . . citing certain folk who seem to have gotten a twitch in their knickers over the fate and dwindling habitat of an extremely rare four-toed salamander. And yet, given the recent spike in property taxes, might they not all have it ass-backward about which local species were most at risk for becoming endangered. Ha! It was brilliant, Ray. I loved that letter, laughed for days out there in sunny California."

His hand is on his water glass, his thumb stroking absently over the narrowing part near the base. "Good old-fashioned streak of the Libertarian."

"Might that be a euphemism?" I ask.

He glances up. "Might be."

What strikes me, of course, is how he says it. How he seems to have learned to take it in stride. I mention this.

He shrugs. "In one ear and out the other."

"Is that how you take, say, just for instance, Huck, and how he goes on about, you know, his views?" I ask this with some delicacy—it's a bit of a strain.

"Huck's who he is," Ray answers carefully.

You got that right, I think.

His eyes on my face are a kind of greenish brown; hazel you could call them, but darker, and that slight scar near his mouth—that scar I thought was new, it occurs to me now that maybe I was wrong, maybe it's been there awhile. He is looking at me like he is weighing what I am saying and what I'm not. Looking like he might add something else. He shakes his head. "It was Huck who wrote that letter."

"No!"

He smiles now. "Yep. Junie was just plain pissed, said if he had his way, he'd lynch about half of them. Huckie drafted that letter up at the Kozy Nook one morning, gave it to Junie to sign."

A wave of unease ripples through me. "There's no way Huck wrote that letter."

"How did you put it? Erudite. Elegant—" He is laughing, teasing me now. "Like I say, Marne. Let it go in one ear and out the other."

"You really think it's that simple."

"What am I going to do? Change their minds?"

"You're never tempted?" The moment the word's off my tongue, I regret it.

He smiles. "Not by that."

I fiddle with the unscrew top of my root beer, surprised the server left it. Past the obvious necessary utensils, steak knives and the like, we are taught, as a caste, not to leave extraneous sharp objects behind.

I think of that tall iris, out front of Pard Islington's house. Ray's hand cupped underneath it, the vivid stain of color shedding through.

I glance at him, his eyes track something, someone behind me. He gives a curt wave, and I look over my shoulder in time to see Denny Morrison slide into a corner seat at the bar. Denny's of the same year as Ray and a regular just about everywhere. Lost his license on DUIs. Still drives his sister's car. Hitches his way here and there. He'll turn up at the restaurant, loaded, around 10 PM every Friday. He's got a glass eye. One with a palm tree painted on it reserved for Friday nights. A few weeks ago I got off work early and was having a beer before I dragged home, I sat with Denny at the bar. He popped out that palm-tree eye for me, swirled it around in a shot glass.

"Guy's got one hell of a liver," I remark.

"Yeah sure," Ray says. "A real testament to miracles."

Then I hear it—those first few notes, unmistakable, on the restaurant soundtrack, between a deluge of bad ABBA and Men at Work,

some bored and prescient employee has slipped in Don McLean—
one you almost never hear in restaurants, more than likely because it's
one of those songs you can't chew mindlessly to—your fork pauses,
midair, food in mid-swallow—hunger is relative, too.

I tell Ray my theory of "American Pie." "You know what it is that
makes this song," I say, "that makes it endless and inescapable. It isn't
just lyrical genius. It's all the vague little utterances he cut in between
the words—all his little glitches and stammerings, his little growls, the
awws and the ohhs and the ands and the buts and the 'Well I, Man I,
So come on now—' "

He is giving me a skeptical look. Understandably so. A slightly different smile, like there's some joke going on just off to the side of me.

"I'm telling you," I say, "you try to sing this song without that con-
nective tissue stuff, it falls flat."

"You've tried?"

"Of course I've tried."

He starts laughing. "Give it up, Marne."

"No, no. I'm telling you, it's true." Realizing, even as I keep rant-
ing on, so insistent on what might seem so apparently irrelevant and
small, I sound like a lunatic, and for a moment I think I should clam it,
quit my raving. But isn't it better we lay out the impasses up front?

"Missy Pie," I say, "would have been a totally different piece if
McLean had tidied it up. Epic still, for sure, you can't beat that story,
but squeaky clean and neat and dull. Not the kind of wild catechism
you hope to impale yourself on. I'm right," I say. "Listen. Listen." And
as the music quickens, moving out of the intro into the main, I reach
across the table, put my fingers near his lips, not touching, though. He
watches me, past my own hand, laughing still, not out loud, but I can
see it in his eyes.

> *and do you have faith in God above,*
> *if the Bible tells you so.*
> *Awww—*

He goes to catch my hand near his face, I slip it back, but smile.

"It's true," I say. "The song is full of those between bits. Every version of it. I've got three different cuts on my iPod, two live, and it all comes down to the same thing. You have to trust me."

His face sobers then. "Alright," he says. "I will."

Uh-oh. Uh-oh. My fuckup.

"You think I'm a nut," I say, backpedaling. "Don't you?"

"Is that what you want me to think?"

"I can see by the look on your face that's what you're thinking."

"Actually it's not."

Oh no.

"Actually," he says, "I was thinking I've never really known anyone quite like you." Which is of course a statement, three words more than I can absorb, that leaves me completely undone.

"I need to be clear," I say. "I am thoroughly replaceable."

He grins. "I'll make a note."

"I can't cook."

He doesn't answer.

"Not a thing," I say.

"There's the grilled cheese."

"That's the extent of it. Why do you think I live at home?"

"Is that why?"

"Work in restaurants?"

He laughs.

"And I kill plants. Indoor. Outdoor. You name it—"

"The gamut."

"You know the old adage, Ray—all the fish in the sea."

"I've heard it."

He leans back in his seat, his eyes dark in the funky overhead light, this stale indoor restaurant light I'm suddenly not so enamored with anymore. There's a baby crying several booths away. A mother hushing.

"You are working so hard to convince me," he says.

It has started again, that thudding in my chest so loud I am sure he can hear it. A different feeling, lower down.

The waitress has brought our food. Bless you. Her name is Karen. Bless you, Karen. Gears shift when the food arrives. Buffer on the table. Intimacy blown back. In the background now, McLean's masterpiece is winding down.

I rein myself in, cut off a piece of on-the-barbie chicken. I cut along the black tic-tac-toe of the grill line. As a kid, I kept my food in piles. Ate in order. Green things first. Then potatoes. Meat last. I couldn't stand anything getting mushed up together. Even touching. Something to do, perhaps, with being my mother's daughter, needing to be unlike her. Just about from the get-go. I couldn't stand it when worlds blended and lines blurred.

"How's your chicken?" Ray asks.

"They don't spare the salt. That's a good thing, though, in my book."

"So tell me more," he says, "about California."

What to tell really? They do a lot of hiking, biking, surfing, out there. A lot of Pilates. But they don't fuck like we do on the East Coast. I decide not to cite this. So what else? The obvious selling point—it's as far west as you can go without falling into the next ocean.

I started in LA. Hooked up with an old boyfriend from my New York life, who rented a basement apartment I called The Cave, after Plato. He was an actor, had been in soaps and a Levi's print ad I'd actually seen. I moved in with him having no other real anchor, no reason not to, but I lasted there less than three months. The sun shining day after day—the slick of the men, the acid-peeled youth of the women—that jaded, interminable sunshine drove me clear out of my mind—I slipped off—a bag of clothes, two boxes of books—slipped north to San Francisco where the moods of the weather were more my style.

I tell Ray this easily. It's practiced, glib, a real-seeming story. True in the factual sense. And he nods, satisfied apparently. I don't mean to do it, to lie, exactly, I don't want to start out on that foot with him. And yet. I spear a piece of lettuce with my fork. It is too much, I think, to bare too much. So much to feel—

Years before I saw Cocteau's film, I read the myth of Orpheus and even young, I understood: she tricked him. Eurydice. Ran all the way back to the underworld to keep herself free.

"I liked California," I say.
"But you left."
"Yes, well, I'm not known for my unassailable logic."
He looks at me—the look I've seen before that makes it feel like he's stepping down on a corner of me, keeping me close.
What can I say that is true?
Sometimes late, when I get home from work and can't sleep, I go out for a run. The world at night is water. Scents. Sound. The less dominant senses, shelved off to the side in daylight, are tall. Acute.
You meet yourself differently at night. You are shadow and breath, and the moon is there, of course, and it is beautiful. It hits your skin, and you are luminous, incandescent, with a borrowed glow that is not and has never been yours. Oh yeah. *There's* a thought to fling across the table at him—
He is more than halfway through his steak. He's telling me now about a bike he has. A '69 Triumph Bonneville. He bought it in pieces—kept the pieces in milk crates in his garage until he'd collected them all, then built it back.
The echo of course is not lost on me. Parallel acts of reconstruction. One brother's milk crates of Bonnie-parts, the other with his scrap metal, his chassis and beer keg.
They are so different, I tell myself. They couldn't be more different.

Ray has always had bikes. Once, in the car with my father, waiting for the light at Hixbridge, I saw Ray come flying up Handy Hill. It was a different bike then, a Kawasaki, I think, some rice-burner. I recognized him easily. No one wore helmets back then. His girlfriend at the time was up on the bitch seat behind him. She had black hair, big tits, played ultimate Frisbee. That day they blew by on his bike, she was in short shorts and a yellow halter top. So much skin, I remember thinking at the time. If they took a digger, it wouldn't be pretty. But Ray Varick wasn't the kind who'd let a girl fall.

He has finished eating. He pushes his plate away. "Can I get you to split a dessert?" he asks.

"Depends on my choices."

He shakes his head, again that half smile, and plucks the dessert menu from the metal clip-stand behind the condiments. He starts reading it off. "Chocolate Thunder from Down Under."

"You're shitting me."

"Nope."

"What else?"

"Sydney's Sinful Sundae."

I reach for the card. "Let me see that—"

He holds it away. "You don't like either of those?"

"Something more simple. Ice cream?"

"Vanilla?"

"That would do."

"Come on. Where's your sense of adventure?"

"Fell by the wayside."

"All of it?"

"Just about."

He waits then, straight-faced, keeping that dessert menu out of my reach. Waits.

"Alright," I say.

"Alright?"

"I want a ride on that bike of yours."

"I want to see you naked."

I burst out laughing. "Well, it's a damn good thing, Ray, you don't lay all your cards down at once."

"Don't worry," he says, slipping the dessert menu across to me. "I don't."

PART IV

THE ROAD

LIGHTBULB

JANE
July 23, 2004

"You know what I love about this game, Janie?" Ada says to me now. "You can have the idea of a word, you can be close, almost there, but you don't quite have the letters you need to make it happen. You're a trifle short. One letter short. And you hope it'll all come together. You reckon without the host and take a chance, hoping you'll draw just what you need. And sometimes you do. Sometimes you reach your hand into the box, pull out that one letter you were looking for. And sometimes, you reach your hand in and get skunked."

She is relaxed now. Chatty. Why shouldn't she be? Seventy-two points ahead.

She unpacks her lunch: a ham sandwich, orange crackers, a ziplock bag of chocolate-covered macadamia nuts.

She won't eat the sandwich. She'll nibble a few of the orange crackers, offer me one though we both know I won't take it, and then slowly, through the course of the game, she'll snack away on those macadamia nuts, her fingers, nails glossed that fire-engine red, slipping daintily into the plastic, withdrawing them one by one without making a sound.

"Sun's bright," she remarks.

"Is."

She shifts on the bench toward the shade.

She starts in again, talking about Huck and the skiff, the argument they had.

"Driving me all over hell's half-acre about that damn boat," she says. "This morning was the worst, him yip-yapping on about the bottom, the rot and the leaks and how long it took this spring for the wood to get tight, so much salt and dirt and paint stuck in those seams, and I told him, if he hadn't tried to rescue that stupid woman in the daysailer gone aground on the flat up the west branch last summer—tore the cleat off the transom doing that, I tell you, Janie—this morning, I almost gave him what for."

"He's nuts about you, Ada."

"He's a pain in the neck."

I move an I on my rack, place it after the X. "You wouldn't know what to do without him."

"I'd have one long glorious stretch of peace and relaxation."

"You get that anyhow," I say lightly. Her hand, moving toward the bag of chocolates, stops.

"That wasn't so nice."

I smile. "You're always the first to say, Ada, no one gets out alive."

"You're just sore I'm winning."

I laugh. "You won't be winning long."

She pauses for a moment. "Why is it you always go to bat for Huck?"

"I don't."

"Always try to sell me a bill of goods about how wonderful he is."

"That's not it," I say.

"What then?"

I don't answer. I remember he fell one day coming out of the wharf store—it was years ago, he was just a boy—on the run that day, trying to catch up with me, to return my book I'd left behind on the counter by mistake. He came flying out of the store, tripped, went sprawling—how confused he seemed, that pained, bewildered look—he was sweet on me, I realized, I glimpsed it in his face. How young he seemed that day, so much younger even than he must have been at the time—I remember his pant cuffs unhemmed.

He wasn't anyone who really crossed my mind. Not in that way. I was older, and he was Ada Varick's son. "That woman." There was another time, though, this even farther back. My father was alive and I was walking with him up at the Head and Huck passed us, gave me a nudge going by, threw his hip out, and his hip caught mine. My father reached back, quick—I'd never seen my father move so fast—he grabbed Huck hard by the arm. I saw his fingers twist, Huck's wrist seeming to melt into my father's closing hand, the skin color turned. My father's back was to me, but I heard him say—"*You* keep away from my girl."

I play a little word, F-I-D. Off the E in T-I-N-C-T-U-R-E, Ada runs M-O-R-E-L back. Edible mushroom. Nightshade.

My mind has begun to click. Seeing words. Combinations of words. Hooks on the board exposed. Colored number squares I can nail a high-point letter to. Thinking ahead. One move, two moves out. Seeing words I can build off words.

I set the X above the I in F-I-D, and make XI twice. On the across, the I tags a pink double word. Thirty-three points.

"There you go," she remarks. "Starting in with your dinks."

"Just like you called it, Ada."

I reach to draw my new letters, her hand reaching to put down her next word almost brushes mine, brief, that touch, half imagined, a dragonfly's wing, flutter of air pushed away.

She sets down H-E-I-S-T for sixteen. I have drawn the J—love it—

another eight-pointer—and I've still got an H and a Y—good balance in my rack between those high scorers and the little vowels you need to make them work.

It's a key. That balance. Hard to keep.

Above M-O-R-E-L, I make H-A-J, the J working twice, J-O—sweetheart—the H nabs a triple-letter square.

"What is that?" Ada says. "Haj?"

"Thirty-four altogether."

"And what the heck does it mean?" she asks, irked.

"I used to know," I say, and smile.

She gives a little snort, sets down an I and an N, predictable, to make J-O-I-N. Doubled. Twenty-two. Not so much.

I lay down C-O-Y parallel to H-A-J, weaving more dinks on the vertical. O-H. Y-A-M. Words interlocking into words. Edging back. Picking away at her lead.

"You're going to build us both right into that corner," she says, her voice casual, but under that veil she is all in a snit. "What is it, Janie, you like so much about a corner?"

I draw an S—desirable S. The second V.

"Two walls at your back," I answer. "What's not to like?"

She shakes her head. "You just can't think like that."

I need to, Ada, sometimes, think like that.

Slight rips in the surface. It's tattered stuff. This world of the seen. Dribs and drabs of the other slinking through. Why not a corner?

I know better though than to pose that reasoning aloud to Ada. Not the sort of logic a woman like her will buy.

I tally the score—close again now—fourteen points only between us.

Ada is studying the board, frowning at the growing asymmetry of it, the upper left quadrant still somewhat open, but the other edges thickening, shunted down. My doing. I take my cheese sandwich from the bag in the shade and unwrap it; wet stains through the paper, tomato seeds in their juice drip. I wipe them on the napkin. A crow shrieks, somewhere in the pine trees.

Her hands touch the word toward the right of the grid we have built thus far. That one she played early on. W-E-L-K-I-N. A lovely word. It must strike her that way as well. More than ordinary. Vault of the sky. She straightens the tiles.

She's only talked to me once about Green. Rarely mentions him by name. Only did that one time, a month or so after Vivienne died. When we met here for Scrabble that day, it was just the two of us, Ada and me. And at one point, Ada groaned about what slow going it was, without the irrepressible Vivi to buoy things up, didn't the game just seem to drag, tiles in the box-lid lasting forever.

She asked me then if I'd ever noticed how one loss seemed to bring up every other. She looked at me, saying it, as she will sometimes, because she knew this would be a thing I'd understand. Loss is exactly this way, of course, and I nodded because I knew, and I nodded because I needed her to go on—a knot tight and sudden in my throat— I needed her to be the one to tell the story, the one who kept telling it. And she told me then how ten days before Junie's boat went down off Georges Bank, she was messing around in her bedroom closet looking for a sweater, a brown cardigan with hand-cut shell buttons she knew was in there, but somehow couldn't find, and she flicked the light-switch on the closet wall, and the bulb flared, then shorted out, and she messed around in the closet some more, and finally gave up finding the sweater and took another to wear instead. She forgot all about that bulb being out until ten days later when she got the news about Junie's boat and the storm they'd run into that took them down, and then it seemed that bulb being out in the closet was all she could think about—Yes, it is this, isn't it? The littlest thing can keep you distracted, a blown bulb, a screen door come slightly off one hinge— some sort of small household thing, fixable of course—you keep your mind set on that so the edges of what you know and do not want to know soften, so you won't lose yourself looking into the glare because the sharpest grief is not dark—it is bright, endless, an insoluble glare.

For Ada then, that little thing to cling to was a blown bulb in her dressing closet, and she started in on Huck about that bulb, asking him to replace it for her and, being Huck, of course, he didn't listen, kept putting her off, and finally she dragged a chair in, climbed up on it, and went to fix that light herself, and as she was screwing the new bulb in, must have gripped it too tightly, because the glass broke in her hand, and she felt it cut her, felt it and didn't feel it both at the same time—and it struck her then, she told me, standing there on that chair in the dark of the closet, that maybe, there was no difference between feeling and not feeling, maybe in fact it didn't matter none at all if a light was out or her hand was cut and so she squeezed and still couldn't feel it, couldn't feel anything, but heard a soft wet grinding in her palm and the crinkling of glass. And it was Huck who came into the room and found her there. "Aw, Ma," he said, "I told you I would get to it." And she turned on him then. "But you didn't," she practically screamed, "I kept asking, and asking, and you didn't, and you know, Huck, it was the one thing I asked of you, the one you promised always you'd look after." And Huck looked at her, and she saw the words, the absoluteness of them, strike into his face and the hole those words made going in, and they both knew it wasn't the lightbulb she was talking of, but Green, and Huck being in the car the night Green died, never trying to stop him. And neither of them said a thing for a moment, then Huck told her to go into the bathroom, and get that glass out of her hand, and she went, and while she was soaking it there in the sink, letting the water run to rinse out the cut, she could hear him in the closet, sweeping up the rest of it, only moving quiet-like and slow, not like Huck, but someone else who took their time. When she came out of the bathroom again, he was gone, and there was a new bulb screwed in, so bright, it was harsh, and she stood awhile in the doorway of that closet, her hand on the switch. She snapped the light out, snapped it on, off again, on again, and she knew there was a fraction-of-a-second lapse, a moment lost, between the time that light changed, and the time it took her eyes to see it change.

So minute, that skip in time, in itself so infinitesimal, you, Ada, me, on again, off, on, and standing on the floor of that closet, it wasn't Junie you were thinking of, but Green, *how one loss will bring up every other*, only Green it seemed somehow, you told me, you could not stop thinking of, like that distance of the twenty years since you'd lost him had collapsed, and everything you should have felt when it happened but didn't—don't I know this?—rushed up from the bottom of where you had stuffed it down, and you were left staring over the brink of how, for example, as a baby, teething, he used to chew on the ends of his sleeves, you'd be folding his clothes, those small baby clothes, matching up the arms, and find the little shirt-cuff ends gnawed to thread.

Like you, Green loved the night, loved the sky. The only boy of yours who did, and older, he would wander out to find you sitting in your lawn chair at the telescope on clear nights when the seeing was good. You would take turns at the eyepiece. You named the stars for him, taught him their magnitudes, their distances, traced out constellations with your hand. But it was the moon he was enthralled by. That nondescript near satellite. It's grandly monikered features: Bay of Rainbows. Sea of Crises. Lake of Dreams. He was a boy of the lunar age, Apollo missions, the space race and the Cold War that it stood for.

There were other things, too, you told me that day. Things you did not know you had forgotten—it can happen like this, can't it?

I remember your face. On it a haunted shredded look. Not you. Not your face as I see it now. I remember how I kept nodding, how I needed you to keep talking, keep telling the story, your story that could have been mine, as we converged, each detail of your story unlocking a small piece of me, set it floating, set it free. As you spoke, I tried to match the things you said about Green against what I remembered. I hadn't known him well. I'd heard he was real smart, but different. Didn't talk much. Kept to his own. Carl told me that Green would crawl into the backseat of one of his older brothers' cars, ride down with them to Horseneck to watch the races they used to hold Sunday afternoons in the off-season, in the new state beach parking lot.

I would see him sometimes, Green, just walking by. Digging his way up to the Head, hands shoved in his pockets, walking alone down the center of the road like he owned it.

Ada has played her turn, made the word E-X-I-T, and drawn new tiles. She is quiet now, her mouth set, studying the letters in her rack. I glance down at the sheet of paper, the columns of tallied numbers under our names. I have not drawn a line dividing them, and it occurs to me that perhaps I should have. To keep us separate, I think.

The shadow of my hand, the shadow of the pen against the page, like the ink is flowing out of the shadow.

"It's your go, Jane," Ada murmurs.

This morning, as I was crossing over the metal draw of the new span, it was Huck that caught my eye, funny Huck working out of his rickety old skiff, upriver. That familiar solitude.

Vivienne told me once about the little hurricane house where Ada lives with Huck now. It was in the mid-seventies, she told me, not long after Green died in Huck's arms wedged together in that crushed car and Silas finally got around to doing what most figured he would and strung himself up in his barn. It was then that Ada had the hurricane house moved from the farm on Horseneck Road where it had washed up on the riverbank when Hurricane Carol struck in '54.

The roof was falling in, that whole little dump of a house falling into itself, but Swig and Junie moved it for her, down onto one of those postage-stamp lots behind the town beach that were selling back then for a song. Ada put a bunch of antiques in and some kitschy stuff, with the thought of renting it. She hired Huck to fix the roof, because he was such a loose cannon, no one else would give him work. Even Junie, who had his own dragger by then, had quit letting Huck fish trips. So Ada hired him to fix up that little house for her. She'd go by every week or so to see how things were getting on, and each time she stopped in, she'd notice another piece of something missing. One week it was a lamp, the next week a clock, then a sterling-silver sugar bowl. She knew what he was doing. She didn't call him on it, though, just watched the rooms in that little house gradually empty and, in the end, she wound up not renting it after all. Huck's wife, the carpetbagger, left him, and Ada let him move into that hurricane house until he got back on his feet. He's been there since.

This morning, crossing over the new span and seeing Huck out there on the river, I paused. Huck still rising from the ashes of all that. I raised my hand, the quirky little wave my father used to give, then looked away, looked west and swore I saw it—the old bridge—the echo of it. Nascent. Like the air still held it, somehow.

HURRICANE HOUSE

HUCK, FOURTEEN
Winter 1962

Colder than a witch's tit, his teeth clacking in his head, as they started walking back toward the Point Bridge, the crunch of frozen grass under their boots—and he could still feel the gash at the side of his temple, the pain smart in it from where that motherfucking nitwit Eejit checked him with the stick—the blood in its wormy trickle down the side of his face gone hard now. The three of them—Huck, Pard, and Robbie Taylor—walked together, the nitwit Eejit dragging behind ten yards, knowing he's out, lugging those sissy figure skates. And Pard asking Huck if he saw that tall man by the tree, who the hell was that and what was he up to—out for an arctic stroll? Yeah sure. Just hanging around, eyeballing them from behind that tree. Saw him, Huck answered, it was that city nutter mick bridge engineer with the duck-butt hair come down to Clerk the Works, maybe thinking he'd kick them off the bog, tell them they got no business playing stick hockey on his state land. He gave a spit. Got no business. Pervert fream.

From his coat pocket, he fished out the broken piece of stick they'd been using for a puck and threw it. Where it touched white earth, it sank, leaving the shadow of itself through the hole where it fell and was gone.

His hands were good and numb, all chapped up, and the sweat on him starting to freeze, a rim of it like crust at the back of his neck, by the time they reached his uncle Swig's house, five doors up from the Paquachuck Inn, and Huck's knocking on the door, banging till it opens, asking Swig to give them a ride home across town. That squarehead Eejit hanging around by the front gate, thinking he'll mooch a drop, too—well, he can just fucking walk, shuckster, two miles whatever, that's his own damn shame.

A seal down by the rocks at the Foot of the Lane, its fat self lolling on the ice as they drive by into the last of the light draining out of the sky. They head north, up Horseneck Road, past the Almy place toward Bald Hill, Swiggie driving. Being a broad-shouldered man, sizable, taking up a good half of the cab, the three boys scrunched to-gether on the rest of the seat, Swig hits out a cigarette, steering with his knee, lights up, smoking, they're all breathing that in, wanting some, Huck asking if they can split one butt between them, and Swig shaking his head with a smile, the tobacco drawn down, that black-flecked orange glow, the cigarette perched out the side of his mouth. They pass the chicken farm, the sign that reads GRAVES DUG AT SHORT NOTICE. Robbie gets dropped off at Skunk Alley. Then it's just the three of them in the car. Swig takes a drag in on his cigarette, keeps his eyes on the road.

"You two keeping out of trouble?"

Huck's throat goes dry.

"Yeah sure," Pard answers for them. None of the three of them speaks for what they all know. Huck feels his head begin to swim, words and no words and the smoke in the car. He cracks the window, lets the cold dusk in. He looks down at Pard's knee pressed against his, sees the patch on the leg his mother, Ada, had sewed on—they were his old pants, he was younger but taller than Pard, when he outgrew those pants, Pard took them on.

They drive the next half mile in silence, drop Pard at his house.

"Poor kid, going home to nothing," Swig murmurs as they pull back onto the road. Huck doesn't answer. They drive past the pig farm, the market gardener's place with that big-ass rock in the shape of a horse out front Pard's always scheming to steal. At the bend, old Mason's crop of cows nose up to the stone wall, snow on their backs, steam rising off them, stubbled corn in a higher pasture, cut last fall, busted stalks poking up through the drifts.

"Due for another round of the white stuff tonight," Swig remarks. He takes a long drag on his cigarette, then passes it over to Huck, who drags in on it himself, deep. It settles his nerves.

"Finish it," Swig says as they turn off Horseneck Road, down the lane, and pull up in front of the farmhouse.

"Go and be a good kid now, help your mother," his uncle says with a wink. Huck hits the door closed, the truck drives off, a snort of gray smoke out the exhaust, snow spun up under the tires, clouds of snow-dust falling through the blue evening winter light.

They are already good and into it, his mother and father—he feels it the minute he walks through the door. His two older brothers, Junie and Scott, gone, up to Charlie's Diner on Route 6 or to that bar down the Cove in New Bedford, where Scott got into the fight last year with a jigaboo, said the wrong thing and got stabbed. Wherever they've gotten to, they're gone, and just the baby, Green, toddling across the kitchen, a knob of bread clenched to mush in his hot chubby hand, and their father, Silas, sitting at the fireplace, polishing his boots, the kitchen full of bad silence, some mess between them he'd just walked into. His mother setting a saucepan on the stove, but setting it down

harder than she had to, the bang of it, the lid clattering, and the hiss
of whatever was inside sloshing out. That was all it took. His father
slammed the tin of shoeblack on the bench and within a moment had
crossed the room, swung his arm, and backhanded her across the face.
She went flying. From the doorway, Huck watched her go. It was the
only time he realized how light she was, his mother, such a force of nature ordinarily, she in her cranked-up moods stomping around—his
gorgeous combustible mother—her eyes that sparked green which
made you think of things at once safe and fearsome. You'd never realize how slight she really was except in this kind of a moment, when she
and his father got into it, and it came to this sort of end—he marveled
at it—the room gone into a deep, almost holy still—the hushed snap
of the fire, and no other sound or motion but her beautiful self in
noiseless, innocent flight—her body lifted as it was, by just the force
of her husband's hand—her body lifted, bare feet skimming over
the floor like some kind of angel—a moment of celestial lightness before she struck against some hard and larger object—in this case the
cupboard—that broke her flight. A vase on an upper shelf jumped forward, tottered at the edge with the thought of falling, but didn't.

Huck moved then. His body uncoiling like a spring across the
room, an arrow unloosed, he shot past the table, past the baby, staring
stupid, openmouthed, past the stirring heap of her to his father who
was moving in to strike her again. Huck did what one of his older
brothers would have done—Junie, for sure—and got between them,
all 118 pounds of him, he shouldn't have, but did, and a mistake it did
turn out to be. His father whirled around and caught him hard, the
slab of his hand made fast to a fist, cutting up into that softer center
spot between Huck's ribs. The room pitchpoled, ceiling spun, the
overhead light swapping places with the floor, and he was down,
curled up in a fetal ball of himself by the table leg, his mother scream-
ing now, their shadows raged across the wall, the orange glow of fire-
light, the smell of dinner burnt, the baby Green wailing, and once
Huck looked up from where he lay, in a puddle of no breath on the

floor, saw his father with his drunked-up, reddened face looming. He pulled himself to. Didn't think a thing. Just ran.

Out of the house, past the barn and the corncrib set up on its stone pegs, over the first gate and down between the fields, past the dutch-cap to the riverbank, the little hurricane house that washed up there, back in '54. It wasn't much, just a step up from a chicken coop really, and all sinking into itself. They'd made a fort of it, he, Pard, Eejit, and Robbie, left some horse blankets there, a few bottles of soda, a tin of sardines, a pile of J. C. Whitney catalogs. He gets inside now, leans back against the door, a fierce throbbing pain in his chest, like a rib got broke off at the small end, poking into his lungs. The floor's wet, ground and snow leaking through the cracks in the boards, so he climbs up into the loft where it is dry, lies down on the old goose-feather mattress that's got the stink of damp and rot in it but is soft. He gets all in, good and burrowed under, keeps his boots on, just in case. His body cold, he can feel that cold working through him, play-ing like tight fingers down his spine, his brain on the numb, his body shivering, and thoughts coming through, like ice, chunks of brilliant silver, thoughts of how someday he'll kill his father, Silas the bastard, someday when he is old enough, he will, not long now. So what if the fault is half hers? She baits him. Always bringing up old things. She shovels out the blame, all on him, for knocking her up at seventeen, shoehorning her into a life she never wanted. She's bucked her lot since, one way or another, but the one thing all their arguing seems to drain back to is that tangle she got into with Luce Weld. Years old now, that mess, it was a bad bad time until Weld got taken care of. There was a respite then. She cried a lot, Huck remembers this, but seemed softened somehow—it was a time of near peace between his parents—almost a family—he was glad of it even until that tell-all skull rolled out of the fill.

Rumor mill started churning then. Talk was his father, Silas, had done it—and he never denied it, seemed to rise to the occasion—who could blame him really, getting square, getting even. Good riddance, most said, back to apple-pie order. But his mother, Ada, man, did she get wild—started picking away at Silas—about what he did or might have done—pick, pick—she brought it up over and over, Huck didn't know what to do—then like that weren't enough, she turned sassy, got up to her tricks. A toss of that proud pretty head to let her husband know she'd go on doing what and who she wanted, and if he got wind of some dirt she was up to, she didn't give a damn. It was her not caring, Huck knew, that did his father in. Made him fly off the handle. She drove him right over the edge with her carrying-on. He'd lash back, shouting that he had poured his life out for her. Drunk, he'd slur on: about how he'd come home from the war, landed a decent job as manager at Woolworth's, taking that work because he thought maybe wearing a suit and driving into the buzz of the city every day might give him a leg up in her eyes. But she was unimpressed, so he quit that job and came home to putter around on his father's farm, and then his father died, and that farm was his, someone had to work it, and whether he wanted or not, he was that someone, so there he wound up: stuck, puttering, paring cowshit out from under his fingernails, picking hay, sweating, swearing, collaring one of his sons to give him a help, drinking down gin like water, while his slip of a wife fell hook-line-and-sinker for somebody else. Scallywag Weld.

She wasn't easy, and they all knew it, her boys. Even so, they worshipped her. That magnificent flare of her moods, and how at times, as well, she could be so beautiful and calm, sitting by your bed on a night when you had fever, she'd sit there hours with you in the small of the dark, giving you sips of orange juice with crushed ice, her smooth hand on your forehead, the perfect gentle cool of it melting the heat and fear down, and that little song she'd sing sometimes on those nights, how does it go, that song? *You and me, Love,* she would sing. *You and me, everywhere.*

Huck floats through this now. His mind peels loose toward sleep but not quite, his mind into that kind of beyond, like underwater, a soundlessness that's full of sound, what God might be if crap luck had another name.

He hears the door creak below.

"Hey," he calls down, "that you?"

Pard's voice answers. A moment later, his face appears.

"Didn't expect you here," he says, plopping down on the mattress.

"It was noisy up at the house."

Pard grins. "Yeah, well I got home, they were both dead drunk, a bowl of cold potatoes on the table. Figure I'd come down here, have a real meal." With his knife, he starts opening a can of tuna fish. "You want some?"

"Naw," Huck answers. "Thanks."

Pard is like shadow to him, the one he can tell anything to, talk about his screwed-up family—Pard's is only worse, and he knows it all anyhow even if Huck don't say a thing. It's been like that between them—how many years now?—where you don't have to breathe a word and it all gets said.

"I'm going to get up early," Pard is saying now, "get down to the store before they open, see what the bread man left in the box, grab a pie."

"Sounds good."

Pard's finished up his tuna fish, he licks out the can.

"Man, that stuff stinks," Huck says.

Pard laughs, throws the can down from the loft. It clanks onto the floor below. He gets under a blanket, the other side of the mattress. That's how it is when the two of them wind up here on the same night, each takes his own blanket, takes a side. No one's looking to snuggle, just don't want to be alone.

They chat a bit, talk back to the stick-hockey game that afternoon on the bog—and what a rat Eejit was, checking Huck like he did, giving him that scratch on the side of his head.

Outside, the night is quiet, the river frozen, the hum of nothing moving under snow.

He wakes at first light, blinded by a whiteness that covers him, a pale glow radiating up from the blanket and at first thinks he's died in the night and this is the heaven he's woken under, the loft around him strangely lit, his eyelashes frozen some, like there was crying in his sleep. He rubs at his eyes to break the ice up, crinkling to cold dust, he blinks against it, and he can see then that a fine sheet of snow has blown through a crack under the eaves. It covers him, covers half of Pard under the other blanket where he lies, still asleep. The sun is on the rise, it slants through that narrow opening, glints of hoarfrost stuck to the wood and every crystal of snow reflects, ignites, a soft fire, all colors awakening in that whiteness, blue, red, a solemn amber glow, more snow still sifting down. It is all so unlikely, such a fart of a chance and yet so lit, so brief, so breathlessly lovely, and he is wrapped in that transient and exquisite miracle like everything is blessed. Forgiven. Like it could be.

Spring comes fast that year, comes right around the bend—boom— and it's there. Only thin bones of snow left in the ruts and the furrows.

It was a sweet soft day in early April, everything busting out of winter forgetfulness into green, buds on the pussy willows, the sun warm. They were in school—didn't want to be—all four of them in the E class, sitting together in their underdog row by the window, which was open enough to let them know what cloud-nine sunshine they were missing. It was Pard's second year in this class, he was chewing away on his tobacco, and once when he had to take a spit, he opened the dictionary, that doorstop of silvery pages, gave a loud ptooey into it, and slammed the thing shut, the sound so loud and sharp like a rifle crack, Missus teacher spun around, her mousy curls spinning with her, lipstick too hot pink for one so plain. A hard glare at each of them to see who'd done it—she knew it was one of them four—then she turned back to her chalkboard and went on scratching out her nothings. They started to fidget then, to titter and fuss, and saw her stiffen, but she wouldn't turn around again, determined not to let them dupe her twice. She just kept up with her scritch scratching, chalk to the board, and one by one, the four of them slipped out the window into the free and glorious day.

They spent the rest of the morning trouting in the creek, then went back to Robbie's house after noon, to hang out in the backyard bomb shelter his father built, not just one of the shit-pulled-together kind, but the real deal—concrete, fourteen-inch-thick walls, a double air-lock door he got from the navy base over in Newport, a hand pump run through a charcoal filter to clean the air. There were sleeping bags, a Geiger counter, crates of canned food, a water storage drum, a battery-powered radio, a lantern, a first-aid kit, and the four of them, their shoes wet and muddied from the creek, sat in there eating Hershey bars, bags of potato chips, drinking soda they'd boosted from the machine at the gas pumps down at South Westport Corner. That machine didn't work right, all you had to do was put your nickel in balanced on the edge of the slit, keep pressing the button, you'd get three sodas for the price of one.

Sitting in the bomb shelter, Huck could feel the cool hard wall through his shirt, and at one point it struck him that above his head, above all of their heads, there was no sky, only dirt, but they were ready. Ready for commies, krauts, japs, nuke-dumping green men, whatever scrod got sent their way. Robbie Taylor now was talking about his sister, who was friends with Susannah Bell, one set of knockers Susannah had. "Well anyhow," Robbie says, "Susannah's been working down at the Point boardinghouse after school, cleaning rooms, and that engineer, he's roosting there. The duck-butt with the blue-tinted frames. What a tear-ass ride he's got, that cool, fast '57 'Vette. Power flip-top. Those silver coves. Must have made money to beat hell to afford a car like that. So Susannah, well, she cleans his room, and she says that on his desk, tacked to the wall above his typewriter, he's got a picture of Jane Weld."

Huck chokes on his soda, fizzy stuff bubbling up, squirting right out his nose. He glances at Pard. Pard's looking at him, that stoned-over look, dull flat eyes.

"Aw for chrissakes, Huckie," he says with disgust, tossing him a towel. "Soda and snot, you better take that rag home."

It was a stroke of black, like tar across his heart, a thick swift stroke. Pure black he felt when he heard, then felt the same again a week later when he and his brother Junie drove down to the wharf to help Swig launch his boat, and on their way they drove past that Tweed Man's onyx car, silver coves and wide whites, squatting by the curb out front of the boardinghouse—that city sucker motherfucker nutter's car—its rich-as-stink svelte shape, just sitting there in its smug lonesome, windows rolled up ass-tight. He saw that car and felt that black again right through him. What the hell right does he have, that Tweed Man, hack, quill driver, barking through town like he owns things, that Leica on a cord around his neck, snapping pictures, busting out his surveying maps, chatting up the locals who think he's a fream, and barking orders at the union crew who've got no choice but to suck up. What the hell right does he have keeping a picture of Jane Weld up on his wall, like she's some kind of a pinup, like he knew her, like he ever could, when she is what they say about the moon, the dark side of it you never see. Huck hated that man now, hated him not for the car or the dapper clothes, or even for that little pad of paper he was always toting around, ballpoint pen he'd whip out like he was taking notes on all of them; hating him for each of those things, and at the same time, none of them, hating him in the end only for that photograph of her. How the hell did he come by it?—hating the thought of it, the thought of him, hating, because she is who she is, the one girl you don't dare to even think about wanting. Don't even think. You don't. Because she is. And it is only her.

Like a nail scraping at the scab sweet center of you, you think of her and everything goes on the tilt. There's a thud in your chest, a light hammering, and that shallow quick beat of running low on air. The thought of her does that, just that and only her. She is. The one thing you can't think about wanting, the one thing you ever could. Don't tell a soul, can't, don't breathe a word. Not even to Pard. Especially Pard. Because she is, and it is her. That beautiful secret you keep. Like when you see her treading through the sunlight down the street, lugging some book like she needs the spine of it soldered to her wrist, or sweeping off the front porch of old Pennypinch's house, that whaling widow she works for year-round who still lays a table for her lost captain every night. You ride by on your bike and Jane Weld might be outside, tinkering with some planting in Pennypinch's vegetable garden, or washing out milk cans and leaving them to sun, or you might catch a glimpse of her on a warmer afternoon, like last Tuesday, out back of her grandfather's place, lying in a crook of the woodpile: reading, wearing that faded indigo dress that wraps like a sea around her. You see her in a moment like that, and she'll never look twice at you, she's seventeen to your fourteen, Dead Weld's daughter, all that. But still. You see her, and everything turns over inside you, an ache in your chest—that kind of yearning ache that if you lay down into it, could kill you.

So you don't. Flick the thought off. You go up with your buddies to the A&W on Route 6—work through a swampwater float, a cheeseburger, a double order of fries, that scrawny carhop up there with the pimply face is sweet on your best friend, and if Pard makes a little time with her, you'll all get the food for free. Or you go out cruising with your older brothers, Scott and Junie, and some of their friends, cruising through T'aintville and down River Road, all around Westport Harbor, shooting rabbits out the car window, picking them off the lawns of the summer homes, those big houses darked up and empty in the off-season, glaring at you from their fat porches. And you're the one always getting booted out of the car to scoot across the lawns to pick up the things just killed, bodies soft, wet, and limp in your hands—driving, shooting, fetching, drive, shoot, fetch, until you're in the backseat up to your knees in rabbits, heading home.

Once, though, it might happen, catch you off-guard, slip past the fear of getting too close, getting caught, you might slow, weaken, think in the flash of a quivering instant that she *is* the one thing, the one girl you'd bend the four corners of the earth for, fold them up right and make them fit, the one girl, the one—you don't dare, couldn't, shouldn't, and maybe that's why you do. It's the joke trick of some toad-bellied God egging you on, the thought of her like an itch in your hands, an itch all through you, like you've caught fire in your clothes, the thought of her just burning you to soot.

You get hold of someone's car. Your brother's or your uncle's, you borrow it or boost it, go out driving that fast new road, twilight thrown down like salt across the pavement, and her eyes are like that road at dusk, that sultry and mystical blue, her eyes, and your foot pressing down the pedal to the floor, driving, she is all you can think about and not think about, all you want, just her, don't dare. And the night is water leaking in around you and you can feel her in the speed, streaming from your skull out through your hair, you pour yourself into that road and drive, faster, like you could drive into her, the forever that is her, go on driving.

HUSK

JANE, SEVENTEEN
Spring 1962

Gray sky. White bird. Wings fold into the seam of a cloud, disappear. Morning noises off the wharf, voices, men loading up their boats—pots, line, barrels of bait—smells of creosote, dead fish, river-muck, gasoline.

Crossing over the Point Bridge, Jane glances west toward the wharf where her grandfather Gid's boat is tied up, that ancient wreck of a thing, still fitted with a niggerhead, manila line, copper- and kerosene-treated wooden buoys he himself had turned.

"Lobsters aren't potting good," he'd told her. "Going into their shed." He'd spent the week moving his lines from the Knob into the colder water off Cox's ledge. She scans the deck of his boat, the pier. No sign of him.

A truck slips by, wash of shadow, smoke from the exhaust, the rumble of old timber planks under the tires. She clutches the book in her hand, hardboard, plastic-wrapped, its familiar width:

The wheel, for example, is a mechanism consisting of a hub, spokes, and rim. A little part of the wheel touches the ground, feels it, then leaves it, to disappear from the reach of the sensations which connect rim, spokes, ground.

But then it reappears.

When that happens to a man we say, "He was born, lived, and died."

The larger part of the cycle is beyond our range of perception, just as the larger part of the wheel is beyond the sensed perception of the ground.

She had read the passage at the kitchen table that morning over breakfast before she left for chores, her face still smarting from the scrub she'd given it with her mother's exfoliating cream. She read it with a pencil, made a note in the margin. Of every passage, it was this one that made her think of her father, reminded her of that late-fall day five years ago when she'd kicked the book over on the floor of his car and saw its cover for the first time. The last time. This passage more than any other. Unreturnable now.

A skiff zings under the bridge, its five-horse humming; in it, two kids who must have skipped school. They zing back and forth, cut three of the four lines a group of Portuguese men have in the water, and when the men realize what the boys have done and that they meant to do it, they start in hollering after them. The boys yell a slur and zoom off, laughing. Wharf Rats, her grandfather Gid calls them, one of them Pard Islington, and the other Huck Varick, both fourteen, already wearing trouble. No good. Huck, the son of Silas and that woman, Ada.

A glint of silver near Jane's feet—a fishing lure dropped, caught between two planks, a half-eaten apple, the skin stripped. Ants swarm it.

On the other side of the bridge at the sandwich shop, some men are finishing up their breakfast—those men no one really knows, union men who have come down from the city or somewhere, dragging trucks and bulldozers back and forth, down that new road, eleven gray miles of highway, farms taken, hills laid open, plucked, leveled off, that road cutting down through the belly of the town like a blade.

It drove strange, that new road, the first time Gid took her down the leg of it they had opened, so wide and fast and endless in its clean paved newness, no face or body to it, no history played out, no houses or landmarks standing alongside to tell you where you were. Driving that road you could have been driving through Anywhere.

It was almost complete. Talk was by late July, early August, the last bit of the new bridge would be done.

She cuts off the road into the woods and feels him rise up in her, her father, his face a reflection in water inside her like he is still there, walking the path ahead, and she is small again, following in her own hooded silence, through the new light blown in this side of the bridge: salt wind, the scent of pitch pine, piss oak, the rank darker smell of the bog. He would take her here, walking, telling stories sometimes as they walked. They'd find a path that opened up to a sudden meadow flush with sunlight. He'd point out the hollowed places in the salt hay where deer had bedded down, the grass still bent to the shape of their sleep. She remembers it, skin on her mind lifting, like she is a shadow in their world, watching a man and his child walk these woods, in and out of seasons, sunsets, daylight, dark.

He came near her when she wrote in the book. She could feel him looking over her shoulder at the scratch of the pencil into the page— his hands had touched it that day in the car, so odd, unintended, but when he was gone this mishap of a book was what she was left with. She writes in it less often now. When she does, she takes advantage of the wide margins, the fat chunks of white open space at a chapter's end. Squatted territory.

She writes only in pencil, as if the words might need to be revoked—borrowed words, for the most part, plucked out of other mouths:

The glacier knocks in the cupboard
The desert sighs in the bed
And the crack in the tea cup opens—

She has reached the bog. The dead thing floating in it. A fox, she thinks it was. She saw it for the first time last November around Thanksgiving, just floating there, dead, but on its front and part-submerged in the dark water so she couldn't make out what it was for sure. Through the winter, whenever she crossed over the bridge, she'd look for it, watching the ice creep toward it, that lump trapped in the freezing. When the thaw came, it moved. The bog flooded with the spring rains, and it moved again. Finally now it had washed up in the north corner, almost unrecognizable unless you knew what to look for.

It was her father's skull that haunted her—the skull they'd determined was him. Not the thing itself or even the public display of how it was found—but the comeuppance of it—that token bullet hole. He had been shot, as he himself once shot a man. Like whoever killed him wanted to ensure, *whatever goes around, comes back around;* his death crafted in that artful symmetry revenge can be.

A mosquito lands on her neck. She feels the bite before she slaps it away. She starts back through the woods toward Bridge Street.

She had done her chores early, then went to pick strawberries in the widow's garden, brought a box to her grandmother, watered the hens. Now she doesn't have to be at work until noon. They are down again, the widow's family from New York, her grandchildren in private school there, let out early for the summer. It is good-paying work, no reason not to want it—except for the girl, twelve now and old enough to give her that smug air, but the little boy is fine, a sweet thing with red fat cheeks, likes to climb in her lap and let her read to him in the afternoons. He braids her hair with his stout fingers, makes a good mess of it.

As she is crossing back over the bridge, she sees the two boys—the Islington boy and Huck Varick—they've anchored their skiff below the concrete forms laid in for the new span, and now they're scrambling up; the Varick boy is in the lead, a spidery thing, moving over the bolted wood, he reaches the top of the form, shimmies across until he comes to the very edge, and stands—the thin ropy gleam of his body balanced there—his arms outstretched rise slowly until his hands meet, clasped overhead.

There's a shout from the shore, Jane looks and sees the city engineer, the project manager. In three long strides, he's come to the rail of the bridge. He's all frosted up—his voice carries, amplified across the water.

"What do you boys think you're doing? You get the hell down from there," he yells.

"You get down to hell," Pard Islington shouts back.

The Varick boy is silent, motionless, poised at the top of the form, a silhouette against the overcast sky. He tips forward, still keeping his body straight, a slow-motion deadweight drawn down; then his head tucks fast, legs shoot up, and he dives, knifing toward the flayed river surface below.

Jane passes the engineer, still shouting. Another car sweeps by. She steps off the bridge. As she walks by Pritchard's store, the gas pumps, she looks again for her grandfather Gid, doesn't see him. His boat gone now, he must have set out. The wharf is quiet, the road quiet, no cars coming down it, everything in a lull.

On the middle pier, next to where the *Laura May*, Swig Lyons's thirty-eight-foot Novie, is docked, Carleton Dyer sits on an overturned nail keg, his shirtsleeves rolled up, mending a section of net. Jane pauses a moment, her eyes following his hands working the needle over the torn places in the mesh he has begun to knit back. He ties off a knot, glances up, sees her there.

"How are you, Jane?" he says.

His cap, she notices, is set back some on his head. The brim doesn't quite shade his face. His eyes are brown, deep solid brown but with some quick shiver of light as he looks over her that makes her skin rustle.

"Fine, thank you," she answers, deliberately, keeps walking, the sense of his eyes still on her, that faint pressure of them resting there. Carleton Dyer. She thinks his name in her head, turns it over once. She had known him, of course, all her life. From down the wharf. From school. He was anyone else. A few years older. Had trouble with penmanship—she remembers this, why?—he was left-handed. Went to sea, the navy. Was back now, so it seemed. Nothing more.

She continues up Main Road. Past the Evinrude shop, the hand-printed sign that reads SKIFFS FOR RENT.

Rain has begun to fall, soft drops on her face, strung through her hair. It is a light rain, short-lived. She likes the cool wet of it, how her skin shrinks.

She stops in at the post office—a line at the window, longer than she wants to wait, but she waits—there's a parcel for her mother, that print she mail-ordered from Sears, to cut for summer curtains.

As Jane steps out of the post office, the package under her arm, she runs into the tall engineer. He is carrying an umbrella and, being the kind of man she has sensed him to be, offers it to her, and because it is too much to explain that she would prefer to just be in the rain for the short distance she has left to go, she accepts. He walks with her, his hand holding the black hooked curl of the umbrella handle, walks with her past the boardinghouse where he is staying, to her grandmother's, two doors farther on. He stops by the gate, holds the umbrella out to her and, when she protests, he waves her off, so cavalier. I'll get it back another time, he says, the clean flash of a smile. Then he starts back down the street through the rain, and she is struck by the pointlessness of it, of being left holding a loaned object in each hand, in one the precious book, in the other, the unwanted umbrella, never having asked for either, but stuck with both now, and wishing he had not insisted, that man, wishing now there was not some link of an indefinite future pending between them.

Not that there was anything about him that was unpleasing. A week ago, he had approached her grandfather about renting the old shucking house that was on Gid's property, down the little slope and close to the river. It had been unused for a number of years. The engineer explained he wanted it as a sort of office, just for the duration of the few remaining months he would be here. There was no outside lock, he explained, on the door of his room at the boardinghouse, and occasionally, upon returning, he'd had the sense his papers had been disturbed. He didn't like that, he said with a brief, self-deprecating laugh, not that there were nuggets of genius worth pursing. He just didn't like the sense of his things being tampered with.

Jane was in her grandmother's kitchen at the time, rolling out a pie, she had overheard most of the exchange.

What surprised her was that Gid had agreed. But the engineer had offered to pay twice what it was worth, and it was, Jane supposed, the money that turned Gid's head.

He was a fine-looking man, very tall, his hair on the gray, streaks of that rich glossy hue blond will turn to. He wore it combed back, in an older style. There was a tone about him, a certain curiosity she'd observed as he stalked around the job with his camera and a pad of paper he'd take out to jot a note down, a certain penetrating curiosity, in excess, perhaps, of what the job demanded. A certain attention in how he listened, looked at things, like he was seeing through them. His speech, too, was different, without accent, every syllable pronounced, a polish to it, not a shine, but rather an exactitude. He reminded her, in an odd sort of way, of that new road—something paved, incisive, immutable about him. Like under his face, there was no face.

She shakes the rain now from the umbrella, closes it up. There is water on the book, not much, but some, seeped into the top edges of the pages. She blots them with a dry cloth, carefully, page by page, but still they dry darker, a ruffled warp left along that upper edge, a tide-line stain.

It was when the engineer came around to pay Gid the first month's rent for use of the shucking house that he gave him the photograph. No work of art, he said, just a snapshot and completely incidental. He'd taken it when he had first come to the Point the summer before. Jane happened to be in it. Without realizing, she had, apparently, walked into the frame.

She didn't like that photograph. She didn't care any that he'd taken it or that he still had it, but she thought it made her face look crooked, her mouth too wide, and it irked her when her grandmother stuck it in a frame and hung it on the wall in the parlor, and she had to look at it, hanging there, whenever she went into that room to dust.

GLOVE

JANE
July 23, 2004

Ada is steamed.

"You've done it, Jane. You wanted that tight little corner, you got it now, good and tight. Got us both boxed in."

It was the turn just past that did it—the play I made—setting a T onto H-E-I-S-T running V-E-T up, jamming that last edge still open.

V
E
T-H-E-I-S-T

A strand of Ada's hair has fallen loose. She tucks it back in place.

"You've been plotting this," she mutters, frowning, her eyes on the board, her face intent. She has two choices now—keep chipping away at things or give in. Sooner or later, one of us will have to give in, and I suspect Ada realizes as well as I do that that one of us can't be me.

She does it then, throws down the glove. She clips a D to the end of T-I-N-C-T-U-R-E, and runs D-I-B across. "There's one more dink for you, Jane."

She knows what she's done: put me in easy reach of the bottom mid-center edge of the board, a coveted dark red triple-word. She knows I'm not the kind of player who'll snub a chance, laid in the hand. Who in their right mind would?

I take U-S-Y, and run those three letters down off the B, and the Y fits so nice, neat and snug, into that red triple square. Twenty-seven points.

I'm nearly caught up.

But then—what I don't expect. She does it again.

"I'm done with you, Janie," she says coolly. "I am done with your tight-fisted board." Off the E in E-X-I-T, she runs R-A-Z-E back across. It's a nervy move, the letters driven into the open, vulnerable there, exposed. And she gets so few points. No number squares—no extra mileage for that Z—she doesn't get much at all. Unthinkable to me—to sacrifice a thing of value for so little.

I know what it is. Bait. She wants me to take it. She knows that if I can, I will.

Wait, though. Wait.

My mind—a moment loosened—spins.

"Get on with it, Jane," she says.

Wait. There's something I'm not seeing.

"You think I'm taking a fall, Jane, don't you? I know you. I know that's how you see it. And it may be so: It may be I'm opening up some good opportunity for you now, but it may also be I'm opening up something for myself down the road."

I look down at the word she has made. Raze. The word that has opened the board—her sacrifice or gamble—a word that in and of itself never asked to signify either, but is only what it is.

I set a B on R-A-Z-E, and run A-B-O-U-T down to meet the T at the end of T-H-E-I-S-T. Twenty-four plus sixteen. Forty. I have moved ahead. Made up my losses. It's Ada's turn again now.

Her hands are on the table, still, fingers interlaced. The ring she wears. The only ring I've ever seen her wear—white-gold S-curve with the sapphire and the two little diamonds that flank it.

Yesterday, Marne was reading that book—*The Secret of Light*. All day yesterday, in every spare moment it seemed, I'd catch my daughter with her nose in it. I watched her and I could see it so clear, how she threw herself into it, resisting and at the same time drawn, as I once was. Such a whatnot, that little book, with its spellbinding premise, rejecting common sense for a beauty that may not exist. Yesterday, I watched my daughter's eyes work across the page. Line after line, left to right. That inescapable order.

PART V

THE NIGHT POOL

SCRABBLED

MARNE
June 22, 2004

I suck at mini golf.

I think to mention this when he picks me up on the Bonnie bike and tells me, as I am slipping his spare helmet on, that he thought we could go up to City View, play a round of mini golf there.

It's always the windmill, hole 7, that throws me.

You look through the slat underneath and think you've got a clean shot—if you can just time it right to miss those three revolving arms. If you hit it straight, it will drop into the hole the other side of the windmill, which pipes down to a second oblong green below.

It seems so benign. So bucolic, that windmill. But I always manage to fuck it up. Hit one of the arms or the top of the slat, because I smack it too hard, or not hard enough, and the putt fails, the ball gets stuck underneath.

Elise Daignault and I used to come here to play, to rev up before we went to Muldoon's downtown, or drove over to Newport when local-range pickings seemed slim. We'd knock those small pocked colored balls around. It was a decent way to kill an hour, and Elise would bring me up to speed on her latest conquest or her next intended victim. I can see her even now, in her skinny Guess jeans, spiked heels poking cuts in the turf.

As expected, it takes me over seven shots to get through the windmill. Ray is laughing. "That was just awful," he says, jotting down my score. I swipe the card from him and tally what we've played out so far.

"I am way losing," I say. "You didn't tell me how steep the damage already was."

"Is that my job?"

"What job is that?"

"Protect you from self-inflicted damage."

"Very funny." I make a face.

He laughs, gives me a light knock on the leg with his putter— I glance at him—that unruly swirling thing in my body again, flush of heat, I can feel it—but I go through the motions. I line up my feet at the starting edge of the next tee, set my little red ball on the black rubber mat, three holes punched into it. That mat has seen better days.

I clock him on holes 9 and 10, under par for both, redeem myself slightly. On 11, I read the graffiti someone has carved into the stand: MICHAEL D IS A WIENER. An X through a rough heart drawn around JIMMY + LEANNE.

"You know the other day I looked up that word," I say.

He is lining up for his next shot, sets his hands on the putter. "What word's that?"

"Scrabble."

I see him pause a moment, I think that's what I see, it's quick though, then he hits the ball, hits it clean, a nice straight thwack.

"Five definitions as a verb," I say. "Four, I think, as a noun. To scratch or scrape. To scribble, scramble, scrawl. Underbrush, too—as a noun, like I said. No mention of that game, though." Another pause, mine this time. I shrug it off. "It was an old dictionary."

He glances at me. "Interesting," he says. He nods to my ball. "You're farther away, your turn."

"You're closer, you go."

He putts gently, drops the ball over the scuffed plastic lip of the cup.

Such a noncommittal word. *Interesting.* Why did I even bring it up?

We move on, the following hole, then the one after that, in silence, a knobby sort of silence.

"Do you ever play with your mom?" he asks.

"Mini golf?"

"Scrabble."

"Me? No. I used to, sometimes, when I was younger, she'd rope me in. She still goes every week you know, to play, just like always. Like nothing ever changes. Do you ever notice that, no matter what actually happens, nothing around here really seems to change? Every Friday my father, he takes her out for breakfast, she takes her walk, and then he drops her off at the COA, just like always, goes and does some grocery shopping for her, picks up a prescription, whatever, comes back for her later." I am explaining this all—logistics, details—more than I need to explain. I can't seem to stop myself. Like the details will justify. "They sort of make a day of it. Even when we had that weird bout of awful heat that second week of May—it must have been pushing a hundred that Friday. You'd expect she'd wilt."

He gives me a curious look, then a smile. "No. I wouldn't actually."

It stops me. How he says it. So matter-of-fact. The smile.

"Things do change," he says.

There are four kids behind us with one mom. She's clutching some Dunkin' Donuts supersize drink. I hope for her sake it's full of caffeine.

Ray grabs the waist of my jeans, pulls me off the path into the gravel. "Let them play through."

"You're getting awfully close," I say.

"Not close enough," he whispers, his mouth near my ear.

"That tickles," I say.

He doesn't let go. "Don't think I've forgotten our trade."

My golf-mind is pretty much blown after that.

He slaughters me by at least twenty strokes. He gets his hands on my body once more, around hole 16, the little crooked house—fingers on skin, where my shirt rides up, I slam my ball off the edge of the green.

He fishes it out of the fountain for me, his wrist wet, water dripping onto my hand as he gives it back.

"Penalty, one point," he remarks.

I shake my head. "Crime of distraction."

"You're contesting it?" His voice is sly and I don't answer. I line my ball up again, line up my feet, self-possessed, give it a whack, and putt it straight off the green yet again.

"This game is so over," I say. He is laughing at me. "I need ice cream. Two scoops, need it now."

"You think that's what you need, Marne?"

"*Stop!*"

"I don't think so."

"You have to stop messing with me."

"You're so fun to mess with."

"Please let me survive this mortification. I don't think I can go two more holes."

"You want to quit now?"

"Grant me some dignity. Let me go out with that. I've always been lousy at this game."

He is laughing, leaning against the edge of a wooden bench set in the pause between tees—that Dunkin' drink the mother of four was carrying, down to the ice cubes.

"Stop laughing at me. *Christ!*"

He doesn't stop. I swoop down, grab my ball off the mat, clutch my putter, walk over. I get right in his face. He's a good six inches taller than I am, and it's dizzying, a kind of vertigo, looking up at him from this vantage point, being so near, this close.

"Stop!"

I expect him to answer, to slip his arms around me. One at least, his hand to come around the back of my neck, at the base of my skull, feel the pull on my hair, his fingers, that touch. But he doesn't move, just stands still, leaning on that bench in his own clear space, looking down at me, that smile in his eyes. Just waiting.

Slightly fucking arrogant, I think. I turn and walk back to the start of 16. I hear his soft laughter behind me. I don't turn around. I hit that little red ball, I hit clean and smart and neat down the green synthetic corridor. Drop it into the white plastic bucket in two.

"Look how well you do when you get a fire going in you, Marne," he says lightly.

"Bug off," I murmur. "You know you've won."

At the last hole, there are three pockets. I sink my red ball into the center one. A light goes off, starts flashing.

"Look at that," he says, "you won a free game."

"Yeah, that's my luck."

I hand him my putter, and he hands them both together to the kid behind the desk, along with the pencil stub. We walk across the parking lot toward his bike. He grabs my hand. The night is rising. The sky that denim worn blue it falls to sometimes in summer, a strip of that weird lucent color in the west near the line where the sun has gone down. The trees are full and black. The chrome on the Bonnie gleams.

"You still want ice cream?" he asks, setting on his helmet.

"In some future," I answer.

He smiles, and that's all he asks. He throws a leg over, and I climb on the bike behind him. He pulls out the choke, kick-starts the en-

gine, and we ride. I don't ask where he is taking me. Right now, I find,
I don't need to know.

As we turn off Route 6 onto the back roads, the air darkens, grows
hushed and clean and smooth, the night and the wind washing down,
my thighs are tight around his hips. Through his shirt, I can feel his
ribs under my fingers, the cotton cool, billowing.

I tuck my head in closer against him, my chin in the cut of his
shoulder. I speak into his neck, his skin, the smell of him that I've
begun to learn, mingled with the dry colder taste of the speed, faintly
metallic. I whisper into his shoulder, knowing he will not hear.
What does it matter? Now, somehow, none of it seems to matter.
He leans the bike into the turns. I can see his hand on the grip.
In the side mirror, I can see the edge of my face. I can see the road
behind us, all of that old back there—my mother, his mother, my
grandfather—that skull—what might have been done—old lives
meshed, knotted, torn, the secrets and the dead—it's all the weight of
moonlight now thrown down on some night pool. No more than reflection now. Collapsed into a mirror the size of my palm. That road
behind us.

* * *

The house he rents is small. A cottage, not winterized. Woodstove.
Galley kitchen. The two back rooms are cramped, but there's a loft in
the front room where the ceiling shoots up, a single big window looking out onto a field.

"What do you do about January?" I ask him.

"Shovel in wood and wear a coat," he replies.

I'm a good fling. No frills. I'm not a snuggler. I don't require a check-
in call. I've endured a few longer-term ventures but, as a rule, I've

shied from men who are viable, not to mention a guy I've almost loved since I was twelve.

He is rummaging through the fridge for a drink. It makes a funny hiccuping sound—the fridge—my ex got the appliances, he explains, along with the house.

Sex—actual Sex—with someone who used to be a fantasy—will never jibe with expectation. It might surpass but, more than likely, it will fall short. You've touched yourself in the dark too many times—conjured sex in the woods discounting the bugs, sex in the dunes with no sand. Your glass dream of him is littered with fractured narratives, scenarios—clandestine, taboo—a secret fuck in a foyer while the Real World where you both ought to be jingles on in a room down the hall. Or the surreal encounter in an extremely public place—a soccer game, a store—everything else suddenly frozen, to sleep or stone, except for him moving toward you, undressing you slowly—

I am overthinking this, then remember what he threw out on our first date, *I want to see you naked,* and the awful thought strikes me that ideals will be shattered both ways. I show okay nude, but I'm no spring chicken.

"I've got beer," he says. "Orange juice. That's about it."

"Water's fine," I answer.

He glances back. "Still your adventurous self?"

"Think purist."

He laughs, running the tap until the water turns cold. He hits some ice into a glass, fills it for me.

In your blood, there are a thousand worlds imagined where he knows how to touch you, just how to push into you—

The tingly rush of that particular thought is more than enough to galvanize my body, so I have to stand up from the chair where I've plunked myself down—have to move, go somewhere, anywhere, and where is there really to go—it's a tiny house—except toward him, under the pretense of accepting that glass of water, getting something, anything, cool and calm in my hand, to draw me back to earth. What I am not prepared for is that, in the process, I will trip over an electrical cord running from the wall to the TV, which slips on its stand, but doesn't fall, except I do, go flying, slightly, metaphorically, crashing into him, the water spills down his shirt, all over me, the tumbler struck out of his hand, ice cubes and glass breaking into wet crystal mess on the floor.

I bend down and start picking up pieces, muttering apology, while he grabs a dish towel to mop up the soak, and I am thinking how I am a bona fide magician for disaster, and if that's not enough, I cut my finger on a shard I mistook for ice, it's bleeding before I realize. He notices. He catches my hand, wraps it in the wet towel, applying pressure, then pulls me toward him.

"You are perfect," he says, his lips on my neck, near my ear.

The exact word running through my head.

But he doesn't let go, he pulls me up, leaving that glass and water melting on the floor, he pulls me to the couch under the window, my hand still wrapped in the dishcloth glove, like Butterfly Ali, and the orchestration of it all is so awkward, so stumbling and real, and as it starts, the thought skims through my mind, *I've been waiting for this*, but thank God, I'm still self-possessed or cynical enough not to breathe it aloud, because *This*—I tell myself—will never turn out like I've planned. Yet just for now, the window is high above us, the cathedral of a window where the ceiling shoots up, and the field at night through it, the grass out there tipped by some bare light that might be imagined but is light I can feel—the shivering tingle of it out there in the dark—I half watch past his shoulder, feel the shiver, light on grass, skin rising to it, he is slipping my shirt off, fingers, mouth playing over me.

The bra will be a sticking point, I think, *as usual*.

He catches my chin in his hand. "Look at me," he says, and as my eyes shift onto his face, his eyes opening down under mine, that unsealed flecked green of his eyes, I realize, *This is what I am not ready for.*

He doesn't let my eyes go, doesn't let me look away, take my flight into the known dark of Out There through the free lofty stretch of the night window.

Sex I love. Love to fuck, to be fucked. Love to come.

As a rule, I don't watch.

As a rule, I do not look too long into someone else's eyes.

It's a searing place. Perilous.

That brink.

"Look at me," he says again, and I do, because this is what I've wanted and not wanted, desired feared most. This.

After two rounds of sex we find ourselves in the shoe-box room—the small bedroom in the back of the house, with an open closet and a small round window. He's left the lamp on. It's an old thing—that lamp—black tin with a Japanese motif—the light it throws is gentle, forgiving—like dilute tea.

Sweat has dried on the backs of my knees, the other stuff down the insides of my thighs. I like the tacky skim of it there—always have. I am cold, naked still. I slide under the sheet.

There's a tattoo on his shoulder—recently inked. A bird in flight, a banner in its beak, his daughter's name. He has fallen asleep, his arm across my body, the weight of it settled. His breathing shifts, slower, more even, his lips part. I watch his eyelids move.

Last week, on Sunday, I worked the lunch shift down at the restaurant. I got off at five. The day was overcast, wind off the ocean, the air rinsed with fog. I took a walk down to the beach. There was a small humped thing lying in the road ahead—some creature, a squirrel, I thought, hit—but it was just an old work glove, stiff, the shape of a hand, but no hand, no wrist, just cloth fingers curled into the shell of a loose fist filled with shadow. That glove lying there reminded me of Huck—and I was annoyed that he should be even the wick of a thought in my brain.

I study Ray's face, it is beautiful in sleep. Not a fair word, I know, to describe the kind of man he is. And yet.

Last Sunday, on my way down to the beach, I left that work glove lying just where it was in the road. On the way back, though, I gave it a smug little kick into some poison ivy. Hick shit. I don't entirely trust the person I become when I think of Huck. That urge to sabotage.

When I was a kid, I stole Alex's skateboard, gave it a shot down the hill and wiped out. The whole cap of my right knee was chopped meat. My mother dressed it, warning me to leave it alone. It healed up fast. Or would have, but I couldn't quit picking the scab. I'd feel it itch, get my nail under it, give it a tug, see how much of a piece I could get in one pull. It wasn't out of defiance, not purely, but rather a quiet, predatory curiosity to see what would happen if—

Next to me, Ray stirs, opens his eyes.

"I fell asleep?" he asks me.

"Not long."

"You still want your ice cream?"

"Everything's pretty closed up by now."

"I'll find you a place." He runs his hand along my hip, the curve of the bone. "What's the matter?" he says.

"What? Nothing."

"Yeah, there's something you're noodling." He touches the edge of my mouth. "You're biting your lip."

There's a gentleness about the way he touches me, the way he comes close to me, so honest and close, I want to die into it. Shut my eyes, walk right out of my mind, let it go.

"You don't want to know," I say, which of course is all that's needed to capsize the boat, kick the door open. I know this. I know it ahead of time, and do it anyway. I tell him about the work glove, I tell him how it bugged me, how it still does.

And he listens, taking in what I say, more generous than I am, I can see it in his face, the lack of judgment. Undeserved.

"You couldn't be less like him," I remark.

His guard comes up, it's subtle, but I see it, a thin veil slipping over his eyes. Not transparent.

"We're pretty different," he says slowly.

Hard-core understatement there.

His eyes on me are wary, like he sees it coming, sees something coming, perhaps more clearly than I do.

"Look, Ray, I need to be completely honest—"

"Then be honest—"

"This won't come out well."

"Spit it out—"

And so I do. I tell him, in not so many words, that his brother Huck is about every walking reason why I can't live here.

His mouth forms a thin line, deliberate. "You are living here."

"Ray, your brother—"

"Your uncle." His voice is quiet.

I stare at that thin line of his mouth.

"What?" I say.

But he doesn't pick up, doesn't continue.

"What did you say?" I ask.

"Just what I said."

And in the pause after, that texture of silence between us now utterly changed, I feel it happen, like a hand, deft, brushed through me. Inconceivable.

"What exactly are you saying?"

He stares at the wall across the room. "My mother. Luce. You know the story."

"Not this part."

"Adds up, though, don't you think?"

"I think it's a load of crap."

He glances at me, a wry smile. "Funny you should put it like that.

That's exactly how Huck put it when Junie told him. Got his back right up. Said there was no way in hell that son-of-a-bitch—" He stops there, shakes his head. "Junie may have been a lot of things, but he was no storyteller."

I say nothing, seeing all. Jigsawed human geography, those pieces, their most horrible fit.

Ray gives a short laugh. "A little nuts, huh?"

That would be a way to render it.

"Who else knows?" I ask.

"You, now."

"My mother?"

"I'm not sure. She might, I guess."

"Alex?"

"I never had a reason to tell him."

"So it must have been your mother, Ada, who told Junie—"

Ray nods. "After Silas died, I guess, one day, she was making up deviled eggs and spilled it. Junie told Huck and me some time after. When Huckie heard, man, did he have a day with her. Said things— he must have—God only knows what—but she sobbed and screamed, flipped her lid, wouldn't talk to him for weeks after."

He goes on, telling me this story of a story, and I am hearing it. Sort of. Half of me is listening. The other half too busy falling off a cliff.

There is a Greek word for this, I think, I grope for it now. Peripeteia.

"To top it off," Ray says, "apparently, when Huck was a kid, he had a crush on your mom. Thought she was something else."

Fuck. Could It Get Any Worse? My mother, Princess Leia, with loser Luke Skywalker.

Rock-bottom. Nadir. All-time low.

"Talk about scrabbled—" Ray says.

Coup de grâce.

It should be funny. It would be, I think, uproarious, under altered circumstances. I would laugh. I should laugh. Let the outrageous farce of it roll off my back. The room has turned slightly, tweaked on its ear, everything on the slide, toward some drain, going down.

I look at Ray's hand resting on the bed between us, the furrows of hair along the back of it, knuckles chapped, a bruise cut through the thumbnail. Shades of black-blue. His hand is inches from the pillow. I study it, intently, it is something I'm needing to memorize, and I don't see his other hand reach out until I feel his fingers brush my cheek. It startles me, the touch, I shift, recoil, trying to keep myself from shrinking back. But it's too late. He's felt it. His hand drops.

"You're going to bail, aren't you, Marne?"

I don't answer.

"You're going to bail over *this*?"

I glance at him.

"You know it's not this," he says bitterly. "You don't even know for sure it was my father who took that shot—"

I shake my head. "Don't—"

"Who really fucking knows, Marne? All the same, you're going to hold *me* responsible."

I can't explain to him that he is right, and at the same time, not right. It's about all of this, and it's about none of it. I should have known better than to climb into bed with a guy so far stuck in this town when there is nowhere I would rather be than anywhere but here.

"I just can't do this," I say.

It happens then. I see it happen. See the words strike his face, the surface of his eyes, straight through.

The upside down of everything.

Half an hour later, he is turning the truck in to the driveway, dropping me off.

"See around you, then," I say.

"Sure." His finger drums the wheel.

"It's not what you think, Ray."

"I don't think anything."

He won't look at me. And of course, at this point, there's no reason for him to.

I shut the passenger door behind me, the truck already moving, he is already pulling away. I go inside. The kitchen is dark. Pans and dishes in their midnight gleam on the drying rack. From the front room, rippling sound, blue wafered light off the TV.

My mother is up. Watching some repeat on the Discovery Channel. Some documentary on evolutionary marvels that I've already seen.

"You're home then," she says, glancing up as I sit down, and in that glance that lasts just a moment, I can tell she has seen the train wreck. The Ray and Marne derailment part at least.

She won't ask why. Should I tell her? Could I? She doesn't know—not about Huck—I'm quite sure. Could she? No. There's a part of me that wants to tell her, scream it, that wants to shatter this room with the scream. The dead are in their precincts, sure. That doesn't mean they don't have their dirty fingerprints all over the lives of the living.

There's a chip in my nail polish. An excuse to strip it.

On the screen, an interview with some prominent ichthyologist. He is what you'd expect an expert on near-obsolete fish to look like—his back-to-the-future wild hair. His eyes are strangely flat, his voice almost antiseptic as he describes the traits of the African genus of lungfish—their svelte and eel-like shapes, their subdivided hearts—how during the dry season they will bore down into riverbed mud, encyst themselves in a mucous sheath that gradually hardens as the water table drops. They lie there, in a dry sleep, digesting their own waste until the rains.

The restraint in his voice, that systematic monotone, can't disguise the fact that he is enthralled by these residual creatures built literally (here he gives a wan smile) into the lives of modern-day tribes settled near them.

I've peeled it. The polish on that one nail.

The TV scene has shifted: rectangular bricks of mud cut and laid into a house. He's still with us, though—our steadfast ichthyologist, in voice-over—as the camera pans toward a black sky, clouds massing, heavy rains striking mud walls. Fish awakened in them, calving away.

It's good and bare, that nail, disgraced against the rest.

Commercial break. Man on a therapist's couch. He's got four alter egos. "Who are you? Nintendo GameCube."

Does she know? My mother. Could she? Is it possible? Even if she did, though, what would it really change? He'd still be a screwball. She'd still be sitting up watching late-night. A bastard brother. A murdered father. Nothing changed.

I stand up.

"You're going to bed, sweetheart?"

I nod.

She pauses then. "I'm sorry, Marne."

"Yeah well, it's how things go."

She studies me a moment longer like she might say something else, but she doesn't. Because we don't.

I go upstairs, wash my face, brush my teeth. Do those minute and necessary tasks. On the inside of the medicine cabinet door, one of those round inset mirrors that swings out on its own and magnifies your face five or ten times depending on which side you choose. I always go out of my way not to look into it, but it's staring at me now—that stifling proximity—flaws, pores, blemished aspects of humanness revealed that afterward of course you wish you hadn't seen.

In bed, I try to read the book about light. I flip back to the front and search out those lines about waves and form, but the magic seems gone. I crease the page down at the corner, tight, and toss the book into the nightstand drawer. I'll go back to it at some point, I suppose.

The night is warm. I fall asleep, woken only sometime after three by the sound of knocking, the sound of the shade hitting against the sill. The wind has picked up. The curtains are wild with it, filled with that restless damp air spilling through. I lie in bed, my body like hammered metal. The curtains snap at me and the sound of that shade knock, knock, knocking.

I slip out of bed and cross the room, lay my hands on the hard cool wood of the sill, then pause a moment as I realize what I am about to do, then go and do it anyway. Like I could shut out whatever it was traveling through me, working its way up to the surface, even after all this time.

BIRDS

MARNE
June 25, 2004

The days lug by.

Wednesday. Thursday. Now it's Friday again. I have to be at work at four, and we're not even pushing ten thirty. My parents are gone for the day, my father driving my mother over to the COA, dragging that Scrabble set, her brown-bag lunch, the new sordid twist in the tale—the star-crossed lovers. Is that how she'd cast it? Ladies Montague and Capulet sitting down for the ritual game.

The tick of the clock on the mantel—tick tock, tick tock.

The silence feels hermetic, unfinished.

I sit out in the sun and fold paper. Four picture frames, four stands. Four African violet pots. Four paper window stars. Colors interlocking, I use more paper than is worth a single star. I am not saving with it. The folds are tight and strong, nothing slips, but I've begun to bite my nails, and the sun feels too hot, and I can't seem to make more than four. I quit for the day and drop them off at Polly's—she's with a customer, no time to talk, I leave them on the counter—on my way to Best Buy to buy an iTunes card—which is more the kind of errand you need to run when you're waiting for life to jump-start. The nineteen-year-old kid who sells it to me has acne and has never heard of Nina Simone. Lena? he asks, trying to be affable, he's got a great smile, and is trying to find a point of connection with an old broad like me before he gives his pitch for some new fancy gadget with a two-year service plan.

Friday-night work. Thank God.

Saturday work. Sunday work. Hours cycling by at a faster clip, brisk, around the weekend corner. Then hit the wall. Two days off. Everything stalled to a screeching halt. Stuck.

So goddamn stuck.

I hurl myself into a late-night movie binge. Wim Wenders. What better way to drown? His Road Movie Trilogy. *Wings of Desire.* Those two angels roaming through West Berlin before the wall came down. Unseen, unheard, they wander. Their work to observe only—*assemble, testify, preserve. Do no more than look!*—until one falls off the wagon, falls in love, and gives up his foreverness for her. He bleeds, wriggles his toes, feels cold, runs into walls, and the film shifts from monochrome to color. Foolish choice, I mutter, foolish, foolish.

The credits unscroll. I glance at the photograph of my mother above the end table, the girl on the bridge.

It must have been effortless for him—that nameless man who took it—to come into town, snap that photo, do his work, and leave. It would have been just another stop to him, another job wrapped up, the fate of the old bridge settled, that quarter-mile stretch of state-owned road at the hell end of the world's end, done—a final report in a manila folder stashed under two suitcases in the trunk of his car, as he drove north up that new single-lane highway for the last time.

I can see it, his hands knuckling the wheel—maybe a tad hungover, a tad weirded out from the run-in I imagine he might've had that night with some local drunk washing himself in gin at the bar. Some local boozer, sitting one seat away, huge hands slinging back drink after drink, starting in with that same story about how he might have killed the son-of-a-bitch he'd caught porking his wife. The locals good and tired of hearing it shifting away and the outsider prey to the tale of how he shot that bastard in the head, dug a hole and rolled him into it, and wasn't he lucky to be near the gravel pit where the digging was easy.

I know it does me no good to run it through my mind, but God, couldn't it have been just this way?

That man. He would have been like those angels. Removed. Nothing taken from him. Nothing robbed. *Listen. Observe. Assemble.* As that lush kept motoring on, his wild story so excessively detailed that, for a moment, the engineer almost believed it was true.

Effortless.

Who was it? Faulkner? Who said the past is never dead. It's not even past.

I make it, miraculously, through the Fourth of July. The family cookout at a cousin's house, and the parade—fire engine sirens blaring, decorated floats scudding by—I am sure I will see him, that I'll look somewhere and see him—wish and at the same time, don't—candy hurled, hoses spraying, children shriek as they scurry, scooping Tootsie Rolls and Dum-Dums off the street.

I start making Polly's birds. Bird after bird. Fold after fold. Body. Beak. Wing lined against wing. I make the edges perfect. They could not be more exact. Creases deep. My nails are down to the quick. I have to use a folding bone.

Bird after bird. Twenty. Forty. Fifty. I make them late at night, in the morning, in the dull flat heat of the day—all different sizes, colors, shapes—a few out of one-dollar bills—some thumb-size, some with movement, you tug their heads, their wings flap, their little feet fold up—I set them all down on the floor of the room upstairs.

Sixty. Seventy-two, and I've spent through my paper, even the Italian gilded stuff that's too expensive and not stiff enough to hold—I put a call in to Kate's Paperie to order more—Express Ship, I tell them—even still, they say, it won't come before Monday.

I can't wait until Monday. I start making my own paper—I glue colored tissue to aluminum foil—they will be exquisite, these Christmas birds—more than she could have wanted, more than she could have imagined.

* * *

I take Alex's kids to the Fair. We go on Thursday because on Thursdays you can buy the bracelets for fifteen dollars that give you unlimited play on the rides.

I get the kids pizza, which they scarf down.

Sebastian is thirteen now, way cool—he hooks up with a group of his buddies, peels off.

"Later, Marne," he says, doesn't even acknowledge his sister.

"Ten PM sharp at the gate."

"Yeah." He shrugs.

Laney stays with me. She has just turned nine and is on the chunky side, wears glasses, she is shy. She slips the sweaty stub of her hand in mine as we walk around, and I tell her stories of her father, Alex, how he could never ride the rides. Puked once all over some girl he was with. I tell it in full gross detail—the kind of detail children love, and she laughs. She's got a little girl's laugh, still, she hasn't been able to shed it, and I might just cry when she does. We ride the giant slide six times, race our sacks down it, then the spinning dragons, then the flying swings.

We wander through the animal exhibit, kid goats nibbling our hands, then we go back to watch the Minis. We've just settled into decent seats on the bleachers, when I catch sight of Huck Varick, sitting with some cronies and his little grandkid, she's wearing red boots, on the opposite side of the ring.

I talk Laney into cutting our tractor-pull-viewing short. She bargains for the Ferris wheel, begs me to go on with her, but this is one ride I won't do. The combination of slow revolution and extreme height. Can't do it.

I wave her off, as the chair she sits in alone churns around. I run into Selma McGuire, who has just set her twins on the same ride. Selma was in school with me and Elise. She gives me a cheek-peck and asks how I've been. We chitchat, and Laney screams my name. I look up, my niece is living my nightmare, stuck at the top in an open chair, swinging back and forth while the gondolas down below load. I smile and wave to calm her.

Selma is telling me now about her new Prius, how she didn't even know she had emissions guilt until she took it out on the highway for the first time and felt a burden lift. Selma has been freed a number of times. Quit drinking cold-turkey, she's a happily married born-again now, and tonight she's arranged to the nines. Her hair in spunky curls, a lighter shade of blond than it ever was in high school, she's got a white lace shirt on, tight, cork platform sandals, capris, still working it—how she dresses now the only residue of what she once was before meeting God and Mr. Right.

Laney is still on the ride. The Ferris wheel's circling now, and she's happy. I drift away and glance down at my watch, I can't see the big hand, I turn and take a few steps to get under some decent light.

When I glance up, I am walking right into Ray. He's startled, didn't see me coming, either, I can tell by the look on his face.

"Hey," I say, but he is already past me, a curt nod in my direction, his eyes cool. His daughter, Anna, who is Laney's age, is with him. She glances back once, but Ray just keeps walking on, not changing his pace. They disappear around the Del's Lemonade booth.

I see Ray once more that night. From the Tempest, as the night sky whirls, the black outline of the woods hurtling toward us, then away, my hair whipped across my face, then whipped back as we spin, our chair thrusts around, Laney shrieks, clutching my thigh, and I look across that twinkling sea of noise and screams and smells, and find him, standing in a break in the crowd near the giant slide, his face pale in the dark. He seems to be looking toward us. Each time we come around, I pick him out of the throng, still looking toward us like across that distance it is safe.

He's gone by the time we come to a standstill. We teeter off. Less than half an hour later I realize I should never have taken that ride. My whole equilibrium has been thrown—it was trying to fix my sight on him, I think, that threw it—if I could have just given myself up to the whirling, I might have been fine. Might have been. There's an awful tinny ringing in my inner ear, and my brain feels crinkly, all scrunched to one side, the other side flung open, way too open.

* * *

I'm up to a hundred birds.

A few days later, my brother Alex stops by the house, I am upstairs ironing my shirt for work when I hear the truck pull in, the telltale clomp of his boots on the porch. My mother comes up from the cellar to see him, their voices drift up through the pipes.

He is telling her about some family camping trip his wife Lisa's try-ing to yank him into; then there's the two-week baseball camp in Au-gust that Sebastian's got planned. Then I hear my name. It's Alex who kicks it off—the do-you-think-Marne-will-ever-get-her-act-together conversation. "Throws herself at my best friend, now look what she's managed to do." I listen to him rant on longer than I should, my mother's gentle replies—in the end it's the gentleness that gets me—I yank the plug out of the socket, leave the iron upright to cool, and go down, making enough of a clatter on the stairs that by the time I walk into the kitchen, the silence is like shocked glass. I cut right through it, throw the fridge open, grab a peach, a knife from the drawer. I walk outside, letting the screen slam behind me—the wood swells in sum-mer and it doesn't fit flush to the frame. I walk away from the house, dust in my eyes, that burning I don't want to feel. The peach is damp in my hand, tawny ridges wrapped through its fur. Thoughts like dirt in my brain.

"A belt slipped, I don't think there's any tightening . . ."

That was how they put it. Those women down at the Point Market when my father took me there one day for a coffee milk. I must have been around ten. He paid for the milk, then went outside onto the porch to have a smoke and a talk with Ernie Mason. I lingered behind in the cool musty dark of the store, thumbing through a rack of super-hero comics by the penny-candy bins. The bell rang, once, twice, someone coming in, someone going out, and there were two women in the aisle, one holding a can of beans, the other buying milk. I didn't know them—they were talking about another woman, whose name I didn't catch, and how she missed a step when she lost that baby, that little Samuel, how tragic it was, that fever he got that flew to his brain, took him fast, he slipped out of the world on the quick, and poor Carleton—my ears pricked up then, curious to know who it was now they were talking about who had the same name as my father—I must have moved a step closer, and one of the women noticed me then, her mouth went tight, and the other who was talking on, sensing something amiss, turned and took me in, and it was one of Those Moments, those two women, strangers both, looking at me with such a queer mix of ashamedness and pity that what never would have crossed my mind suddenly struck home. I gripped that bottle of coffee milk so tight I could have twisted the cold neck of it off and I walked outside to find my father.

I kept the secret (what else would I have done?), never asked, either one of them, did not mention it to Alex, about our brother. But I ransacked the house on the sly, scoured closets, dressers, attic trunks, books she read, pages for some scribble in a margin, a photograph, scraps of paper, some proof bearing his name, and found none, not a trace of him, but realizing still, without having the words to bind the thought, that *he* was those small clothes in that old bureau drawer I had seen her once folding, unfolding; he was the fleeting stuff, one of those blurred un-things you see on occasion move quick at the corner of your eye, and realizing, too—this more slowly, as I began to piece the years together—that I had been born to replace him. It wasn't until I was older that I went to look in the obvious place and found his name and dates on the small stone.

I told Alex, knowing by then he had been old enough to remember.

He met me with a shrug. "And—?" he said, then, "Hey, did you take my keys?"

I sit on the bench by the garden and wait for my brother to leave. Inside me, darkness, my mind scrubbed. Sun nicks my feet and the frayed hem of my jeans. With the knife, I peel the skin from the peach. I've never liked the skin. The fuzz texture, the mealy rub of it. I watch the fruit in my hand shrinking under the blade, I pare the skin in such a way that it unfurls in one long, continuous piece.

Sunday. Monday. Tuesday. My paper arrives. I split the packing tape open. Boxes of it. Sheets and sheets. One hundred and twenty birds, one hundred and thirty. Smaller species now. More homespun, familiar. Sparrows. Starlings. Stubby bodies grown fat by summer's end on insects and bayberry fruit. Birds I have seen all my life, seen and never seen, on their migrations through. They cluster in flocks on the floor of the room upstairs with the gulls and the Japanese cranes. The room so full, I worry for a moment, it will lift, wing away.

I drive down to the restaurant to pick up my check. On the way back, I take the highway. I'm driving slower than I should—there's a silver Altima on my tail—a young girl driving, and she's tapping at the wheel, impatient behind me, she's got a little scowl on, she nudges out into the lane, trying to find a blank stretch with no oncoming traffic so she can pass. She presses closer, gives me a honk, which I ignore. I glance at the speedometer.

There's a rip in my jeans near the knee. That pair of jeans I wore the first date night of down-under before it all turned wrong-side up. As I drive, my fingers trace the tear, the white softness around the hole, free skin through it, and I think of him, that shiver when he touched me.

At the red light, the Altima pulls up alongside, on my right. The girl in it doesn't look at me, just stares right ahead, like she's pissed at the road. There's a dent along the door on the driver's side and I know what she's plotting—the grim set of her face is so easy to read, a certain familiar wreckage I can glimpse even at profile. The light turns. She guns it. I put the gas to the floor. She's not a day past eighteen. I shouldn't test her. It's a junker she's driving, I can hear the groan of the muffler as she keeps up with me even as the lane she's traveling in narrows, tighter and tighter, still she clings, her tires hitting over the serrations that demarcate the edge of proper road, in another five seconds she'll be off it.

I touch the brake just enough with my foot to give her the room to squeeze in. She slips onto the single lane ahead of me and speeds off, her window unrolls as she goes, an arm—lovely, alabaster-pale— coming through the open space. She throws me the finger.

The rest of the day dribbles by. I work on Wednesday. The restaurant is unusually busy. The season's kicking in. On Thursday, I am up before eight, casting about in the kitchen with an Irish soda bread mix I dug out of the pantry. My father has already come home from checking his pots, and he's eating the breakfast my mother fixed for him, a bacon, egg, and cheese sandwich, while she steams the five lobsters he brought in. She stands at the sink when they are done, shelling out the meat, casting the split-open boiled red carapaces into a pile.

I am in her way. I know this. With my wooden spoon and soda bread in a mixing bowl. The directions on the box are foolproof. Preheat oven to four hundred. Knead gently on a lightly floured surface. She finds ways to step around me when she needs to. They talk here and there, my parents, mostly to each other.

I've just slid the lump of dough into the oven and sat down at the table with my toast when I hear the truck pull in, assume it's my brother, then glance out the window and see that it is Ray.

He's looking for Alex, he says as I walk outside, wiping my hands on a dishcloth. He's been trying to get hold of him since Monday, left three messages on his cell, went by the house, but there was no truck, no sign of him there, of anyone.

"They went up to Maine," I say. "They left on Saturday."

He nods. "That explains it."

"Some cottage by a lake up there. Lisa insisted. Kind of hauled him off."

"When's he back?"

"Saturday, I think."

He looks through me. "Well, tell him I came by, would you?" He's got a paper coffee cup in his hand, he starts to turn away.

"It was pretty last minute," I pipe up.

He glances back.

"Lisa got some good deal—you know how Lisa loves a deal."

I sit down on the porch. He is still standing there, paused at the bottom of the steps, his hand on the square cap of the rail, those light freckles along the bridge of his nose, they seem to have more color now. It's summer, I think. Summer. Don't go. He's on the verge of leaving, I can feel it, I can feel him, on the verge.

I start chatting on, about how there was someone else trying to reach Alex as well, some customer who got a bill in the mail, wanted it itemized, had a few questions, you know how people can't seem to quite trust you when it comes to paying up—"I don't think there's phone service in that little cottage they're staying in up there—have you got somewhere to be?"

"Work," he answers.

"Where are you working?"

"Finishing up a job."

"Around here?"

"Fairhaven."

"So you have to be there."

"I'm on my way there."

"Now?"

A slight pause. "Just about now."

Some coffee has spilled out the little triangle drink-hole peeled from the plastic lid of the cup. He sips it off.

"I hate that," I say. He glances up and I nod to the cup. "When it leaks out like that."

He takes another sip of coffee. Then lowers the cup.

"How are things going with you, Marne?"

"Oh," I smile. "Somehow."

He gives a short laugh, and I feel a *pop*, slight, like someone's just pulled back a vacuum-packed seal.

I consider pointing out that here we are again—on my parents' back porch—like everything of import has to happen here. Or maybe I could mention, in an off-the-cuff sort of a way (is there such a thing?), that tomorrow is Friday again, when my mother will go in search of his—looking for a chance to lay everything down on the table, play that ultimate seven-letter-word to say it all.

Like you ever could.

"What was that?" Ray asks, and I realize I was speaking out loud—how much out loud?—I feel a flush spread through my face, and deeper inside, things coming apart.

"I didn't mean to—" I start to say, start to explain—then stop. My throat is tight. He is looking at me—that look in his eyes like before—isn't it? and I can't really say anything, look anywhere else.

He's still holding that coffee cup. He takes the four steps up onto the porch where I am, and sits down.

PART VI

SALVAGE

COIN

JANE
July 23, 2004

"So what's the damage?" Ada asks me now. "No no. Forget about it—I don't want to know." She eats one of her chocolates, grinds the nut in her teeth. "Alright," she says. "Tell me."

"I'm ahead."

"I do know that. By how much?"

"Twenty-four. Not so much."

"You're a bug," she says and laughs. She is happy now. I have passed her up, but the board is open, flung wide enough that it will stay open. The board is how she wants it to be, and I can feel the happiness coming off her—a humming in the silence between turns.

Off K-I-P, she runs S-W-O-O-N down.

"Drew both those damn O's after the fact," she says ruefully. "Could've used them, even just one, and done a little something more with that Z." She shakes her head.

I add up her score. "You've passed me by two."

"You've got a turn yet."

"This is quite a game," I say.

She does not answer.

She has not drawn her new letters. Her hands rummage through the tiles in the box-lid like she is looking for the right ones, like her fingers will know when they touch their blank sides.

She gives me a look, faintly ruffled—some old thought, of my father perhaps, or some other unspeakable crossing over between us, then it's gone again, and her face, her eyes, are clear. She is like this for the most part. Ada. Doesn't let things stew. Only Huck, it seems, can swamp her.

"I know you might think it was wrong of me to do it," she says now like she's read my thoughts. "And perhaps it was, pitting one against the other, but you know, this morning, he just wouldn't leave off. Kept yapping on about how that old skiff's past saving and needs to be glassed in—all the leaks and rot and the 'this' and 'that'—

" 'That boat needs a new bottom is all,' I told him this morning. 'And if you weren't such a lazy good-for-nothing, you'd go and cut a few planks to size, slap a new bottom on and, come to think of it, since you don't seem to have half a mind, I'm going to ask Ray to do it for me.' " She pauses. "That shut him up, Jane, for a minute. He was some sore at me, I could tell."

Ada is harsh with Huck. She always has been. Calls him her trouble. Smoking cigarettes by the time he was five, born with the corner of his right ear folded over, it damaged his hearing in that ear, enough to keep him out of Vietnam.

He never did leave town. Stuck around, stayed right underfoot. And Ada has always been tougher on him than the rest, always saying "That Huck, he's the spit of his father, hidebound like his father was, sulky like his father."

She'll throw me a look when she says it, a kind of queer look, like she's checking in to read my face, to see what I will say, if I'll agree.

————

I set a D at the end of B-R-A-Z-E.

"Rubbing it in?" she remarks. "What a waste—that Z."

"I'll milk what I can." I laugh. "Your go."

There are things that you learn when you play this game often.

You learn, for example, that some letters can work more than one way.

Unite. Untie.

Heart. Earth.

Pare. Reap.

Those are obvious ones.

There are others you might not think to look for.

Listen. Silent.

Angel. Angle. Glean.

Chaste. Cheats. Scathe.

Waiting in a doctor's office once, I picked up a magazine and read about a fire that started in a small Pennsylvania mining town back in the early sixties when some trash, burned in the pit of an abandoned strip mine, caught an exposed vein of coal. The surface flames erupted and were doused, supposedly put out, but that fire got loose, got off on its own, and kept burning, for decades, underground.

I read that and thought of Ada's middle son.

On fine nights in the summer, Carl and I will see him, Huck, parked down at East Beach, his F150 backed in near those heaps of cobblestone the highway department will bulldoze up into a loose wall to keep the sea from washing out the road. He'll sit there parked, for hours. Just Huck, alone, that wild odd elusive thing about him you can't pin down long enough to name. He keeps an Adirondack chair set in the pickup bed, and he'll sit in that chair, facing the ocean, whittling a loaf of pine, drinking through a six-pack of orange Fanta, and freeing the shape of some creature from the hard of the wood, making shavings of it.

"I suppose it was a little heavy-handed," Ada muses now, "my saying that to him about Ray." She moves a letter on her rack, knocks it between two others. "Ray hasn't exactly been such a glory lately—all in a wrinkle over your girl."

She says this, and I remember then, I have not told her yet. About yesterday and what happened when Ray came by. I want to tell her. I am on the verge of telling her. Then I catch myself. She'll just scoff— say some dismissive thing.

It was yesterday morning. Carl had just come home from pulling his pots. Marne was up, early for her, fussing with some quick-bread mix, then she sat down at the table in the same chair where she used to sit to eat her lemon ice. She loved that lemon ice when she was young. She'd kneel on the chair and work through a cup of it with three or four of those little baby spoons, and leave a sticky mess in the corner of the table. I used to wonder how it was that one person, so little herself, would need to use so many little spoons.

It can be hard, having one like Marne. A child you never quite seem to learn. Wrapped in her own dark cloud, rattling around. She's nothing like Alex. She never has been. Alex was my easy one. As a baby, he'd cry and I could soothe him. With Alex, it seemed, I always knew what to do.

Yesterday morning in the kitchen, I was thinking this. I was thinking about those paper birds that Marne's been making, it's been almost a feverish thing with her—a need—I've watched her at it, how she takes that sharp tool to the paper, makes a crease, hard, exact, her strong fingers twisting a brilliantly colored paper square. Watching her hands you feel she's on the verge of shredding it—astounding then, to see how she can make some creature of inestimable grace emerge.

Yesterday morning, in the kitchen, I could feel the restlessness coming off her—not so unlike Huck really—that thing in her that can't be smoothed out or contained.

You don't want that for them. You want to see them settled. They grow up, grow away, and you still want to know they're tucked in their beds when you go in to turn out the light.

I was thinking this when I heard the truck pull in, glanced through the window, and saw that it was Ray.

"That girl won't change," Ada's saying now. "I told Huckie just the other day: That girl your brother Ray's stewing over, she won't come around. Don't I know her kind?"

She says this so casually, so offhand, like she's remarking on it to herself, like she's forgotten I'm here, like she's forgotten that my father was my father, and Marne is just as mine. She hasn't forgotten. It's intentional, what she says. Meant to sting.

Her fingers that have been drumming lightly on the table stop. Her eyes are cast down, the shadow of her lashes on her cheek.

I glance past her shoulder, toward the distant corner the other side of the wall by the swamp woods, a few rows of stones there, stubs really, that white marble they used to use, some of those stones so old the names have rinsed away.

Ada plays R-E-N-T, nipping the double-word square. "In case you needed one more chance."

I smile. "No. I'm looking elsewhere."

"Some other corner?"

"Maybe."

"I'm down, aren't I?" she says.

I nod.

She makes a face, drawing her letters. "And up to my ears in vowels."

I look at the board, and it occurs to me that I already know the outcome. I have had this sense before, in other games we've played, games that were close as this one is. It is there. The outcome. In the grid of what we have already laid down. In these last letters that still remain unturned.

Yesterday, when Ray came by, Marne went outside. We could hear them on the porch, their voices sifting with the light breeze through the window screen. It was stilted at first between them, clunky and awkward. Then they seemed to settle in. Ray was asking her about California, about why she came back, and she told him how it wasn't such a bad life out there, people started work at 7 AM to finish up at 3 so they could go sailing or hiking or skiing. Once, she said, she took a little boat out with a friend into the bay off Tiburon, and as they tacked, she looked back and saw the houses on the shore. They were so pretty there, she said, those houses, but she had the sense that she could poke her finger right through them, and that was it, she knew, for California, she was all done. She has never said half that much to me. She fell quiet then out on the porch, and for a moment Ray was quiet, too, then he asked if she thought she'd stick around. "Don't know really where else I'd go," she answered, but it wasn't quite so casual. Then neither of them said anything for a bit, and I just sat there inside at the table with Carl, eating an oatmeal cookie. I looked around the kitchen, no cupboards still, only shelves, and above the sink, the pipes running down the wall as they were laid, and I thought about the first year we were married. We had no running water that first winter, just a privy out back by the old corncrib, and a well that kept freezing over, we had to break the ice up with a stick. There were two stoves in the kitchen then, one kerosene, and one of those early refrigerators, a Kelvinator with the motor on top that worked only some of the time. That first winter we lived here was a brutal winter, and we moved around each other through the cold of the house with the electricity of strangers.

Yesterday, at one point, Carl glanced up once from the newspaper and nodded toward the window.

"You hear them out there?" He kept his voice low. "He laughs at her jokes." He smiled at me. Outside on the porch, they were talking again, Marne and Ray. He was telling her about a boat he'd raised the week before, out past the Devil's Bridge; he was telling her how the mast of that boat was stepped with silver dollars and the man who owned it, his father had built it, had stepped those coins himself around the mast, eighteen of them altogether, he wanted all eighteen back. "But when I got down there," Ray said to Marne, "and cut the mast I found nineteen." Marne answered something, her voice too quiet I couldn't make out the words. I saw Ray's shadow through the window, his shoulder coming up as he dug into his pocket. "Here," he said then, and there was silence, and I knew what he had done. He had given her that coin. I glanced back at Carl, and I could see in his expression that he knew it, too, and something in how his eyes stayed on my face reminded me of that summer the highway opened, the summer before they took the old bridge down.

Back then the sky, the fields, the trees, the light on the river belonged to us, all of it, we had grown up in that place and it was ours. It never occurred to us it could be different, it never occurred to us we were already caught up in the draft of something else, some new future, a speed we had no warning of and did not understand.

Yesterday, sitting in the kitchen across the room from Carl, I thought of this, I could see it so clear: the hinge that summer was. His eyes strayed from my face, his eyes slipping over me. My body goes to water, still, when he looks at me that way.

PEA-SHOOTER

HUCK, FOURTEEN
Summer 1962

So far the season was tame. They only went through
one bunny nest with the mower, rabbit babies flying
out, chopped by the blade to squeaking pieces, going
just everywhere. After that, it was all good drying
days, then one long week of picking hay, forking it
over to get the green out, rowing it up. One long week
of driving the rake, his foot on the tripper, his father
Silas-the-bastard bossing him on, shouting at him to
keep them rows straight, calling him every name for
"stupid" under the sun. His two older brothers, Scott
and Junie, both fishing now, Junie laying up lobsters,
working that boat out of Fairhaven, and Scott swordfishing down at the Dumping Grounds, so Huckie
now was the only one left underfoot, the only one
Silas-the-bastard could still keep his thumb on, roped
in to do the bull work. And it was one long week of
that work: getting that first cut of hay up into the barn,
sweat pouring into his boots, blisters on his hands, the
air in the loft thick and blue with haydust—haydust in

his throat, hayseed down his back and in his clothes, around his crotch, making him itch, his face tattered gray, that seed stuck all to his skin for that one long week of work and wondering what the fuck is it all worth. One long week when the only thing he had to look forward to in a day was the end of it—at best some good thing his mother might have cooked up for supper, slumgullion one night, another night codfish and potatoes with those cream of tartar biscuits slathered in strawberry jam. One long week of squinting into the sun and knowing there was no way in hell he was going to grow up to be a hayshaker.

Then on Saturday when his mother took the skiff downriver to the wharf to meet her friend, Huck went with her, hooked up with Pard down there, and they spent an hour shucking out four dozen littlenecks for Pritchard, Mr. P, who owned the fish market and the store. The littlenecks were for some garden shindiggedy luncheon up at the old Valentine Estate. They'd called in the order the day before, they wanted only the small ones, no cherrystones, and wanted them cut on the half shell on ice. It was Huck who got the idea, every eight or so, to leave one connected. He and Pard took turns at it, chose one quahog and cut it near all the way through, but not quite, leaving a sinew attached.

"Can't you just see it?" Huck said, cracking up, "some sucker tilting back that shell, slurping away, slurp, slurp, juice drippling all down his chin."

Then the work was done, and Mr. P paid them, gave them each a coffee milk, too. They drank those down, then jumped in the river, took the tide down to the Yacht Club, hung around there for an hour, looked at some girls, then when the tide turned they floated back to the wharf on the flood.

Early afternoon by then, Pard had to get off, up to his job at the gas pumps. And it was as Huck was coming around the corner of the Evinrude shop, his hair still wet, the salt drench and weed smell of the river still on him, he came around that corner and saw it. The car.

That sweet flip-top car belonging to the duck-butt clerk fream. That car just sitting there alone, parked out front of the Paquachuck. Empty. No sign of the nutter himself. Huck took a stroll by it. The top was down and on the red leather passenger seat, he spied a camera. He took a quick glance around and, seeing no one looking who would care, leaned in and grabbed it. He'd drag it back to the hurricane house, go pawn it or stash it somewhere. He cut behind the outboard shop, then paused a moment in the shade, looking down at the lens. He could see his own face, hair peeled back, only his face, skull-like, distorted there. The shade was cold. He shivered and walked back out into the sunlight, down to the little sandy beach where his mother was wading in the shallows with the baby, Green, on her hip. She was babbling away with Vivienne Butler, their voices carrying to him on the breeze, Mrs. Butler saying something about how she'd heard they'd pushed back the time of opening the new bridge now to August, saying there was something in the draw they couldn't seem to get working right. Then his mother getting that tone in her voice, saying how that new road'll do nothing but bring the town to rim-rack-and-ruin, shaking her head, her hair piled up and some loose curls of it falling down to touch her sunburned shoulders, his gorgeous mother, bands of thin clouds reflecting in the shallows where she walked. Huck snapped off a photograph. They had not seen him yet. They were gabbing now about something else, some recipe for piecrust Mrs. Butler had come across and how the secret of it was in the cider vinegar. "Can you believe it, Ada?" she was saying, "something so household and simple—"

An egret passed behind them over the water. As it rose, its reflection thinned, flying away from itself. Huck snapped a photograph of his mother's boat staked to the marsh, then another, the click of the film, winding, winding. A shrill whistle came from the docks, and the women turned their heads to look, seeing something there, but Huck did not look, only watched his mother through that small clear window of the viewfinder lens, his mother captured in that frame, she was less than the size of a periwinkle, her long arm wrapped around the baby on her hip to hold him set there, and her dress in a swirl around her as she waded deeper in, not caring if the water soaked past the hem, her dress like some pale yellow flower, a butter-and-sugar snapdragon opening, and the toes of the baby leaving darker prints of wetness across her hip. He snapped off one more shot and then somehow, for some reason, didn't want to look anymore. He melted away behind the shop before they saw him and with a funny twinge of something in his chest walked back to that smug car, still driverless, windows still open. He tossed the camera back onto the front seat where he'd found it. Let the nutter scratch his duck-butt head bald over that one. There was a pack of cigarettes on the shift. Lucky Strikes. Now, there's a different story. He reached back into the car, boosted the pack, tucked it into his pocket, turned around, and ran smack into Mr. P, who in one glance let Huck know he'd broke the golden rule, he'd been caught.

"I've got to run those littlenecks up," Pritchard says, his voice knowing. "I was just coming to ask if you'd mind the register for me, for an hour or so."

Huck felt his face burn. "You can trust me, Mr. P," he mumbled.

Pritchard laughed. "I think as long as we both know I can't, we'll be fine. Give me an hour. The cash is in the drawer. Counted."

And Huck was just sitting there, in the muted cool quiet of the store, picking his toenails behind the counter, when the door opened, chimes rang, and Jane Weld walked in. Just her. He nearly fell off the stool, brushing off his hands on his pants as she walked to the back of the store. She picked a tin of sardines off the shelf, then a can of beets, then she came back up to the counter and set those two things down, and Huck could feel the cold and sweat all over him like it was two hundred degrees in the Arctic.

She was right there across the counter, eighteen inches away, the other side of the world.

"Is there nothing—I mean, anything, you need? Anything else?"

He rang up the sale, he rang it up slow. His fingers shaking pressed down on the keys, numbers rolling around, popping up into the register window.

"That'll be forty-three cents," he said. She didn't answer, didn't reach for the money, didn't seem even to hear him. Her face was turned away, slightly toward the window, she seemed to be studying an imprint of dried salt collected along the edge where the glass fit to the wood, and the sun coming through struck the bridge of her nose, lit the plane of her cheek, and she was so there, so beautiful and solid and present, that he was suddenly thrown by the sense that although she was standing right there across the counter from him, at the same time, she was somewhere else entirely, and the body of the girl he could see was more shadow-like, more unreal and insubstantial than the other part of her that was removed. He cleared his throat, maybe too loud, because she glanced at him, a startled expression in her eyes, her beautiful eyes, her face very still, like she had accidentally left the door of it ajar, and he was falling into her through that open door.

"So, uh, is there—?" he muttered.

"What?"

"Anything else you need?"

She just looked at him. "No."

"Alright then. You bet."

"How much did you say it was?" she asked. "Did you say?"

He went to answer, cracked his mouth, and some queer stale noise whizzed out, and her face was closed again, and she was just a girl standing on the other side of the counter. She glanced at the numbers on the register window, counted out the money, took her things, and walked out into the blaze of the overturned world.

He stared at the door just where it was, soft and shut against the jamb behind her, and knew it then. He loved her. Like he'd never loved another living thing, like no one ever could. He knew it. Like he knew daylight.

He felt stupid. Ashamed. Young. So impossible, loving her. Such ugly and stupid impossible shame. He glanced down, so frosting stupid it was, then his eye caught the book on the counter—the plastic-covered library book—hers—she always had it with her, that book, and now she had left it behind. He didn't think a minute, snapped it up, jumped the counter, and ran. He shot through the door, caught sight of her ash hair, gave a shout, and she turned, startled, as his toe caught the edge of the door, and he tripped, flying forward, he staggered, caught his balance nearly, then lost it again, and fell, his hands scraping hard over bleached shell and the book sailing out of his grasp, landing splayed open on the ground. She walked back quickly, picked it up, and looked at him a moment.

"Not your day," she said, a little smile that made him just crazy, made him go right to pieces. "Are you alright?" she asked.

"Earthbound fine," he said. He couldn't look at her. He picked himself up and slunk back into the store. His toe was a mess, the nail dangling, he ripped it right off, there was a nasty cut on his hand from some dumb piece of shell. He picked the grit out. But it hurt like the devil that cut, so deep and bad, the hurt, like the devil, the devil, the goddamn fucking devil.

Two weeks later, a heat wave struck, a set of real scorchers, day after day topping ninety, the air so humid you could skin it with a knife. By nine on Saturday morning, the traffic was already backed up Main Road as far as the gas pumps at Aiken's corner, car after car stuffed full of beach chairs, towels, sand toys, kids, everybody loaded up with coolers full of lunch and cold drinks, bulging and pushing to get out of the city and down to the breeze off the ocean. They got nowhere fast, just stuck on that winding country road, bumper-to-bumper, cars snaking past as fast as molasses, and the four of them—Huck, Pard, Robbie Taylor, and Eejit—were lying belly-down on the roof of the Point Market, lying on the shady side, peering over the peak, down the pitch into the line of cars in a slow creep down Main Road. Wheels turning once, brake, stop. Somebody leaned on a horn. The four boys had their pea-shooters out, their pockets stuffed full of hard peas and good chewed-up bits of paper wadded into tiny balls. They loaded them into the shooters, blasted them down into the open car windows and the folded-back tops of convertibles.

"What the heck is old Vernon thinking trying to get somewhere now?" Pard said, giving Huck a poke, nodding down to where Vernon Soule was backing his green tub of a DeSoto out his driveway into the traffic. He waited patiently until some courteous driver waved him in, and then Vernon backed out slow, backed out his driveway and into the street until he was crosswise in it. Then he put his car in park, got out, and ambled around to the front of it, popped the hood, and started tinkering with something underneath it. The boys just stared. Everyone just kind of stared. Then Pard started to laugh, he started laughing so hard, he was rolling on the roof. And when the DeSoto didn't budge, horns started to blare, somebody shouting, and old Vernon straightening up from under the hood, dug a finger into his ear like he couldn't quite hear, then leaned down again over the engine. Pard was still laughing, he and Eejit laughing. Huck loaded his shooter, pegged a guy in a red convertible T-bird, nailed him good right behind the ear. And as he was loading in another bit of chewed-up paper, he suddenly noticed Jane Weld across the street, standing on the sidewalk, out front of Mary Johnson's folding table of lemonade and zucchini bread for sale. Jane was just standing there, one of those rotten summer kids she looked after, the little boy, he had her by the hand and was pulling at her to come on, but she wasn't moving, she was just standing still there, looking across the street at something, not old Vernon's DeSoto, but something on the porch of the store. What the heck was it? Huck couldn't see, it was down below the overhang pitch of the roof where he was lying, something though had caught her eye fast.

Pard jabbed an elbow into Huck's ribs. "Give me some of them peas, I got a good shot, and I'm out." Huck dug into his pocket, drew out a handful, still not taking his eyes off Jane standing there, still staring at whatever it was.

"That Mustang there," Pard was saying, "knucklehead in the Yankees hat, he is all mine."

What the heck was she was staring at?

Farther down the street, the same side of the street where she was, Huck spied the tall engineer, all dandied up, white shirtsleeves and tailored trousers, slick-shine shoes and those blue-tinted rims, that sucker Clerk of Works, that adman hack, that ghost. He was walking toward Jane Weld, he was, had his eye on her, motherfucking nobusiness nutter, he did.

Huck spit the balled-up wad of paper from his shooter and dug into his pocket for a stone. The stones you took your time with. You picked them with care. They had to be the perfect shape, perfect size. You wouldn't often find a deserving use for them, but you'd keep a few on hand just in case.

The ghost was ten yards from Jane Weld now, his ballpoint pen a dark jab sticking out of his shirt pocket, that Leica swinging on its black ribbon from his neck, walking toward her, his eyes on her, like what the hell right did he have?

Huck loaded the stone into his shooter, aimed it, fired, fuck it, missed.

GLANCE

JANE, SEVENTEEN
Summer 1962

She was starving that night, at supper, filled her plate
with three slices of cold ham, potato salad, corn, diced
tomatoes, ate that up, then filled her plate again, her
mother, Emily, looking across the table with some surprise as she kept on eating, squirreling that food away.
It was unlike her. She knew it herself, but could feel
only hunger—a sudden wild hunger.

She broke a heel of bread off the loaf.

"Are you alright?" her mother asked.

"Yes fine."

Emily looked at her doubtfully.

Jane nodded at the butter. "Pass me that please."
Her mother did. "Why wouldn't I be fine?"

Carleton Dyer. She thinks his name again. Why think
it? Just for how he'd looked at her across that morning
street and the way that look poured through her. No
good reason. He was sitting on the front steps of the
Point Market when he caught sight of her, on the side-

walk across the road, his eyes fell on her face, stayed there, and time
ended.

Carleton Dyer. She remembers now, growing up, she'd see him
down at the wharf, or on his way there, he had a kind face, even young,
skin used to weather, he always smiled when he saw her. His father was
a fisherman—one of the few her grandfather Gid thought well of—as
good with an iron on a swordfish as the Norwegians working out of
the Vineyard. He kept pots as well, set seine for herring up at the little sandy place, fall-fished for tautog. And Carl was his only son, always on the water like his father, just had it in him as some did. She
remembers this now, remembers, too, how she'd see Carl early mornings helping his father load up the boat when she'd run down to the
wharf to bring Gid his dinnerpail, which he always managed to forget
though her grandmother left it right with his boots at the door.

She never thought much about seeing him there. He was anyone
else. Wasn't that true? At school he sat with Zeke Cash and Danny
Wilkes, near the woodstove in winter, potatoes they'd brought for
their lunch baking on that heat while they learned off their long division and, at recess, as she and Sue Thomas skipped rope, Carl and the
other boys would play mumblety-peg with a pocketknife, and once
when Carl threw, Danny Wilkes tried to grab the knife midair and the
blade slashed his hand. She remembers how the blood ran, fat and
glistening into the dry dirt, all the boys laughing, even Danny, all but
Carl, who tore a piece off his flannel shirt for Danny to wrap his hand
in. There was that other time, too, when they were a little older, five
of them messing around one night, they broke into the old Cory store
that had been shut down, no one knew exactly why, boarded up for
forty years. They found their way through a window into the basement and went all through the place, the sail loft on the top floor, sails
laid out, half finished; the main room downstairs that had been a post
office and a tavern, drinking glasses still on the bar, a table set, like
someone had just stepped out, and locked the door behind them,
never intending to be gone all that time. Along one wall were the pale

slashes of letters in the post boxes furred with dust. That night the five of them agreed each would take one thing: Sue Thomas took a sugar devil, Danny Wilkes, a whalebone-handled corkscrew. It was one of those letters that Jane wanted, addressed but never opened, that no one had come to collect, and Carl, being tall, reached across the counter to draw one out for her—

All of this, somehow, she had forgotten. Details burned away into the colorless time of her father's disappearing, the long flat plain of After-ward that gradually effaced every other before. Had she read that let-ter?—that scrawl with no recipient? She must have once. What had it amounted to? Just another instance of putting her hand through cloud.

She mulls this over now, sitting at the dinner table with her mother. How he'd looked at her this morning—Carleton Dyer—that quick sudden light she saw break across his face when he looked up and took her in. Her fork scrapes the plate, an awful noise over the skid of food still left. She gets up, clears the table, and fills the dishpan. How he had looked at her, staring through the blue flow of the mov-ing street, looked at her and did not stop, and now these buried things about him rushing out of corners she didn't even know she'd tucked them down into. Her hands feel through the soapy water for the cut-lery, a brown scud of grease rims the dishpan's edge, and she thinks about how it's like a rock you walk by for years and never notice, never wonder what might be hidden underneath, what strange free life, if you were to kick it over. Wings sudden in your chest, alive in a way it never struck you to be. Just standing on that hot baked morning side-walk, and the traffic tied up, that DeSoto blocking them all up both ways, the old man in his red suspenders fiddling around with nothing under the hood, and you are hearing nothing, seeing nothing, only Carleton Dyer looking at you like you were all that was in the world.

She pricks her finger on a knife tip. Swears.

When the dishes are done and dried and put away, she and her mother come to read in the front room, as always, her mother vanishing into some novel, and Jane with a book of poetry she'd picked off the shelf, the consistent rhythm of verse, meter, some refuge, order, to tame the unquiet.

> *Round her trailed wrist fresh water weaves,*
> *With moving fish and rounded stones.*

She glances up at her mother sitting there, in the green upholstered chair, its stuffing gone alump—the fair beauty of her once, now care-worn and alone. Same old story: Nice girl. Loved a bad man. Married him. The end.

Isn't that how it breaks down? Just a pair of old shoes matched together in a closet. After the bruised, irresistible sweetness of the early time, what will you be left with then? There was a doom to it.

It never struck her before it could be any different.

She does not seek him out. Not the next day or the day after, not, at least, in any intentional way, but seems to see him everywhere, like her eye is just drawn. And it is Wednesday, the following week, when she walks out of her house to go down to the widow's for chores, and Carleton Dyer is sitting on the cemetery wall with one of his friends, having a smoke, and for a moment she feels like she would just as soon leave her bones in a pile on the sidewalk than walk by him but, at the same time, wanting only that. As she passes, Carl glances up.

"Hello, Jane."

"Hello," she says and keeps walking, past them on the wall, like she has told herself she would. Carl jumps off and falls into step beside her.

"You on your way down to the wharf?" he asks.

She nods.

"Mind if I walk with you?"

"Don't mind," she says.

"Why do you do that?"

"What?"

"Walk by me so fast."

"I don't."

"You do," he says, smiling, "you always walk by me fast like that, say nothing."

"I said hello."

"That's it."

"Not much else to say really." But now she has started to smile herself, to laugh a little even, like she doesn't want to but, at the same time, does, a fluttery kind of lightness like a bubble in her chest nudging up. She keeps her eyes on the sidewalk, the cracks split through the concrete, a fallen branch in front of him, he steps around it, his shoulder brushes hers, and instinctively she moves away. He stops then, catching her by the arm, swift, and without thinking she looks up and he is looking down, and her eyes are under his, that light in them, his eyes, that raw clean light that gives everything away. The sky has gone small and the street is quiet, all the sound drained out, and he is close to her, his hand on her sleeve, close, and she feels something blown open inside her, then fear, a wave of it, and he must see it cross her face, that fear, because his hand drops from her arm and they just keep walking, not looking at each other now. Some summer kids ride by on their bikes, shouting to one another, laughing, so free, every carelessness about them, and for a moment she envies them, that they can have that.

They pass the Point Market. Joan Slane's cat darts across the road, pauses on the opposite curb, its tiger-striped head swiveling to watch a car go by, then it sprints back across the street again.

"That cat'll be dead by the end of next week," Carl says.

Jane shakes her head. "That cat's been slipping fate for ten years."

"Bet?"

"What?"

"I'll make you a bet," Carl says, "that cat's dead by the end of next week."

Jane starts to smile again, she can't help it really, the smile. "Alright," she replies.

It is an ordinary day. A drift of haze still clings. The lawns, trimmed, have begun to give up some of their green—it's been so dry—clouds promising rain, no promise kept. Just an ordinary day, but the light cuts through, there on the stone wall, and on the newly painted whiteness of that gate.

They reach the widow's house. Jane pauses a moment before she turns onto the walk.

"See you around then," he says.

"Sure. See you around."

That was all. Only that. He walked away. And she went and did the chores, then to work, and at the end of the day, when she came home, she found a note from her mother saying she'd gone into New Bedford, shopping with Mary Ellen Reeves, they would be back late, and not to wait supper.

Outside, the wash is still on the line, the sheets, a summer dress, nightclothes, pillowslips; across the river, the sun dropping now behind the scrawl of hills on the opposite shore, the water holding every failed and fallen color of the sky, and it occurs to her that the river has never looked so beautiful, and she is alone with her shadow turning its own lovely way on the ground, in the soft air cooling now. She begins to take down the sheets. As she unsnaps a clothespin from one corner, the end gets loose, the sheet blows in against her body, and for a moment, it all feels clear.

Impossibly simple and clear.

MEMORY OF WATER

JANE
July 23, 2004

A shadow moves. Ada's hand. She picks a speck of
something off one of her nails, then moves a tile in her
rack. "Looks like I've spent through my luck," she
mutters.

I've taken my turn. I glance at my watch. Past two
o'clock. From the swamp woods back there behind us,
a bird calls. Weep call. A jay. Is it? Wait. No. The call
again, shorter, more grating. Mockingbird.

"Clear up to my ears in vowels," Ada says, still
looking down at the seven in her rack.

I lift the pen. The curve of the script, a doodle I've
made there, at the border of the page, like a vine, that
doodled script, no word or thought exactly straight or
held to its own closed and self-contained shape anymore.

Ada leans forward, without looking up. She shifts
her elbows onto the table, rests her chin in her hand. I
glance away, waiting still for her to take her turn. On

the other side of the cemetery wall, the soft emptiness of the deep summer grass growing fast, faster now than they can keep it cut, and the sun still high in its place above our heads, soaking down through that summer green like the light is growing up from the ground.

"It's your go, Ada," I say.

"I know that," she murmurs. "I know."

Yesterday: After Ray left, Marne was restless. She flung herself around the house awhile, then went down with Carl to the garden, and I got to the wash, dragged it up from downcellar, and brought it outside to hang on the line.

It was early afternoon, this time of day, but hot, yesterday, no breeze, the air so still and white and stifling, you could see the heat settled into the trees, and when I came back inside the house, there was sweat all through my shirt, and I went into the front room, into where it was dark and cool, Marne's sweater tossed pell-mell on the sofa—that little red sweater, summerweight. I picked it up, matched the arms, folded it neat, and set it back down, then stopped when I noticed the book about light. She'd left it there, the inside foil from a pressed gum wrapper marking the page she was on. Just waiting there, underneath that photograph hanging on the wall.

It was seeing the two together that threw me. The proximity of one to the other. Like it had been planned. Marne would not have known. I've never said a thing to her about that book, what it was to me once, or where it came from. There's never been reason to. She didn't know my father. Barely knows his memory. What would it have meant to try and explain? That book was how I found my way back to him—a man despised, whom I adored—Marne wouldn't understand that. I've never come up with the right combination of words to lay it down in a way she could. But seeing that book there on the table below the photograph of the girl on the old Point Bridge, I thought of that last summer, 1962, the summer I fell in love with Carl. The last summer I wrote in the margins of that book. That's when I remembered the cigar box upstairs.

Put up in the attic, in a trunk of other things I'd taken from Gid's house after he died and my mother put the house up for sale. The whole complexion of the village at the Point by then was on the change. The old ones gone, most of them, fallen under or moved away, and my grandparents' house still with their things in it, dresser drawers still full of folded clothes, photographs and paintings still on the wall, and dishes in the sideboard, but all of it just so empty, that house so empty, except for the something more than silence I could feel, hawking around the battered screen door.

I helped my mother clear it out, helped her sort through the relics and the kitsch, all the salt junk Gid had collected. He'd kept everything—used tinfoil, flour sifters, ice picks, sugar devils, sinkers cast out of sand, mugs with no handles, old churns, needles someone had used once to mend sail, a pail of square clothespins. Flags. There was a tree swallow's nest I found deep in the hall closet, near perfect, the rounded shell hollowed out with only feathers, the softest stuff. Once while my mother and I were in the kitchen, she looked at me, her eyes filled, and she sent me from the room. I went down to the old shucking house. I found the cigar box there, set up on a shelf, and I knew right away who it had belonged to.

Yesterday, when I brought the box down from the attic, I took it out onto the porch and started going through it. It struck me then, how curious it was, these were the things that bridge engineer had left behind, discarded or forgotten, his refuse in that box. His chaff. That small heap of everything had meant nothing to him—those cast-off bits that revealed so much of what we were. They were nothing to him, and he was no one to us. He had slipped in, slipped out, nameless, featureless, as wind.

Still Ada has not taken her turn.

"Are we going to have to start playing with a timer?" I say.

She doesn't answer. I glance up. She isn't there. I look around. No sign of her. She must have needed something from inside.

This morning. Earlier. As I was crossing over the bridge, there was a stain of fish blood on the concrete. Dried.

I am thinking this. Remembering. The girl I saw, that girl I was, the imprint of her like a weight on the surface of the river, the ebb tide pulling through her hair.

Ada slides into her seat on the bench across from me. I raise my eyebrows at her.

"Where did you get off to?" I ask.

"Went for a pee. Thought you could get rid of me so easy?" She smiles, teasing.

I search her face, but her eyes are in the shadows. "You haven't taken your turn yet," I say.

"No. I've been mulling things over."

I slip the cigar box from the bag, pass it across the table to her.

"What is it then?" she says.

"You'll see."

"I don't like the way you say that."

"Just open it," I say, and so she does, sees the photograph first—it is on top, I placed it there, I couldn't quite bury it under the rest. I can see how it stops her, takes her breath. For a long moment she does not say anything, just looks at it, her fingers tracing lightly in the corner the petaled warp of a water stain.

"I don't remember this," she says.

She touches her knee in the water, pushing out in a ripple, her fingers pause before the face of the child. Not touching.

"It's Green, isn't it?" I say.

She does not answer right away. "Yes. Where did you get it?"

"That engineer man," I say. "It's a box of things he left. Scraps of 1962."

She nods, her fingers moving now onto the foot of the child, hanging off her hip, his toes brushing the river surface. A mother and her baby. I looked at this photograph yesterday, I looked at it and could not look. I looked at it and could not stop.

"How long have you had this?" she asks quietly.

"A while," I say.

"Why didn't you show me before?" It is not an accusation in her voice that I detect, but something deeper, past that. I'm not quite ready to answer. "Are there more?" she says. She looks up at me, and by her eyes I know what she is asking.

"Not of Green."

She lifts that snapshot then, and sees the one beneath—of the little boat, her skiff, staked to the marsh. I see the smile.

"Look at that," she says. "What would have struck that funny engineer boss to take these shots?"

"There's another of your boat," I say. "Farther on. There's a few of the old bridge, one of the kids turning the key and the draw swinging open, some of them hanging on it. There's one of Swiggie and a fish he brought in on the scales—"

"Is it all photos?"

"No. They're just tossed in with other stuff."

"What's the rest of it?"

"Old menus. One from Tattersalls. One from the Paquachuck. A gaming schedule from Lincoln Park. There's some newspaper clippings, typical job reports, drafts of letters to the state. From the state. Some scrap notes he scribbled."

"What sort of notes?"

"Snippets of conversation from the looks of it. Bits he overheard. He seemed to jot down what struck him, you can't tell really why—it's a mess of junk."

Ada smiles. "Junk."

"There's a few drawings. Charcoal sketches. Cattails. Another of the flats scaled back. Houses. Not much else."

She starts sorting through the things in the box. Some of the pages were completely watermarked when I found them in the shucking house, a leak in the roof, no rhyme or reason to what was ruined and what slipped through unscathed. Some of the snapshots were all pocked up, the images distorted, or they'd dried stuck together, and when I tried to peel them back apart, they tore.

Ada has paused on a sheet of notepaper, she turns it toward her to make out the cramped handwriting, and reads it through.

"Is this an *i* or an *e*, Janie? This word, what does it look like to you?"

I peer past her hand. *"Homily?* No. It's an *e*, I think. *Homely."*

"Ah, yes." She goes on reading. When she gets to the end, she gives a little chuckle. "Oh that's funny—he must have overheard that one. Can't make that stuff up—I wonder who, though—" Her voice is soft, strangely soft, almost a whisper, some wild quiet like the wind in my head. Past her shoulder, alongside the yellow shed, the trees seem to spin through the sky.

"Why today, Jane?" she asks me, turning again through the pages. "Why did you bring this today?"

I have no answer. How can I tell her I don't think there'll be another game?

She is not listening for a reply. She is studying an image of the street, looking north up Main Road from the wharf. You look at that snapshot and at first glance, you might think it's the street as it is now, a designated historic district, it ought to look the same, and at first glance it does, and you might not notice the difference unless you went to stand in that same spot and looked north from there. Then you would see how the houses are larger now, lumpy second stories, dormers, ells, odd overlarge appendages built off the old saltboxes and the half Capes. They are caricatures of houses, poofed-up flower gardens, squared stone walls out front.

"All we wanted then was to be left alone," Ada says, laying that photo of the street into the pile of what she's already gone through. Then again, "Why did you bring this today?"

"It was just a box of things I came across."

"But why today?"

How can I tell you?

This morning when I told Carl to drop me at the lights so I could walk the bridge, it was you, Ada, I came looking for. But as I was crossing, it was Huck I saw, out there, tonging from that boat of his, that boat I know that holds so much, out past the Point of Pines.

"Did you see the sky last night, Janie," she is asking me now, "—that sky last night, it was like a river. Whole week's been that way, all good-seeing nights, everything clear and bright and still, the stars seem to ring. On a night like last night was, you look up into that sky, and the blackness of it all seems so settled, so stable, so serene, you can almost forget what you know—"

She pauses. "There was a night once," she goes on, "over a year ago. A river sky just like that, I remember, it was a Thursday. On Thursdays, Sara used to go to her stretching class, her pilots yoga or whatever, so that night Huck had his little grandbaby Augusta, and it was evening time, and I was at the kitchen sink, washing up the dinner things, when I felt a tugging on my skirt, looked down and there she was, in her little cotton nightgown, her coat, and red cowboy boots, her hair done in its ponytail, some of it tufting up because she'll never sit still long enough for it to get done right. On her cheek was a black smear, chocolate from the cookie Huck had given her. 'Gammy come,' she said. Can't quite speak her r's. Her little fingers messy with that chocolate, tugging me toward the door as I dried my hands on the dish towel, she pulled me outside onto the porch, into the porch swing, clambering up into my lap. 'Gammy, the Moon,' she said, pointing up. 'Open it for me.'

"That night, sitting outside with her on the porch swing under that sky, I didn't tell her what I could have. About the moon. That it only pretends to shine. Got no light of its own. Just a cold stub of rock. Bone-dry. No memory of water.

"I couldn't tell her that, any more than I could tell her that every year I go out to sit in the night, and find some light-object up there that is the right distance away. Twenty, thirty, forty years—that light I see has been on its journey, I mark out time by that. Count one more year I've traveled. Some star just doing what it does, burning through its life, throwing off light, with no thought of me. Just burning itself away, not knowing and perhaps not caring none whether I will be down here looking up to catch its light as it falls.

"I couldn't tell Augusta this, and by the time she's old enough to hear it, more than likely I'll be somewhere up there in that black space falling down through time just like the light is now.

"So that night, instead, I told her to find me the Big Dipper, and she did, put her hand up, her little fingers and thumb in an L, then she took my hand and did the same, fit them together that way, my finger to her thumb, and my thumb to her finger. She made a frame around those seven stars, and I told her that five of those seven were born together. They were a cluster once, a family, and only over millions of years, slowly they've begun to drift apart. And that's not all, I said, see over there, and I pointed with my other hand to the opposite side of the sky—that bright bright star, just over the scrub oak, by the edge of the dark that's the dune, that star is called Sirius, I told her, the dog star, and once it was a part of the same group as those stars in the Big Dipper. Don't seem possible, does it, when it looks so much farther away? It isn't, though, not really so much farther, only seems that way to us because we're driving straight between them.

"Augusta, she got quiet then, real quiet, and I could see she was thinking it over, trying to get her little mind around it all, and we stayed out there that night, her and me on the porch swing, rocking some, and she was quiet. I kept my eyes fixed on the moon in those trees until I could see it for how it really is. Not the moon going into the trees, but the trees passing up the moon. Eight hundred and some miles an hour in these latitudes, that's how fast we're turning, those trees on the earth turning fast and the moon only seeming to rise, only seeming to beat its track across the sky. We're the ones turning into it. And when I looked down again, it might have been a half-hour later, I could see that Augusta had fell asleep, there in my arms. She was asleep, her sweet little face, little mouth falling open a bit with that smudge of chocolate on her chin, her sweet warm breath, and I thought about how, just a week ago, I was her age, not more than five or six. I used to go down below the fields, took the path there between the dutchcaps to the old stoned-in burying yard. I'd lie down there and take a nap, it was all my people buried there, and my pa, he kept the grass cut nice, trimmed short, so it was soft against my cheek. Later in the afternoon, I'd wake and hear them yelling for me from up the house. They didn't know where I was." Ada glances at me. "Didn't matter none. I knew where I was." Her eyes are green, very green, that blood-rimmed corner. "All turning so fast, Janie. Don't feel it, though, do you? Don't feel the wind on your face."

She says this and I see it. More than think it, or remember. I see it. Once. He was just out of me, the little one Samuel, just born, and I woke one night in the new hour and found his eyes fixed on my face, skinless there, his eyes, no shell to them, just the deep of him there on the surface, and it was like I was looking into a well of dark nothing filled with an unnamable something, and the bed where we lay was a white speck, falling, slight pale skull, his hair like bone, that skin baby smell, and how when he laughed in his sleep (have you heard this?) the sound like bits of rind cut from the sun.

The nib of the pen digs. The tip pressing in, this way, in this spot, goes deep, hurts. Ink spreading out in spokes.

It wasn't what they thought—

It wasn't that the world came unglued after.

Once, too, him stomping through the yard—eighteen months he must have been then, not more—it was before his hair was cut for the first time. Before. He was stomping around, this way and that, wearing those yellow rain boots although the sky was parched, no sign of a cloud in it, and his little fist clutching a brown-paper bag full of peas he'd plucked off the vine. That one curl. At the base of his sweet neck. That stubborn curl. So perfect there.

You see it—in the evanescent once—see it, more than think it, more than feel it or remember. The imprint the dead will leave. That impression of a life, still in this life. How the air is pinched around the outline where someone used to be.

"Shhhh," Ada says like she can hear my thoughts, that click, click, click, of thoughts like drilled bits of fired clay strung on a wire—

It wasn't what they thought—

"Shhhhh."

I am not saying anything, but she smiles, softly shakes her head—more gentle than I'd expect—her half-dreamt face through the casual shadows, that smile like she knows I am lying.

Once, I believed there was a grief I could touch, a grief I could dig down to, I believed if I dug deep enough, I would find it, and it would be solid, it would be something I could pick up and carry, a weight in my arms—not this.

She says my name, her voice a whisper stripped, like winter, her voice like a river pulling down through stones.

It wasn't what they thought. It wasn't that the world came unglued after, but that it always had been, and only after that I turned and saw it as it was. You could lose yourself there, in the perishable brightness of a moment, moment after moment. You are the blink of a lamp, the quick sudden shine of a life thrown, falling, into the dark flowing dark of the endlessly flowing world.

This then, in your arms only, wind and water moving—

But that one curl.
    At the base of his sweet neck.
    So willful and forever. That one curl.

Slowly Ada sorts back through the pages, replacing them into the box, in the order they were—stubs of paper, water-smeared, snapshots, odds and ends—until she comes to the first photograph, the one of her, Green on her hip, his toes still trailing in the river.

"Keep it," I say. But it is like she does not hear me. She touches the edge of it again, that odd petaled stain that muddies the grain at the lower right corner. She sets it back in with the rest. It feels heartless, somehow, though I know it is not. I should have known better than to want it otherwise.

There are shadows on her wrists, on her long fingers, shadows of the oak leaves above us that wrap her hands. She closes the box. Pushes it back across the table to me.

PART VII

Parables
of Sunlight

THE BLUE HOUR

MARNE
July 22, 2004, 6:30 PM

I can feel the coin in my pocket, that coin he gave me, the dig of it into my thigh. Through the window, the woods across the yard, the unmistakable stillness that comes at the end of a day. That quiet, desperate hush. On the sofa next to me, the book about light—I am nearing the end of it:

> Those seemingly motionless clouds are moving at the speed of a thousand miles an hour without the slightest evidence of that swift motion recorded on our senses. The earth also—

Down the hall in the kitchen, I can hear my mother messing around, starting up supper, the oven door closing, the timer set, a knife drawn from the drawer, the snip-ting of the blade, vegetables—carrots or the green beans that we picked—laid on the cutting board.

There's a pull on the arm of the sofa where I sit. A thread loose. I tug at it, gently, unraveling. And still the dig of that coin in my pocket.

It was after that last dismal blunder—speaking out loud, and then realizing I had without knowing how much or what I had said—some desperately garrulous rush, no doubt, to keep him stalled there, to keep him from walking away—it was after he and his paper-cup coffee with the plastic leaky cap had taken the three steps up and sat down on the porch next to me, and I was thrashing around in the silence, that shiver of feeling him there with me, close, a slim chance to maybe undo, atone, not knowing though where to pick up what we left off, or something like that. Then he cleared his throat, backed up a few months, before sex and other revelations, and asked me, "So Marne, why did you come home, from California?"

And it was true, almost—the answer I gave him about sailing in the bay off Tiburon and looking back and seeing those cardboard tulip-hued houses on the shore and thinking how I could stab my finger through them—

It is never entirely clear. What draws you back to this sort of a place, a gorgeous backwater rump of a town. You might like to think you know for sure what didn't: a mother, for example, that nail-bitten memory of her sitting on the floor of a room upstairs, so intent on those small clothes, so lost in her folding it felt like I was the one who had disappeared.

So what was it then? A phone call from Alex soon after Christmas. That phone call me gave a little jerk, brought me home. How could I not? But just for a moment, I told myself. Not to stay. I never thought I'd stay.

All of this, of course, was nothing I could have begun to lay out to Ray sitting on the porch, and so instead I gave him the answer of Tiburon, and then there was a silence, a funny, tippy silence, and I looked across the yard to where some sparrows had been nesting in half a dozen unused lobster pots stacked by the shed. Those pots have sat there all spring, some of them busted up, paint chipped off the buoys, autumn olive growing out through the holes, and those sparrows keeping house. Watching them flick around there, I thought about my parents—I thought about how when you see them together, you can feel that they are still within reach of each other. Body, hands, eyes. He loves her, my father, he has always loved her, the way you can love only, perhaps, a rinsed sky.

I have never understood it. How he—so capable, level-minded, fatalistic, and wise—could have chosen her.

I considered remarking on this to Ray as we were sitting there, in that funny flung-over silence that had begun to feel unbearable. I considered mentioning the book about light, in an offhand sort of way—that passage I went back to last night, late, read and re-read, the one I started with that has left its glittering like footprints through my head. The one about how light holds all things—matter, motion, time, dimension, change, the living and the dead. I know it's night logic. A truth that was never true. But today on the porch, I wanted to ask Ray if he has never noticed how it can happen: that something you know is not true can sometimes feel more real than what is.

It took me half an instant to think all of this, to say none of it, and by then the moment had passed, and Ray was asking me if I remembered Stevie MacGregor (yes of course I did), and he told me that Stevie was working as a salvager, too, but down in Tennessee, where he made the bulk of his living diving for river mussels, selling the shells to Japan where they get crunched up, smoothed down, turned into the stuff they use to irritate oysters to grow pearls.

There was a foot of empty space on the step between us, and it suddenly occurred to me that it might feel more right to have my shoes on, so I looked around and found them on the step below the one where we were sitting. I slipped them on.

Ray glanced at me. "Where are you going now?"

"Oh," I said. "Just nowhere."

And he gave a little laugh and smiled like he knew that place and how to get there.

It was less than half an hour, that time of sitting with him on the porch steps, but the grass was sun-touched, the pavement and his face near me suntouched. I could feel that glow in him I feel sometimes, that glow that comes from somewhere deep in him.

"You're up early today," he remarked. I got it then: He'd come by not expecting to run into me.

"Just that sort of day, I guess." Creeping anguish.

He laughed. "What sort of day would that be?"

I didn't have an answer, exactly, and he seemed to sense that, because he laughed again, more gently, dug the toe of his boot against a pebble on the step below the one where we were sitting and shot that little rock off the edge. It fell into a clump of daylilies. I heard it, quick-falling, through the leaves.

From the trees by the shed, a catbird shrieked, and a handful of those sparrows sprayed out of the brush, like shot, and the yard and sky were like a Van Gogh print, everything caught up in the wind-struck throes of some violent motion.

I could feel a pressure in my chest, like it was my turn, and he was waiting for me to come up with something to say, but all the things I might have wanted to say, or should have said, I couldn't, and so instead I asked if there was a salvage job he had coming up, and he told me about the job he had just finished, and gave me that coin.

Then there was absolutely less than nothing to say—nothing, except everything, changed.

"Well, I'll see you then," he said, and took his paper-cup coffee and left.

The weight of that coin in my hand hurt—the perfection of it, so simple, so slight. I shoved it into my pocket and went back inside. My parents were in the kitchen, sitting at the table, and they both looked up as I walked in, and I felt a heat go through my cheeks because I could see they had overheard and, in their minds, were playing it again—the what-if? game. Tough to win—that game. The soda bread I'd thrown together was already out of the oven—wrapped in a tea towel—nothing left for me to follow through on that front, either. I sat down in the chair where I'd been sitting before Ray showed up, half a piece of toast left on the plate I for sure didn't want. I picked up the book about light, found my page, pushed through a line or two, then set it down, picked up a Cabela's catalog, and started thumbing through that instead. And when my father mentioned he was going down to the garden to pick beans, I decided I was feeling a little too edgy to hang around the house, so I went with him.

And as we walked down the hill into the shimmering heat of the green, he was humming that song, that bluegrass song, about the '52 Vincent Black Lightning and the man who owned it, the thief who fell for a redheaded girl.

My father took two baskets off the fence post, gave me one, and we started in, gathering beans, working down the rows. The weight of the sun lay hot across my shoulders. I could feel my hair stuck wet to the back of my neck, clots of dry earth breaking under my feet, and my father still humming that motorcycle song, that free and happy song that has a sad end, and as I felt for the beans through the infrequent shade of the vines, I thought about how he used to go out lobstering, on one of the longer trips, when he might be gone a night or two, my mother would often ask me to drive her down to East Beach. We would sit there, parked on the stones, her eyes just on the ocean, watching the horizon, like she could feel it shudder, like she could feel him out there, on the verge of reappearing on that line, beyond the range of ordinary sight.

At the end of the third row, my father straightened up, took off his cap, wiped sweat from his brow with his sleeve. And it was as he was setting his cap back on again that I asked him. In spite of what had happened on the porch, or maybe because of it—I have never asked him, and only today I did—standing in the green light-soak of the garden—I asked him if my mother ever mentioned that boy, ever spoke of him at all, that son of theirs who died, whose name was Samuel.

It was the name that stopped him. I felt it more than saw it, felt something in him catch. He looked at me, looking directly into the scorch of the sun that came from behind me.

"No," he said.

"Do you think she's forgotten?"

"No."

And that was all. He started working down the next row. Strange. After years of wanting to know and not knowing, wanting to ask and not asking. It was that simple. I had asked, he had answered, it was done. I took a breath.

"Why did you marry her?"

This time he did not stop, he did not turn or look at me, he kept on working down the row, twisting beans from the vines, his hands calm, efficient, swift.

"There was no one else," he muttered, loud enough for me to hear, his voice with a gruff indifference like he'd decided once and for all just to say it straight-up, dash any romantic inkling I might have had and just be done with it, give me the unsweetened truth as it stood, since wasn't that what I was asking for?

I felt my throat close. No one else? No other half-reasonable option?

He looked up, still working down the row, and saw me stopped, just frozen there, staring at him.

"What the hell's wrong now?" he said, his voice kind of annoyed. It was unlike him, that tone. He tore off a bean, taking vine with it, and shook his head. "You're looking for a fancy answer. Well, Marne, you should know better, you won't get that sort of answer from me. That's just the way of it. There was no one else but her. Never was before, never since."

* * *

The woods now, blue. This side of evening. The lengthened shadows of the trees wrung through the yard. In the kitchen, the timer rings. I hear her opening the oven door, the baking dish slid from the rack, a muted thud as she places it onto the counter to cool. Through the window, the world steeped in sapphire—stones, trees, grass—drunken over in that blue, soaked down.

A faint scent, from a flower in the sun-window.

My mother has a gift with things green, which is why I felt quite sure she'd have no trouble with that orchid. But when I look at it now on the end table where it's kept—its stripped, failed self—I wish she'd get along and junk it. Let go of what's past losing. Move on.

From my pocket I draw out the coin; its edge is smooth, unridged. I wonder if it was always that way, or if it was the unseen workings of the sea that wore it down.

Above the orchid on the wall, that black and white of her—the girl on the bridge. I see that snapshot now and it's clear to me. She was looking right through the camera—right through the man—whoever he was—who took it. She was seeing *something*, though. You can see that in her eyes. They are not empty, not flat at all, but filled. That unusual expression in them—her mind like moving water, wind, sky—so much of what I know.

Outside, it is still not dark. Long summer twilight lasting. Just going on. I can hear my father down back, behind the shed, splitting wood.

Do you think she's forgotten? I had asked him down in the garden.

For three years in my twenties, after New York but before California, I lived in Taos, New Mexico, I worked in a café near the Rio Grande gorge that served breakfast burritos all day, and almost made the mistake of getting married. It was a long relationship, a bad relationship that ended badly, and when it was over I came home for a month before I threw myself at LA. And one night, during that month I was home, my mother, Ada, and Vivienne Butler were going over to Newport Jai Alai. Vivi asked if I wanted to come along, and I went.

It was a seedy place, that Newport Jai Alai, everything laid over with a fake-gold grime. We sat up in the lounge, looking down through the glass to the courts where men hurled that ball around with the long sticks banded to their arms. We sat in a row of chairs, my mother at one end, an empty seat beside her that soon was taken by a man, some slick-haired natty, alone and not unhandsome. He offered her a cigarette, which to my astonishment she accepted, he lit it for her, murmured something, she laughed. Smoke glowed around her hair.

There was an air about her that night, as she sat casually drinking her liquor from the cheap plastic cup, with her betting stubs in her hand, her cigarette, next to the well-dressed stranger who kept trying to chat her up, she kept blowing him off, but that air about her—that lovely, disenchanted air—disdainful even, yet intimately so—how at ease she seemed, more at ease than any one of us, even Ada, in that seedy glint of a place, as if this, all along, was the sort of life she had been intended for.

At one point in the evening, as I was watching her and thinking this, she turned and her eye caught Ada's, a look exchanged between them, complicit, sly, then her gaze shifted to me, and what unnerved me was the composure in her face as she considered mine, before she turned away back to the courts. It was a look that, as I considered it later, bespoke a certain clarity of mind, a lucidity and intelligence that I knew in that moment I had not accounted for, and still failed to understand.

What do you think she knows?

I glance at the book about light, closed. Inside though, between those pages, in the scattered notes, pencil smoke, stale ash. A drift not meant to be gleaned, as good as unwritten, unread, not meant, maybe ever, to be. From the kitchen, the smell of onion, the smell of chicken baked and on the cool, sharp smells, smells of home, on a draft come through an open window, a draft that has touched her hands, and is touching me now.

My head hurts, not in the usual way, but like I can hear a whole sky of stars.

Footsteps then, hers, soft down the hall. She walks into the room behind me.

WINDOW

JANE

July 23, 2004

Ada is looking at something over my right shoulder. It takes me a moment to realize what, then I do.

"You know what it is about those lilies?" she says. "It's not just them themselves as much as how they bloom this time of year—when the world reeks of summer, and every smell reminds you of some other summer come before."

I know the smells she means: blueberries, corn on the ripening, the smell of hay, just cut—smells so dank and rich, so much of this place, no other. And when the wind comes around, as it will in the afternoons this time of year, driving out of the southwest, driving in that cooler, sharper salt tang off the ocean—sea-muck, fish, the mudflats at low tide—by those smells, you know just how it looks: the river laid out, all gloss rippled silver against the black static masses of the marsh islands: Little Ram, Lower Spectacle, Ship Rock.

It's how you know a place, isn't it? By its smells. Year in, year out. It's not a thing you learn. It's a thing you know—the differences, for example, between the smells of a dry summer and the smells of a wet one. You map the changes in a place by how those smells change.

Ada takes her turn. She drops two letters, two vowels. Makes the word A-N-E. Six points. She must have crap in her rack to play such a dinky dink.

"I never used to question it," she says. "When you're done, you're done. There's no little part of you left over. It was always so cut and dry for me before. I suppose it comes with getting older, Janie, the future starting to look a little skimpy up ahead." She pauses then, a soft reluctant smile. "This morning, though, I woke up early, so early, such a still and lovely morning, a perfect day. I took my coffee out onto the porch, and as I was sitting there, in that beautiful lonesome morning, I thought about a window in the house where I grew up, that window with the beveled panes on the south side. Every time my pa walked by that window, he swore he saw an Indian woman sitting inside smoking a pipe by a fire he knew wasn't there. 'You've gone pixilated, Ernest Lyons,' my mother would say, 'clear around the bend.'

"As a child, though, I looked for her. That woman. In between chores, milking cows or filling the woodbox, I'd hunt up some excuse to go by that window ten times a day, hoping for a glimpse. Never did see her."

Her fingers drift back to the tiles in her rack, touching one. We are always, it seems, touching these tiles.

"You asked before about that summer, Janie," she says, "the summer they opened that new road. That was the year before I left Silas, before I moved with the boys into that ratty old Colonial down the street from you." She glances up, I nod, and she goes on. "One night that summer, I remember, I went out driving with Junie. It was just him and me in the car. He'd done something crazy to his '59 Galaxie Sunliner and wanted to take me for a drive. He knew I loved to go fast. We took the highway. The new road. They hadn't yet opened it all the

way down, but we couldn't keep off it—eleven miles of drag strip—
none of us could keep off that road. That night on the highway, we
took the hill and he punched it, buried the speedometer. We hit the
rise at full speed. All four tires lifted, I swore it after, we were on
air—"

Her voice breaks off. And it occurs to me that this is how it happens, how every story will come back to the one you cannot tell. I
know that she is thinking about Green. She never says it. But I will
feel it, sometimes, between us, like the air is drenched.

One afternoon, when I was pregnant with Marne, there was a storm.
Alex was just six. He and I were alone in the house. He sat up at the
table in the kitchen with his coloring paper and crayons. I was peeling
carrots at the sink. The rain beat against the window, it started coming down hard, and we could hear how the time between the lightning
flash and the thunder grew shorter as the storm drew near. Once,
when a flash of lightning struck, the yard outside turned a sudden
white. The overhead light trembled. Alex left his crayons, and I sat
down in the chair. He crawled up into my lap. "Mommy," he asked,
"what makes thunder happen?" His hands were tight and damp
around my neck, his breath hot, and I knew I could give him some answer about fronts, about waves of warm air meeting up against the
cold and, at the same time, I knew all he was really asking was how not
to be afraid.

He was nine the night Green died. It was later than I should have let
him stay up on a school night. We were downstairs, Alex and I, on the
sofa in the front room watching television, three-year-old Marne
asleep in my arms, and Carl had just called from the wharf to say his
boat was in, he would be home soon.

We felt the car pass by, the rush of air lifting the night, and when
they struck the pole a quarter mile north, there at the corner, the

lights snapped out and we were left in darkness, waiting for something without knowing what that something was. We heard a woman calling her son's name, and we knew then who it was in that car. Soon after, Carl arrived home. We told him, and he left again, drove down to see, and when he came back, some time after, he just looked spent, sad, a slight dark soak where sweat had spread around his collar. He kept shaking his head. "Green was driving. Only thirteen years old and they let him. They'd been racing on the highway, tried to take the same speed to the back roads." He couldn't seem to stop shaking his head, saying how nuts it was, how unlikely, that Huck, who they had to pry out of the car with Green, had come clear of the wreck near unscathed, just a cut on his forehead, his elbow dislocated, and Silas— well, he had sailed right out the open window on the passenger side, sailed scot-free, then rolled, struck the ground and passed out, dead drunk as he was, not a single bone broken.

I did not sleep that night. Lay awake to the smooth black running down the window glass, and sometime that night, Marne awoke, frightened, I heard her feeling her way down the hall, the crack of light at the door, her footsteps on the rug, she crawled into the bed between us, pressed herself against me, and I held her, tightly, her small soft sweet warm body like a heaven held against me. Next morning, I left her there asleep, the speck of her alone in the big bed. I went downstairs to fix breakfast, to get Alex off to school. I buttered toast, poured juice, like it was any other morning, and I sat with Alex outside on the front steps waiting for the bus to come around. It was fall. Early October. A beautiful fall day—that ache in the light—and the wind soft, the dry scrape of leaves on the road, the sound of the tractor from the Wales farm next door, the air full of the smell of plowed earth, the lighter scent of apples. Alex was quiet. He scuffed his toe into the seam where the doorstone met the dirt. I saw the school bus coming over the rise and felt my chest tighten. I didn't want to let him go. No, not that morning. I kissed him good-bye, and he let me, like he knew.

I straightened his coat, went to smooth it once, but he shrugged loose and walked down the drive to meet the bus. I watched him go. Only nine, already gone from me.

I picked grapes that morning. Took Marne with me down back. There was plenty of other housework that needed doing, but the smell of those grapes, that dusky smell, was ripe and close. We stripped the vines, took every one we could, our hands stained by the time we were done, her little mouth and teeth bruise-colored from the juice.

The sky weeping. All that fall I remember. The taste of ashes in my throat. Cloud shadows moving through the grass.

I would see her drive by. Ada. Almost every day, it came to seem, she had some reason to drive by our house, to drive that particular stretch of road to the corner. She was looking for Green, I knew, trying to find her way back to the moment before everything changed. Each day she drove by that spot, whether or not it was on her way to wherever she might have been going, if anywhere—to get her nails done or up to Vivienne's house on Blossom Road or shopping at the Star Store downtown. I would see her pass by, the window open, black pin curls of her hair escaping from the scarf wrapped around her head, dark sunglasses on, and one long hand draped over the wheel, hell-bent, it seemed, on driving that stretch of the road, no one ever with her in the car. Just Ada alone. Fast. Her eyes fixed on the road, like she could stare it down. Day after day. Taking a knife to the string.

I came to recognize the sound of her car: her engine, and how she took the hill, her foot to the gas, coming over the rise past the glen.

Once that fall, I ran into her. At the post office. She was at her box, messing around with the little screw thing, finally got it open, scooped out the letters inside, then turned and, when she saw me, stopped a moment. I could feel the hollow bend of air around her, and she looked at me, and I looked back at her, the space between us bent like the air was caving in, and I saw it in her face, how we were each only just a mirror for each other.

You don't get past it, her eyes telling me that day, though she must have known I had learned it myself. You go on, of course, but you don't get past it. You don't stop loving them just because they're gone. You don't stop, except the part of you that has stopped, the part of you that was your heart outside your body, stopped, stuck there in that before of what you lost, stopped, turned, looking back, like Lot's wife on her hill gone all to salt, looking back toward the hour of a life when you were sunlight. You didn't know it then. How could you, then, have known it?

She fiddles with her nails, a little cluck, cluck noise, her tongue against the roof of her mouth. "Get on with it, Janie," she says, impatient.

"It's not my turn."

"Is so. Check the score." She leans forward, looking at the paper. "Did you give me my six? You didn't yet, did you?"

I glance down. No.

"Little sneak."

On the paper, her name. The numbers in their clean ordered columns tallied, under the solid dark line beneath her name. I write down 6. Add it to her score. Two sixty-seven now. To my two ninety-two. And my turn.

In the box-lid, I count the tiles left. Eight. Soon, within half an hour, less, they will be played out. The game will be over. Every word that we will make today will have been made. I will take the board by the edges, bend the two halves toward each other, make that gully in the center, and lift it over the box, tilt it so they go on a rush, that strike of lightweight wood to wood, letters, words, washing into one another, rinsed away.

It is a sound I love. A sound I have always loved.

She has left a hook exposed. The A in A-N-E, the last word she played. It dangles, that A, a niche open to the left of it. I go to set down my M and run E-M-U down, then realize. The Q is still out there. In Ada's rack or in those tiles still unturned, the Q at large, along with the last precious blank. And three of the U's already played. I am holding the fourth.

I put that U by. And use the M in another spot, farther up on the board. I draw my letters. Wish. Wish. First draw: A. Wish again. Yes. There it is. Q. Ten points. And in my rack, a decent setup for it. Q. U. I. A. L. O. E. So far, so good. I can win this.

Once when Marne came home from California, she brought a T-shirt she'd found at some fancy hardware restoration store out there. She told me at that store, you could also buy mahogany-inlaid Scrabble boards, two hundred dollars a pop; for fifty more, you get your name inscribed. The T-shirt was black, on it written in bold white letters, WHO NEEDS U? and under that, a list of Q words that don't require a U. I didn't know there were such words, I said. Marne lent that shirt to me, and I wore it the next time we met here to play. Vivienne was still alive then, claimed she knew about some of those words—qoph, qat, qwerty—she'd seen them in the updated *Scrabble Players Dictionary*—a dictionary we never kept as a standard for our games. Vivienne got a kick out of that shirt, but Ada had no use for it.

"Yuppies," she scoffed. "Had to go invent new words because they'd come right apart if they drew a Q in the eleventh hour of a game and all the U's played."

Yesterday, once, as Carl and I were sitting in the kitchen, and Ray and Marne were out on the porch, I glanced through the window and saw the shivers pass through my daughter's body when she stole a look at Ray and found he was already looking back at her. I saw it then, how she looked away quick, that shine in her eyes she tries to hide, that quiet secret smile.

I tell Ada this now. I tell her all of it, expecting she'll bristle, say something harsh, unkind. But she doesn't. She just listens, as I tell her about how Ray stopped by yesterday morning, unexpectedly, looking for Alex—how he and Marne sat out on the porch—how my tough little moxie daughter was all in disarray.

Ada chuckles. "And wasn't it your Marne who said that thing once about love—it was Marne, wasn't it—how did she put it? About love being just another four-letter word? Ha!" She laughs. "So doesn't it all come back around?"

I hesitate.

Then I ask her. "Luce," I say. "My father. What was he to you?"

And that is all I say. It is, I know, all I need to say. She does not answer. For a moment I am not entirely sure she has heard. She is looking down at the letters still untouched, the scattered pool of them remaining, their blank faces in the box-lid. I see it pass through her—the thought of him.

"He used to talk about you, Janie, all the time. Your father."

She falls silent.

I wait.

Her hands resting on the table are strangely still.

"Was it Silas who killed Luce?"

Her eyes rise. I have caught her—at last—off-guard. She does not answer, only looks at me. With that look, her eyes filling, some fast steep tide running in.

All these years I've come to play and wondered. I've waited for some slip on her part, for the door to open, for there to be a chance, this chance, now.

I am not entirely alone. I know this. I knew it the day Vivi called me out of the blue and invited me to meet them on a Friday. They met every Friday, she explained over the phone, a little old club of old women. "You'll be our young one," she said, and laughed, ebullient Vivi laughter. I went. No hesitation. There was no question, ever, in my mind that I would go. Ada had lost her son by then, and I'd lost mine. She knew the difference between what could be absolved and what could not. It was Ada, I knew, who had told Vivi to call. It was Ada who'd come looking for me—to play some word, to lay down some last story, the one you cannot tell.

"Do you know?" I ask her.

"Silas would have," she says quietly. "And it's better, don't you think, we even say he did."

I don't answer, and she does not say more. She will not. I know it now.

Her eye has shifted. She is studying the board.

"Curious," she remarks. "And I almost went and spent them out last turn, but something told me, 'Hang on a minute, Ada Varick,' and so I did, and there it is. My spot. That S I needed. Right there. Just like you knew it, Jane. Knew that S was what I'd need down the road. You aren't going to like this," she says. She starts dropping her letters, one, two, three, no, not all of them, no. Four. Five. Six. She sets them down, all but one. "Joker's a T," she says.

□-R-A-N-P-A-

I can't even see where she intends to set them in until she has done it. How has she done it? Laid that word, using the S that I set down five or six moves back, and R-E-N-T, she weaves her six letters into the skinny space, making room where there was none.

T-R-A-N-S-P-A-R-E-N-T

She can do this. Ada. This is her gift. Whereas I will look at the board and see the words that fill it, she will see the spaces still left open in between.

It is not so much: the letters themselves at face value. It is not a high-scoring word—or particularly remarkable. It is a word in common use—a word anyone might know. But how she has done it—slipped it in there.

"That's good, Ada."

"Only six letters," she answers, ruefully, "I wanted another boodle."

I am adding up the score—that one longer word, and the other incidentals made crosswise off it. Points scored in all directions.

"You're going to win," I say.

She shakes her head. "No. I've done it out twice in my head. It isn't enough."

"It will be."

"I don't think so."

A play like that, I want to tell her, so gorgeous and deceptively sly, doesn't it have to be enough?

She glances at me, her smile—touch of mischief, touch of the quick—so much her, that smile.

"Well," she says, "it's not quite over yet."

THE WORLD

HUCK, FOURTEEN
Summer 1962

On the table up at Charlie's Diner: some dirty plates, the nib of a roast beef sandwich, coffee cups, and a *Life* magazine left behind by whoever was there before. Huck grabs the magazine as the four of them slide into the booth. He starts flipping through it, and the waitress comes by, asks if can't they take another table, one that's already been cleared. "Naw," Pard answers, "this one's good." Waitress frowns, a punk look, then she starts clearing, cups, dishes, silver, clanging and banging, because she's ticked, her red hair pulled back tight, she's an older broad, mid-thirties maybe, still has a body on her, but her face deeply lined like she's seen her share of bad road.

She wipes the table surface down. They put in their order. Then she's gone, and Pard's looking out the window, watching the outside tables and the walkway that runs alongside where they dropped the wallet.

"Anybody coming by yet?" Robbie asks.

"Naw, not yet."

Eejit's elbow bumps Huck's, and the *Life* magazine page he's holding tears.

"Watch it, Eejit!"

Red The Waitress walks by their table, carrying a tray piled high with someone else's food. Pard follows her with his eyes until she's out of range, then from his pocket draws out an empty pack of cigarettes, peels the tinfoil from the inside, folds that piece of foil up, and slides it in behind the jukebox keys, jimmying it right, so the thing shorts out, lights up. He starts punching in numbers.

"Play one seventeen," Eejit says.

Robbie growls, "That is such a tweet song." Huck, still flipping through the magazine, pauses on a full-page advertisement for Maxi-Pads, a woman dressed all in white; with his eyes, he traces the slope of her waist. The three others are arguing now, into it good, Robbie saying that Jerry Great Balls Lewis is head and shoulders above Roll Over Beethoven Berry, and Pard snapping back that Lewis at his ultimate best isn't half the musician Berry is, only Berry don't get the airtime Lewis does and never will on account of his being a nig.

"One seventeen, Pard. Put it in. C'mon," Eejit says again. Pard ignores him, his knuckly fingers working fast, punching in those numbers, punching them hard. One forty-five. Bill Haley and His Comets. One forty-six. The Spaniels. One fifty-one. One fifty-two. One fifty-four. Elvis. "Love Me Tender." Elvis. "Jailhouse Rock."

"One seventeen, Pard."

"Mum up, Eejit," Robbie snaps.

"One seven-teen," Pard trills, pushing those last three numbers down, slow and with intent. Then he sits back, weaves his fingers together, his knuckles crack. He hits out a cigarette from his working pack, lights up, glances through the window. His voice drops. "Alright, boys. Here we go."

Huck glances up from the *Life* magazine as the three others shove toward the window. By the outside tables, a man has stopped, chinos, a pressed white buttondown shirt, he is looking down at the wallet they planted there beside the walkway.

It's an old trick—always works. One of those tricks engineered by Pard who gets off on seeing how far people will go to fall. Kind of a dumb nasty trick, Huck thinks now—though it's never struck him as such before. He only saw the prank of it, but now watching his three buddies crowded at the edges of the window, jeering at that unsuspecting fellow outside, he just wants to be gone.

"Come on, man," Pard whispers, "pick it up. You know you want it."

Pressed-white-shirt man looks around. Sees no one.

"Greed, man. Feel it. Beautiful greed."

Man bends down, slips the wallet quick into his back pocket, then walks into the diner, and crosses to a booth at the other end of the room where a fine-looking woman sits waiting, a brunette, her hair teased, all lipsticked up. He slides into the seat across from her.

"This should be so good," Pard says.

"What if he don't notice?" Robbie asks.

Pard smiles. "He'll notice."

Huck glances back down at the *Life* magazine, starts turning the pages again, a page of all text, then another advertisement, then a longish feature story about the Bay of Pigs, that mess down in spicquito Cuba—page after page, he keeps turning, no wait, there, stop, back one, the page slips, then he gets it. There. A full two-page black-and-white photograph of a highway running along a seacoast. Title in block white letters: THE NEW CALIFORNIA. His fingers pause.

The jukebox song that was playing ends, the machine ticks, a soft grind, its skinny arm moving, a new 45 picked out, set down, starting to spin. The voices of the other boys ricochet off the strains of the next song starting up, arguing, laughing, distant-like, other voices too folded in and flung together with the greasy scent of food and the electric light climbing the scabby walls. Pard is talking some shit now, his voice strikes deep and bold, no question in it, ever, no doubt. That sure sane tone of his voice enough to tell he never looks around, too deep in, or back. He knows what it all comes down to. He's waxing on about Marilyn Monroe, a little eulogy to that something-and-again woman, dead as dead now as of last week. There are some things, he says, that are tragedy in the true sense of the word, and the loss of a woman like her from the world, well, don't that top every list?

Voices, music, smells. Robbie whining now about how long is it going to take for that pressed-shirt man to realize there's a scoop of dogshit in the fold of that wallet he picked up, how long now for that stinky wet stuff to start seeping through?

Huck hears it all and hears none of it, his mind on the lip of a shell, he touches the photograph, the free winding forever silver of that road running along the California coast, twisting its way down the edge of the page—touching that paved shimmery silver, then jarred out of that, remembering his father's finger pointed at him as he was walking out the door earlier that evening, unpared tobacco-stained nails, that dirty slab of a finger nagging—

"Five AM, Huck, you hear me? I'll be kicking your sorry ass out of bed. Top of the morning tomorrow, first thing, we'll be at that hay—" And Huck muttering back, "Okay, Dad," pushing his way out the door into the evening cool and onto his bike, down the drive, past the front field with the corn already tasseling out—pedaling, pedaling, pedaling—get out, away, get gone.

Waitress Red has brought their food, is setting down the plates, Robbie almost knocks over Huck's soda, and the jukebox strikes up the next tune, and Eejit is asking Huck to pass the vinegar and salt, and Huck's arm doing it, the glass saltshaker moving across his line of sight, his own hand not his own, his hand like the rest of him, mechanical shadow.

He can feel the wind on his throat, the wind and the soft speed of driving that silver California road down the edge of the page, the photograph spread open on the table by his left elbow. Some ketchup has spilled into the glittering sea. He blots it with his sleeve, still driving down that West Coast highway. She is with him: Jane Weld, in a cool, fast car, the top down, his hands on the leather-wrapped wheel, her skirt blowing around her knees, driving through inexhaustible sunshine; peach trees set alongside the road, orchards where they will stop to wander through and pick the fruit whenever they get hungry or just have a notion for a bite of that delirious sweetness, no one will mind. You say her name, Jane, Jane, Jane, and she is with you there, in that car, driving through silver gelatinous sunshine down that photograph, just you and her, warm wind on your face, Jane, and the unclenched blue of the sky silking down.

"What's bugging you?" Pard says, his voice almost a hiss, low enough the others won't hear—that tone of his voice, Huckie knows, is reserved for him, and on cue he glances up. Pard's looking at him, a dull, flat look on his face, that stoned-over look. Huck knows it. He shakes his head. "Nothing." He digs into his food.

Every night this week there's been something getting into the trash. Night before last, it came around, some creature scuttling through the garbage cans, metal lids rattling. Huck went out onto the porch to have a look, spotted that bushy black-and-white tail as the skunk made its way off in a waddle around the side of the corncrib. Easy enough, he'd thought at the time, to wait up for it, there on the porch. Skunk don't move quick. Take a shotgun. Finish that thing off.

It's what his older brothers would have done—what they would always say—something comes poaching onto your property, starts messing around with what's yours, it's your right to take it out.

He feels a chill. A pit in his stomach, bits of himself gnawed away.

It's all been getting worse. Storm brewing, worse, his mother pregnant again, still picking back over old things—their midnight fighting louder—loud enough sometimes to wake him; those threats thrown around, not unlike years ago when Deadman Weld was still alive, pulling on their mother, that business between them wrecking the peace—the boys would overhear, how could they not? Her threatening to leave, their father threatening much worse—they were all home then—Junie home, and Huck being small would find his way into his oldest brother's bed, Junie's arm tight and strong around him, listening, eyes open to the dark, his face set.

Different now, Huck's alone in the house, only him now and the baby Green. Different now, how his father's grip on her has begun to slip. She's on the edge of done, dealing from the upper hand. Just last night through the wall, he heard her say, "You were happy, Silas, with me thinking he'd picked up and left. Got news for you though," she taunted. "I was never yours to begin with." There was an awful silence then, Huck knew that breed of silence, and waited, his body braced for the familiar sound of his father's hand across his mother's face. He waited, but the sound didn't come, didn't, maybe never would, and it struck him then what Silas must have already known: She was gone for good this time.

"What's bugging you?" Pard asks again, low stone voice.

Huck doesn't answer this time, doesn't look up.

Across the diner at the counter, a glass falls, the sound splintering, loud, ice cream soda splattered, a scuddy mess on the floor. The whole place gone rock-still for a moment, everyone turning to look. The food in Huck's mouth tastes wrong, dry, a tarred, rubbery taste—all of this wrong, a nasty trick, his being here, anywhere here, all wrong. He takes a gulp of Coke to get it down.

Pard pushes his plate away, maybe a little harder than he has to, the edge of his plate strikes Huck's, and suddenly then, across the room, the hair-teased brunette belts out some kind of shriek, and the guy who nabbed the dog-cookie-loaded wallet is standing up, wiping his hands on napkin after napkin, then walking fast toward the men's room, and Pard drops his share of the money they owe for their food onto the table, Eejit still shoveling down french fries, and Huck, paid up as well, gets Eejit by the collar, saying, "We're done, let's get the hell out of here."

Then they are outside, the four of them, heading down Route 6, Huck a beat ahead and the other three walking behind, still laughing. Smith Williams drives by. Pard gives a shout, flags him down, and they pile in. He's into the sauce already, they can smell the liquor on him, the reek of it filling the car. He tells them he's just coming back from that bar down the Cove. "Saw your two older brothers there," he tells Huck, and Huck murmurs something about "don't it figure." Pard talks Smith into stopping at the Congo package store to buy them two bottles of ginger brandy. He holds out the money, some extra as well, and Smitty answers with some cobbly, half-slurred logic about how the government's got no right to tell people of any age what they can or cannot drink or buy or sell. At the Congo, he leaves them outside in the car still running, and Pard debates aloud the pros and cons of whether to borrow the car or wait for the booze, when Smith comes back with the brown-paper bag Pard asks if he could give them a lift down to the Point Wharf, and Smitty says, sure as hell why not, he's got nothing else doing, just cruising around.

They take the new road. It's open now all the way down to the State Beach Reservation the other side of the new bridge. Pard sits up front, yacking on with Smitty, telling him about the buttondown-shirt sucker who picked up that wallet, and they are laughing, talking, carving through the night down that new highway, sheets of fog blown across, bruising the dark. In the backseat, Huck leans his face against the window. He can feel the trembling shudder of the glass, the trembling shudder like it is inside him, his cheek against the body of the night, like a hunger, an unfinished country. He cannot think. He cannot tell her. How could he ever tell her? He closes his eyes and he is driving, still, down that other road, that other coast, with her.

Smith drops them down at the wharf, and they sit on the edge of the town dock, their legs hanging over. They break out the first bottle of that nice ginger brandy, pass it back and forth, a nip here, a nip there. They kill that one, then start on the second. Huck can feel the tingle work through his brain, warming him. He glances toward the bridge, the crowd of men fishing, packed in, lined up shoulder-to-shoulder across that old iron-and-timber span, while behind them in the night rises the brash hulking gleam of the new—they fish the tide, so their backs are to it, seeming unaware of that arched wash of steel looming up behind them.

"Slim pickings," Pard's saying now, in the middle of some new illumination. Some soapbox rant. "These are the facts. See—" And Huck decides he's had his fill of listening to what he hasn't even heard. He strips off his shirt and dumps himself off the side of the pier into the river.

Cold. Even in the summer night, the water like pins all through him. He holds his breath, sinking down, down, until his feet touch bottom mud, he crouches there, in the fierce pulsing silence of the dark underwater, holding his breath; he can feel the burn come in his chest, lungs slowly crushed, he holds still, old air like a blade, breath escaping, leaking out the side of his mouth, the high-pitched broken whistle of it, shrill. Bubbles rising. Could he stay here, down in this night world? Stay down long enough for everything the other side of the surface to change? His head spins, breaking. He pushes off, his body taut, shoots up through the skin of the river back into the known summer night. The other three have stripped off their shirts and jumped in, they swim around the docks, Pard in the lead, calling to Huck, the crook of white arms, splash, disappearing, voices echoing among the close, intimate black oiled shadows of the piles.

Huck lets himself start to drift, downriver, floats on his back, looking up, chasing the sky. He feels some slithery thing come up from underneath him, a hand grasps his hair, *what the hell*, he starts to sit up, thrash, spitting water. It's Pard.

"You dumb fuck," Huck says, sputtering. "That was no joke."

"I know what it is," Pard says, his voice low though there's no one else near. His hair is wet, plastered back, he treads water slowly, not seeming to move, his head just above the surface like it's only his head bobbing there, pale, skin like bone. "You need to let it go, man. It wasn't our fault. Who knew he was gonna turn?"

Huck just stares back. They don't talk about it, have never since that day, it was just cloud between them, a moment so rushed and bewildered, it might not have even happened. He dives, against the current, comes to the surface, he starts swimming back toward the piers.

After midnight, the other three take off, head up to Robbie's aunt's house for the night to crash.

"Come on, Huckie," Pard says.

Huck shakes his head.

"You think you're going to walk all that way home?"

"Got to," Huck says. "Tomorrow morning, I got to help my dad with the hay."

And Pard, because they are best friends, their lives fused that way, one the shadow of the other, always there, gives Huck a look like he might say more, but the other two are still hanging around within earshot, and he doesn't. He leaves with them, walking up Main Road toward the church. Huck starts over the bridge, wondering who might drive by at this hour he could thumb a ride from. Halfway across the draw, he glances back toward the wharf. He stops then, his eye caught. The pencil-thin gleam of a mast. The *Laura May*, his uncle Swig's boat, tied up in its berth. He stares at it, stares, his mind brittle, seesawing, beating like an insect, unstill.

* * *

Voices wake him, the rub scratch of burlap against his face, his neck cramped up. Voices in the wet dark, still bluish, before dawn, smell of coffee, smell of salt, cool air off the sea.

They are out on the deck, his uncle Swig and Carl Dyer, who works for him. Pitching in high school, Carl threw a fastball that became legendary. Pard as a rule has no heroes, but has dubbed Carl The Iron as he can strike a swordfish like nobody's business. From the corner of the wheelhouse, Huck can see his uncle and Carl, leaning against the rail, drinking their coffee. They talk about hunting, some trip Carl took last fall, going after deer through the big woods down Maine, the edge of Allagash.

"Eighty miles in, they're cutting. Virgin timber," The Iron is saying. "You walk into those woods, you can walk for days, weeks, and not find your way out. Mountains up there'll throw a magnet, you never know for sure if your compass reading's true." He's got a low voice, Carl Dyer, strong hands, you notice his hands, you know what they can do with that harpoon. They wrap his mug of coffee now, steam rising off. "It's not like down here," he is saying. "Sure there's plenty of deer to drive, but down here, you know you'll always come out somewhere, some brook or wall or road, and know just where you are."

Swig murmurs something, an assent, then silence awhile, both men leaning on the rail, looking out.

"So what do you think?" Swig says at last.

"It's going to slick off," Carl answers. "I say we go swordfishing."

Swig turns around, his eyes fall on Huck curled up in the corner of the wheelhouse, a momentary flicker of surprise. Then his brows crease. "What trouble are you into now, Rat?"

"None. Swear it."

His uncle gives him a smile.

"Let me go out with you, Swiggie."

"Haven't said we're going yet." Swig looks at Carl. "Are you fierce to go?"

"It's a good day for it."

Swig nods, glancing back at his nephew. "Alright then. Five bucks, Rat. For every fish you spot if we land it."

A perfect day. Occasional clouds boxing in their packs like great white fists. The sea is glass, a slow-moving swell. They go south, southwest of Noman's, twenty miles, to the Dumping Grounds, and Huck is up in the mast with The Iron; other boats already there, steaming around. One to the east of them, half a mile or so off, makes a sudden hard turn, smoke belching out, the dory lowered, shooting away.

Huck scans the sea, the mirrored surface of it, looking for a thin darker mass lolling about, a fish come up to sun. And the world, from this height, is vast—all world, all divine brightness, sea and sky unmapped blue stretching out in every direction away. To the north farther off, he can see the humped shapes of the islands, beyond that lies the mainland, a low dark scud.

It cannot touch him here. That mainland. Not any shithouse mouse strutting over it. No old bad things, midnight threats, nagging father's finger. All that sums up to nothing out here.

"Sun's hot," he murmurs. The Iron doesn't answer. Huck steals a glance at him, his square sun-darkened jaw, a day's worth unshaven. He is tall, good looking in a straight-up sort of way, like he hit life and it all just went forward from there. He's got his sight focused on something, near one o'clock off the bow, something he's seen, his keen eyes, Huck looks, and sees it then himself—a flash, tiny, off the glare.

"Go on," Carl says quietly, "you make the shout."

"Fish!" Huck yells. "One thirty." And Carl takes the upper wheel rigged in the crow's nest, swings the boat around, and they steer onto the thing, Huck keeps his eye trained on the fin, Carl calling down to

Swig in the wheelhouse below until they are near enough that Swig has it in sight himself.

"See you then, Huck," Carl says, setting his boot on the lower cable. He grabs hold of the upper one, slides down between them into the pulpit, and grabs the harpoon. From up in the mast Huck can see the fish floating, the widening dark mass of it below, and there's a moment as they are steering onto it when the shape suddenly changes, seems to rise, fin, tail, the whole of that fish in mirage pried out of the water, levered up by the sun's glare, like it's floating there, suspended. Carl draws the harpoon back, throws it, his left hand in a loose grip guiding the pole, the iron drives through the surface, the lily sinking into the back of the dorsal, just alongside, and that fish, good and struck, sounds. The line runs fast, paying out of the tub as she goes, Swig cuts off the engine, swings the boat to starboard. When the line has run out to the end, Carl Dyer heaves the keg overboard.

Not much doing then, but to wait for that fish to tire out and die. They keep an eye peeled for another, but there isn't one and an hour later, they search out their keg, haul in the line, rope a noose around the tail, hoist that swordfish up. One huge staring eye.

"Get back, Huck," Carl says. He takes a knife to the gills, severs them. Gallons of blood rush into the water.

Almost evening when they come back into the harbor, dead low tide, they keep in the channel. As they round the Lion's Tongue, the Point comes into view, cedar shake houses huddled together, the jut of the piers, a few boats already in, off-loading, fish being gutted, weighed. A crowd has gathered on the wharf, summer kids, white T-shirts darting, one girl with a sword dodges a boy on his bike, women laughing, gathered by the scales, waiting for a cut of fish to bring home for supper. Old-timers, milling more slowly, a few just sitting on the bench out front of the Wharf House, doing nothing and not wanting to but watch a day slip by.

As they pass Crack Rock, Huck sees her. Jane Weld. Isn't that her? Standing on the town pier, alone and facing away, toward the old bridge and the brash lit shine of cars passing over the new. She is there, and it is just her, near the end of the pier, the perfect perpetual stillness of her, waiting on him like every dream he has ever had, the dusk gloss of the evening sliding over her bare arms, the curve of her neck, where her hair has blown to one side.

Turn, Huck thinks as they approach. *Turn*. He thinks it hard, the thought a burn, a magic. *Turn*, and then as if she hears him, so she does, she turns and her eyes touch his, that strange glimmering distance of her sweeping through him. The throng of the crowd around her moves, breaks up again. Gulls wheel, circling the boat, they shriek, wild for the smell of that dead fish strung up. She lifts her hand, shielding her face from the light, her shoulders thrown back, a certain strength in how she stands, something bold and unexpected he had not glimpsed in her before, and everything around feels overcolored, bright cheap waste, everything but her, and she is there, and it is only her, the still point of stillness, lifted apart from every other moving thing.

How will he tell this to her? How can he love her and not tell her? But how to explain? It was just meant to scare him, send a bullet past his ear, scare the daylight out of that son-of-a-bitch—the gun a .22 they kept down at the hurricane house, took turns with it shooting rabbits, squirrels, tin cans. Huck had been griping on to Pard one night, griping on about Luce Weld—how his parents were fighting nonstop, all the grief that bastard caused. "We'll fix it," said Pard. Just like that, so matter-of-fact. He made it sound easy—such a simple plan: track Weld down in the woods where he hunted, Huck would distract him while Pard took aim, pushed a bullet past his ear. They'd send that bastard packing. It wasn't meant to unfold as it did and wouldn't have. Except that Weld turned, took a sudden strange step, almost lurching into the path of the bullet intended to stream past his face.

It was any other freakish stupid thing. Like throwing stones at a car passing by. All you see is the moving target, metal and glass. It never strikes you there might be something more to lose inside.

When he fell, they ran. He could have been dead, but maybe not, they didn't stick around long enough to find out. The fall woods spun, and they ran through those trees spinning upside down. They kept close together, and once when Huck tripped, Pard reached back and grabbed his hand, pulling him up, and they kept running like that, a pair of dumb fools clutching hands. It was Swig they went to. He was the only one they could have gone to then, and when they told him he asked, "Was he moving?" and Pard looked at Huck, and neither of them really knew. It was Pard who Swig took back with him to the gravel pit. And when the boys met up together later down at the hurricane house, and Pard said nothing about it, Huck knew, but didn't really know, didn't really have to know, sure as shit didn't want to, until that skull rolled out of the fill.

He will confess it some night in her sleep. Jane, he whispers. He can never tell her. Jane.

The boat slips against the dock. Swig throws the engine into neutral. And she has turned, just barely, her eyes following them, her eyes wash over the deck, over him, a softening, her mouth touched by a smile, looking at him, but at the same time, through him, past him. No, no. There is nothing past him. Empty river, empty sky, the sun a worn-out shrivel, nothing past him. No one. Only Carl. No.

Then he knows. In one shrinking moment, without turning around, he knows.

A candle guttered, his dream of her, sun-shivered-road-driving sunshine, snuffed. His heart is paper, in the sudden wrench of falling toward a future he has no place in, her beautiful face looking past him, looking into that future, the man behind him, her beautiful face, not meant for him. Ever. Without turning around, he knows.

BOY

JANE, SEVENTEEN
Summer 1962

She did not notice the Varick boy until he stepped off
the boat onto the pier, sprang quick over the gunwale,
practically leaping into her line of sight, forcing her
eye to follow. He strikes toward the road, but his way
there is suddenly blocked by a wave of summer kids
swarming over the pier toward the boat just touching
in. She sees him stop, caged, the slowly gelling crowd
from every direction tightening in, and his uncle Swig
in the wheelhouse is yelling after him to get the hell
back, and the boy not hearing, or not minding, only
looking fast around, bewildered, like looking for a
way out, but every way is blocked except by going
back, going past her, there's a narrow channel open
there, but for some reason he has not looked that way,
has not seemed to notice; then his eyes catch hers for
an instant, and she is taken aback, how astonishingly
pale they are, the color so fierce, almost unnatural, unreal, and something in his face raw and undone.

He has realized the only way off the pier is past her.

He does not want this—she can see it in his face as he starts toward her—a set in his jaw hardening, almost cruel, and she shrinks, that old fear in her startled up, his elbow like a whisper, fatal, brushing hers as he strikes past. Then he's gone. She does not turn. She does not look toward the fold in the crowd where he melts in.

"Forget it, Swig," someone says. Carl Dyer. His voice is starboard side now, the side nearest to her. He is tying off a line, looping its end around the cleat, pulling it back through to make the knot fast. He glances at her and smiles.

"How are you, Jane?" he says.

"Fine thanks," she manages. "You?"

"Still at it."

She laughs.

"That cat's not, though," he says.

"Yes, so I heard."

He smiles at her once more, then turns back to the work at hand.

Two days later she hears Nate Wilkes tell her grandfather Gid about how Silas Varick, loaded to the gills, tried to get rid of a skunk that had been hanging around the farm, went and doused the thing in gasoline and set it afire, skunk ran straight into the henhouse, and the henhouse went up in flames, all the chickens in it, burnt flush to the ground.

"Would've been too easy to take a gun and shoot it," Nate Wilkes remarks. "He's a real beat-er-up. Not wrapped tight."

Gid shrugs. "She drives him to it."

It is overhearing the story that reminds Jane of the Varick boy, that evening on the pier, the son of the woman, Ada.

> *And I saw in the turning so clearly a child's*
> *Forgotten mornings—*
> > *Through the parables*
> > *Of sun light*

The lines stick with her, fractured, words like glue to the boy's face. Strangely familiar. That boy with his pale eyes full of nothing. And she wonders. She mulls it over, the story of the skunk and the henhouse burned, that Varick boy and his mother. They are splinters of a thought rattling around in her, vaguely, as she picks through the tomatoes in the garden, lobbing the rotten ones over the stone wall, as she braids the garlic, as she adjusts the piece of looking glass set in the rows of corn to spook the crows.

Boy with his eyes full of nothing; under that nothing, a world.

She sees him once more that summer, the following Saturday, down at the wharf with a friend, bodies rising from the white dazzle of the river laid out behind them in the late afternoon. They are walking up the road from the Point as she heads down. On spotting her, the Varick boy stops, again that look, not quite as hard though. He stares a moment, then mumbles something to the other boy with him, ducks away.

And again she wonders, glancing toward the line of shed he disappeared around. She wonders if what she had seen in his face that evening on the pier, the half-lit contours of a truth, was not, in fact, what she had seen. It sticks with her, though. For a day or two, she wonders, then does not, anymore.

Birds flock away. The town empties. The air has begun to awaken, to find its way back to itself, the marsh on the turn; the light has shifted, toward that long sharper ache that comes in fall.

It is the end of September, still warm in the Indian summer, when the Andrews woman who owns the boardinghouse calls Jane and explains that she still has guests who were planning to leave at the end of the weekend, but she herself has to drive up to New Hampshire; her sister living there has had a stroke, is on the downhill. And would it be too much trouble for Jane to come around the next three mornings to set out the breakfast things, and then at the end of the weekend, when those guests have left, to pick up a bit, get the place back into some order? And Jane had said yes, of course, it would be no trouble at all.

Late in the day Sunday, she was just finishing up, cleaning the last traces of them from the rooms. They had gone, all of them, gone back to where it was they went back to, all that is, except that engineer, him staying on, still, she wondered how long he would stay. Soon enough, she expects, he'd be off, moving on, another job, another new piece of highway, another town. She stripped the rest of the beds, emptied the wastepaper baskets; found a woman's scarf under a bureau, silk, teal-colored, a jagged streak of black run through—she put it around her neck and looked at herself, there, in the mirror. There was a perfume on it, faint, vanilla or some other crushed scent she could not name, and the girl in the mirror looking back at her was pretty, her eyes with an unfamiliar wayward to them, her hair straight. She took the scarf off and was herself again, folded the scarf into the pocket of her skirt, and went back to piling up the sheets and pillowslips and towels in the hall at the top of the back stairs, when she heard the knock at the front door.

It was coming up on evening, the sky a soft blue dust through the window, just lasting, as she went downstairs. The house was empty except for her, coming down the hall past the front table with the metal letter basket and the vase. The knock came again, sharper now, like someone annoyed. "Will you hold on a minute," she murmured, cross that whoever it was couldn't just wait, then she opened the door, and it was Carl Dyer standing there on the porch steps, behind him the sky on tender fire in the pale floating rush of the sun going down, his cap set back on his head like he wore it, his hands shoved into his trouser pockets, turning away like he had finally decided no one was going to answer, then he saw her, and went real still.

"How are you, Jane?" he said, that dark his voice got, like always, that she was never quite prepared for, that dark when he said her name, like he had said it a thousand times, already, her name.

And he was just standing there, the free and thoughtless beauty of him on the porch, his eyes with that raw light she recognized, moving over her that certain way. He smelled of wind, of work, he smelled of the sea, his shirt collar tugged open, she could see the hollow of his throat, the lighter sheen of sweat along the bone.

"So you want to come on then?" he said.

"Come where?"

"With me."

He said it just like that, and that was all, like she would know just what he meant, his voice with that dark way in it she loved. And she did know. And she went.

WELL

LUCE
October 1957

He woke in a sweat. Dead man dreams. The room felt
pinched, suddenly close. He lay back down—it was an
old bed, springs creaked—he flicked the lamp on and
just lay there, watching tree-branch shapes scuff
and jab through the shut window. Silent. Lamplight
thrown, rings within rings on the skin of the wall.

* * *

Scratch of dawn, and he's thinking of her. Ada. Don't
it figure. Can't think about her. Can't not.

He gets up and shaves, the straight razor working
slowly over his jaw, the face emerging from the lather
and scruff, unfamiliar somehow. Once, the blade slips,
blood wells in a lean fine line below his ear. With a
towel, he blots it.

The wind has freshened overnight, a cold front come through. A gust catches in the door, rattling. He glances up. Nothing, no one, there.

As he fixes his coffee, it strikes him that tomorrow when he meets Ada down at the cranberry barn, assuming she shows, she'll be asking for that book, the one wrapped in library plastic she left behind last week in his car. And he'll have to tell her he doesn't have it—conjure some lie or just tell her he gave it to Jane when she kicked it over on the floor of the passenger seat. Won't Ada light into him for that, giving away a borrowed thing that wasn't his to give.

He knew her. She'd be all over him for that small thing. It'd been touch and go between them for weeks, it seemed. She'd look for anything to scrap over, anything to wash her hands of him once and for all.

Silas had threatened her, she'd told him last week when they met. Got wind of something.

She has bobbed her hair. All one length now, a sweep to her shoulders, the color of lampblack. Her body has grown pale, tan lines gone. Last week when they were together, he'd noticed it. How the sun had fallen from her.

They had met down at the cranberry barn as always, but she was restless, cranked up, said she wanted to take a drive, and so they drove, took the Buick down through T'aintville, down those windy roads through Little Compton, out to Scunnet Point. He'd screwed her there, they were all smashed together in the backseat of the car, he got behind her, got her up on her knees, her back arched down, he gripped her hips and she pushed back against him. In the faint light shedding through the rear window, he could see the bones of her spine.

It was on the drive back that they fought. Those twisting roads. He had tried to explain to her, tried to put it into words, that apart from Jane, how he felt about her, Ada, might just be the one stake in the world he had that was good and honest and pure.

She was smoking, her feet up on the dash, bluish clouds on the exhale.

"Nothing honest and pure about what you're doing with me," she answered, then laughed. It was the laugh that incensed him. The penetrating scorn. She could do that. In an instant, diminish, spurn any effort he tried to make.

"How does it come to this?" he said bitterly. "That it's my locked sealed fucking fate and destiny to be tormented by a snapper like you?"

Her head spun around. "What did you call me?"

"You snap at me, snap it on, snap it off."

The anger melted from her face, a new expression, curious, amused. "That's more out of you at once than I've ever gotten."

But he was past it by then and retorted back, called her another name, not quite so catchy. That did it. She whipsawed, got ferocious. They fought for the rest of the ride back into town, her raging at him.

He was all done by the time they hit the bottom of Handy Hill. All done, he told her, and she quit then, just got cool. He stopped the car and let her out. But as he drove away, it flowed over him, regret, the pullback. This was what she could do. What he felt on her account: desire, lust maybe, but more than that, a sort of dizzying faith he once thought might be enough to save him.

He turned around, picked her up, and without a word drove her to her car. Before she slipped out, she leaned across the seat to kiss him, hard, she caught his lower lip between her teeth and bit down. He felt the sharp warm rush of her breath into his mouth. Then she let go. Neither of them, of course, giving a thought to that book she'd left behind on the floor of the passenger seat.

On the table near him is an old Bakelite radio. He never used it anymore. Wasn't even sure it still worked.

He hits out a cigarette. Lights it. He should get that book back for her. Go to Jane and explain he needed it back. Jane would understand. It was never his to give.

Damn you, Ada.

* * *

And so he goes, that morning early, into the awakening sky. As he is driving down Main Road, a hawk flies out from the trees on the left, flies low across the road in front of his car. He goes to hit the brakes to swerve, but his foot, of its own will, pauses. The car coasts, the body of the bird close enough for him to see its chest, the spread of wings, feathers through the windshield. It swipes past him, just missing the glass. He glances in the rearview. No sign of it.

He parks down the road at the Methodist church—no reason to make a stir—and when he reaches the house, he slips around back, goes in through the old horse barn, and waits just inside the barn door, watching, until he sees Emily leave.

It's Wednesday. Still half an hour before the bus will come around to bring Jane to school. He is about to go up to the kitchen screen and knock when his daughter steps out. In one hand, she carries that book, in the other an empty pail. She sets the book on the porch rail and crosses the yard to the well.

He goes to step toward her, but stops. Something in him stopped.

The barn is cold. The shadows stiff. He stands at the edge of them, a cobweb spun across the door, light nicking his boots.

She cannot see him. He knows this. Even if she were to look toward the door to the barn, the light would strike her eyes, blinding, she would not see him. The yard is filled with brightness, the wind blowing through the trees; leaves torn from the branches, dazzling, catch the light as they drive down. He breathes quietly in the chill dark hush while out there, in the yard, it is all movement and warmth, sunlight glinting off the seams between the well stones, the marl, the roofs on the laneway below, wind working with the sunlight through his daughter's hair. She has pushed her sleeves up to the elbow, her hand on the pump handle, the smooth even motion of her arm, water rushing into the pail.

And as he watches her, as his eyes move over that familiar and perfect geography of her, he has the sense that he is seeing her more clearly. Nothing mistaken. No detail overlooked. He has never been so aware of what's to come, has never felt it so keenly like it is a future already transpired. Years later, he thinks, he will circle back to this moment. His daughter already grafted into an older form, but engraved in his mind at this moment now, and that certain aspect of her, that curious expression in her eyes he knows is there although he cannot see it for how her head is turned, even so he knows, that look in her face, in her eyes—and the leaves falling everywhere. The light is ravishing, underfoot.

As a child, when she slept, her hands would reach out, float through space, touch nothing, her fingers moving like she was knitting the dark to the dark.

He would watch her do this, he remembers. In that nip of time when he was a tenant in her life. So commonplace, so mundane. A child sleeping.

The pail is filled. She carries it back across the yard and disappears inside. The screen door springs shut behind her.

She has left the book out on the porch rail. The glint of the library plastic.

Forget that book. Let her keep it. Let Ada fret and bitch—light into him—fine—she'd come to, get over it, eventually. Or not. And if she flung him off for good on that account, well, so be it. It's just a book.

* * *

Late that afternoon, he parks at his mother's house on Pine Hill Road. He takes a shotgun, a box of shells, a fishing pole, takes the skiff across the river to the creek just below the gravel pit on the Drift Road side.

Bony light. True autumn. A thin coat of dusk. Sunlight, cold and unclaimed, leaking through the trees. Shadows skittish, thrown down on the dry leaf-litter. Goldenrod. Aster. Red scorch of the swamp maples, the banks of the river in flames.

He takes the loop he always takes to hunt—from that spot where the creek dumps into the river, up through the woods, to the edge of the cornfield. He'll walk alongside it, then cut back down. He rarely goes out looking for anything particular. Rabbit. Pheasant. Squirrel. He'll take what comes his way.

As he walks, he thinks, as he often does, of Ada. He thinks of how when he lies down with her, it's like lying against the ribs of the earth. Both sense and senseless. Beautiful and treacherous. Honest and there. He thinks of her, his hands on the shotgun, tight. He smiles to himself. It won't last forever. He knows this. She'll get bored, leave him. Eventually. She's no stick-around.

Sometimes when he is with her, her legs wrapped around him, he feels his life burn away, the strange terrible wealth of it, burning.

A twitch in the brush. He stops. Listens. The sound again. A light rustle. He looks through the trees, toward the blurred gold edge of a clearing. A slash of movement. Deer.

He slips between the trees, noiseless, until he is in range. Their bodies sleek and brown, three doe together, nibbling brush. He marks the one he wants, raises the gun to his shoulder; the gun stock smooth, wood like flesh against his cheek. He can feel sweat cooling on his skin.

·

He hears a click. The sound from behind him. He freezes, then whirls with the gun, his eye catches on the boy, her boy, the one called Huck. He has stepped out from the trees to his right, his eyes are extremely pale, familiar, an odd mix of clarity and fear in his young face. But his hands are empty, the palms turned open, like an offering. Luce lowers his gun and there's a moment where time drops, the distance between them collapsed, and the world feels suddenly skewed, turned a beat too fast, too close, bewildered. He cannot take his eyes off the boy's face, her boy and—dawning on him, then he sees it—his.

He stares, transfixed, as the moment shreds. He does not notice the other boy. He would have recognized him. He would have seen the spark of resolve in Pard Islington's face, taking aim to the air near his head.

He takes a step toward his son.

A shattering flash. Heat.

It is a strangely failed step, almost a lurch, as the ground seems to rise, seems to flow up against him, the distance between them not meant to be crossed. Huck doesn't move, he stands still, only one hand, fingers open, reaching slightly toward the man falling toward him.

The deer are gone, fled deep to the woods, their hind legs tossing dry leaf to the shadows.

FIRE

JANE
July 23, 2004

Down to the wire. The score close. I am ahead still,
but only just—

No letters left to draw. The box-lid empty. I have
set the bottle of ginger beer inside it to keep the wind
from carrying it off.

Ada is waiting on me to take my turn. Her eyes
rest, their green-brown stillness, just resting on my
face, light strung through her hair—that sparkling—
like tiny diamond bits, crushed glass, salt, a crystal
sprinkled there.

"Go on, Jane," she prods. Gently.

It can all turn at the end. You don't expect it will,
though. No. You never do.

We approach the end of a game differently, Ada and I.
We always have. Come to it each in our own style.
Whereas I am saving with my letters, doling them out,

one, two at a time, maxing out the value of each, Ada will try to drop all she's got in one shot, go out early, and win that way.

My eyes search the board.

I slip Q-U in against an open A. Q-U-A. In the character of.

Ada nods. "Didn't want to be caught holding that one, did you?" She smiles. I tally twelve as she drops a G on a double word square by an O, then spells G-L-E-N in the abrupt wedge of space running down.

She gets twenty for that, creeping up, a step closer. I set an O onto V-E-T, L-O across, for eleven. At the bottom of the board, she makes E-Y-E, for twelve. Only four points between us now. She has left the bag of chocolate-covered nuts halfway across the table, still in the shade, dark smudged on the inside of the plastic, one piece left, small-ish, near the slit.

I do it quickly, before she can stop me, I think, my hand slipping through, but she is faster. She has pulled the bag away.

"Such a little thief, Janie."

"You won't eat it."

"I might."

"No." I shake my head. "I know you."

She gives me a smile but her thoughts, I can see, have turned away.

"You know, this morning, Jane, when I was sitting with my coffee outside on the porch, everything was still, so still. It was just the sunrise. You couldn't hear the sea, couldn't hear even the slap of a wave coming over the dune. Not a breath of wind, and by that, I knew just how that sea would look, all calm out there, flat and smooth, laid out like a table." She moves a letter on her rack. "It happens sometimes, doesn't it? You find yourself in a morning like this one, some dumb-luck stunning miracle of a morning you've just stumbled into—the whole world touched—a day so lovely, a world so lovely, it don't seem meant for everyday use."

She glances down at the board, then back again at the letters in her rack. "And that's where I was," she says, "just sitting out there, having those kinds of thoughts, my own private snivel for that sunrise. And that's how he found me. He came marching outside and launched in whole-hog about that skiff. Had his list of reasons all lined up, he just started firing away—about the seams and the hole in the transom, the gunwale this and the leaking that, blah, blah, blah, and how long it takes each spring, each spring taking longer, to get the thing tight, and it never really does get good and tight. Go and buy your own boat, I say to him, do what you want with it, but no, he says, he wants that one, and what the hell's wrong with me, and so it went, on and on and on, and nothing I said this morning would put an end to it—I sure as hell wasn't going to tell him that skiff was your father's; even after all this time, I'd no idea how that would fall; still, when I think about it close, more than likely, he probably knows, how could he not really? And isn't that our secret, his and mine, a secret too close to say out loud—but this morning, he wasn't going to give me any room edge-wise, just kept up his wrassling, and by then it didn't matter none what I could have said, my sweet peace and quiet was all busted up— my beautiful rumination—smashed right to smithereens—and still he didn't quit and, finally, I threw up my hands—I was so steamed— 'How does it come to this?' I shouted at him. 'How does it always seem to come back to just you and me, stuck here together in this scrap stinking house going at it this way?'

"It caught him up short. My yelling. And he left off then. Just stood there a minute, my middle-aged trouble in his shirtsleeves, just stood there stock-still, looking at me. Then he grinned.

" 'Cause that's all there is, Ma,' he said, grinning away. 'Just you and me, Ma. Everywhere.' "

Ada shakes her head. "Damn kid." She is smiling though, trying maybe not to—"So I've been mulling it over since, I guess. Been thinking maybe I should just give in to his malarkey, give in and hand that old skiff over, such a beat-up thing, my stupid heart in that boat, I should just hand it over, let him go do with it what he will."

She smooths a word near the edge of the board, lining the tiles so they fit neat to their squares. Just so.

"I could," she says, shaking her head, a faint smile, her face soft-ened, gentled up. "I could, but then"—she steals a glance at me—"what would we have left to fight over?"

"Ada." I say.

Wait, Ada. Wait. Something else. Let me tell you. Something else about yesterday.

This is new, I say, I have not told you this.

Yesterday—it was after seven, that grit of evening, the air had begun to cool. I was in the kitchen when I heard a noise, faint-like. The cat, I thought, come to scratch at the door to be let in, and I went into the front room to see, and found Marne sitting there, on the sofa next to the end table with the orchid on it, that coin in her hand, that silver coin Ray had given her. She was looking at the photograph, the girl on the bridge. As I came into the room, she closed her hand, that coin, a flash disappearing into her fist.

"What?" she said.

"Just thought I heard something," I said. "It must have been noth-ing."

She nodded. "Must have been."

I sat down in the chair across from her, by the window. She looked away, back at the photograph, or through it to the wall, and we just sat there awhile, my daughter and I, in the silence of the front room marked only by the tick of the clock on the mantelshelf, and the dark came fast, it pulled in through the window, fell across our laps, until it cloaked us, and we were full in it, our faces in shadow from each other, and once, in that new dark, I saw a flash in her hand. The coin.

Then she spoke. "You know," she said. "Sometimes I look at that photograph, and I wonder who you were."

I didn't answer, and she was silent for a time, then she asked, "Why do you keep that orchid I gave you?"

"Why wouldn't I?"

"It's dead."

"No," I said. "Just the frost touched it."

"Maybe it would do better somewhere else."

"It likes that spot."

"How do you know?"

"They're fussy things," I said. "They get notions. Don't like to be moved."

She didn't answer.

"Some things, you know, really belong to one spot. They're meant for staying put just there."

She heard me then, I could feel it, though she did not answer.

"It will come back," I told her.

"How do you know?"

"It will."

"You can't know."

"I trust it will."

Then there was silence again, and by that silence, I could tell that she did not believe me.

Her heart was breaking. I could feel it. I could hear it in her voice. And I knew that it was Ray she was thinking of. She loved him and didn't want to. She has never wanted to let herself love anyone, to risk that broken place, to risk that losing, but still she did. She loved him, and so her heart was breaking.

I wanted to tell her, You just can't think like that. I wanted to say to her what you, Ada, would have said to me. I wanted to tell her about the gray horse, about prayer-flags, about watching the trees pass up the moon. I wanted to give her something to hold on to, something fierce, something with fire, a few words she could hold like stones, something you would have given to me, something that might be enough to offset the weight of what she felt—the fear. It was mine, that fear she was feeling. From the time she was a child, I had wrapped her in it like wet shadows.

I wanted to tell her what I had never been able to. I wanted to give her the promise that all would be right with the world. I wanted to say it in a way that she could hear it. I wanted to tell her what I see in Ray, that strength, that same blunt strength that reminds me of his mother every time. I wanted to tell her that love is only this: A tiny nothing. A slip of the tongue. A glance. A world can be built on a glance. I wanted to tell her that the hope you feel at the beginning of a game is a hope worth playing for.

"She's trying to hold on by her fingernails, isn't she, your Marne?"

I hear you say it. Ada. It is you and not you. Your voice. Isn't it? Who else would it be?

"It's going to work out between them," I say. "I can feel it. You think I'm a fool, don't you? I know you do. You think I'm loose-headed to believe that I can know."

I see you shake your head. "You can't know."

Ada. Wait. Let me tell you also this.

Last night, after supper through the screen, I saw the lightning bugs, and at first I mistook them for shooting stars. Then when I realized they were only what they were, I stepped outside and sat on the porch steps to watch as they hurled themselves down, their lights like tiny blades taken to the night, and I thought to myself, Tomorrow I will go and tell Ada this. Tomorrow. And she will say something like, Good Lord, Jane, shooting stars? Will you wake up and die right?

Last night, though, I could not leave them. Those little fire-bugs. Somehow. I could not go back inside, that flutter inside me like I was string, a wiry tremble that only the dark was vast enough to hold, and I understood then what it was you have been trying to tell me, I finally began to grasp what it was that you have always loved about the night—not the light of the stars or planets or the moon with its stubborn and holy routine, but the unthinkable reach of the millions of miles of darkness between them, and every possibility that might exist there, and I sat on the porch, in that sudden and clear understanding, feeling that night all around me writhe and crush and breathe like a sea.

I can still feel it, even here, now, at this table, in this hard polished daylight, the board laid open between us, so filled. I can still feel it, that flutter of thinking about Marne and Ray, thinking about what you would say when I told you, how you might shrug, Whatever happens, happens. But wait. I see you shake your head. Ada, wait, isn't it true that one way or another, their lives are still laid out, so young, parables of sunlight, like fields for walking into, as ours once were. Last night, I sat out on the porch and thought of this. I watched those lightning bugs dive in their fever through the night and I thought of how I had to tell you all of this.

A sudden movement, a darkness, shifts at the corner of my eye. I glance up. She isn't there. Her seat is empty. Two tiles left in her rack. Two pieces. Unplayable perhaps.

She's gone. And it occurs to me that in fact she has been gone for quite some time. I have known this, though, haven't I? Funny, how it happens—a quirk of the heart—these things you know but cannot own until, all at once, you do. When was it I saw her that final time? Winter. Yes, it was winter. I remember that day. The morning of Christmas Eve. A day of fog when I walked over the bridge—that day I saw Huck, just like I saw him this morning—out on the river working through that thick low-lying whiteness torn to threads, that old skiff with him in it floating there, a thumbnail of blackness drifting just beyond the Point of Pines. I remember, when I saw him that day, I thought to myself, I will go and I will tell Ada this—that Huck is out there, working the river when no one else is.

It snowed that afternoon. It was the first snow. And I came around the house and found you lying on the great white pillow near the woodstove, your eyes filled with the sky. Huck's house. That little hurricane house, behind the dunes you had given him when the carpetbagger left him and took everything else. You gave him that house when he had so little, when he needed, perhaps more than anything, to know that you forgave him, and when the tables turned and you fell sick, he brought you home to die. And I came by that day, last Christmas Eve, to bring you a gift. I had brought the game as well, but we did not play. I only sat with you awhile, held your hand. I looked down once at the blueness of your veins raised up like riverbranches under the pale of your skin, and you told me that the bliss we have is to go on loving what we love, knowing we will lose it, let the sunlight and the rain wash over us and wash us down. Then you fell silent, looked away, and it was winter again outside, a bowl of water on the window ledge, snow falling through it, and the echo of someone chopping wood in the yard next door.

You are gone then, Ada. So you are. And everything you've told me since—in words or by a glance—did I pull it from the air or breathe it out of what you were? That echo of you.

I stand up from the table and collect my things.

Carl is waiting for me on a bench in the hall just inside. He sits where it's cool, in the air-conditioning. As I reach the door, I pause a moment and watch him through the tinted glass. He turns a page of the newspaper, his elbows resting on his knees, then he looks up as if he feels me there and his eyes are what I know, in the late afternoon, that softer brown, flecks of raw light still in them. He smiles as I push through the door. It feels cold inside. I shiver.

"You're done then?" he says. I nod, and he closes up the newspaper, folds it under his arm, and we walk together out into the day, puddles of sun slick on the tar, the air in the parking lot kinked with heat. Halfway across, my heel catches on a stone. He is quick. He grasps my elbow, steadies me, shifts the newspaper into his opposite hand, and tucks my arm through his, and holds it there, the pressure of his hand on mine, firm but gentle, as he has always been with me, and we continue walking. White glint off the hood of a car, ours, the door handle hot to touch. I slide into the front. He closes the door behind me, the windows open, and we drive.

"Can we take the long way home?" I ask him. I know he will say yes. There is nowhere in particular we have to be. We're in no rush to get there. We drive through the village at the Head, and up the hill. We cross over the highway, and at Booth's corner, he takes the left-hand turn onto Main Road. We drive through Central Village, past Lees, the fish market, and the Grange, past Hix's Corner where the Knotty Shingle church once stood before it burnt. The road curves and dips, then begins to rise. I watch the fields pass by. It is later in the day than I had realized. At the Santos farm, the corn is on the ripening, crows fight through the fields, the hay has been cut, kicked over, spread to sun. It lies now, the blue and silver color of the sea.

As we are coming up on Dunham's Hill, I see them ahead. I see them even before the road bends by the tall spruce, and they come into view: the loose cluster of them there, lining the road past the brook, and another patch I don't remember seeing there before, they must have escaped from the rest, grown up on their own.

"Slow down," I tell him, "Carl, slow down." The breeze softens through the window, thick with the damp reek of the swamp woods and the shade, the sweet white scent of grass, and he slows the car, just then, as we pass that little clearing, near the old half-sunken wall, where the wild lilies open, for their one day, into fire.

AFTERIMAGE

MARNE

July 23, 2004

I had heard them this morning, my parents downstairs in the kitchen, their hushed voices drifting up through the hollow of the pipe chase. Early still. They did not want to wake me, my father asking where she wanted to take her walk today. "The bridge," she answered. Then silence. "Are you sure, Janie, that's what you want?" he said, like he knew already then what she would find there.

First light nudging in, as it does, touching the familiar outlines of everyday things.

I heard the car start up, the engine on idle as he waited, the door closing softly below, the tap of her shoes on the porch. Then they were gone, the house empty. Empty. I could not fall back asleep. I finished reading the book about light—no notes on those final pages—I set it, closed, on the end table, the last few words, still a glow, forsaken, at the edges of my mind.

It happened as I was brushing my teeth in the bathroom. I spit, rinsed my mouth, let cold water spray down the basin; then, glancing up, I caught my mother's face. It has happened before. I've passed a mirror quickly and glimpsed her face, there, in mine. It's startling when it happens. This time, though, more so. I reach for the faucet, twisting it closed, without lowering my eyes, the water slowing, slowing stopped.

I go downstairs into the front room and take down that photograph from the wall, the black and white of her. Printed on the back of the frame is handwriting in soft pencil—not my father's left-handed scrawl, not hers, either—someone else had written, GIRL ON THE BRIDGE, 1962. I sit on the sofa, the snapshot on my lap. The focus is blurred at the edges, an almost spherical ring, like a print made from a pinhole camera—that odd infinite depth of field a testament to the fact that light, left to its own, travels in straight lines. I have looked at this photograph a thousand times. But the eye trims, the eye compensates, skims over what it does not need to see.

I tilt the frame so the light falls off the glass, and the image of the girl is distinct. I seem to know her, this girl, so much younger than I am now—traces of the woman she will become, beautiful in some changeless, unrestrained way. The river is behind her, the horizon level. The tone of her eyes matches the sky, and her hand, the angle of her arm merges, like it is all of a piece with the bridge rail. It is her. And at the same time, not her. The pale stuff of a dream that slept in her, a place glimpsed once, seized, in that fleeting inadvertent image of her face.

By the time my father brings her home this afternoon, I will be gone. On Fridays, they are never home before five. I have to be at work by four. They will come home. She will set the game on a shelf and drop her bag on the mudroom chair. She will stand at the sink in the kitchen before she starts supper, and let the water run over her hands, like she is washing the day from her hands. Holding the frame, I tilt the photograph again, tilt it just enough so my face is visible as well—transparent—like I am staring through the ghost of my face and seeing her.

I call Ray. I call him at home, four rings and his machine picks up, I leave a message, then call his cell. Ring, click, voice mail. His voice. I leave another message—why not? what have I got to lose?—*Hi, Ray, it's Marne, I was wondering if—I was wondering, you know, if—call me back when you can, please.* I set the phone back on the cradle. In the room upstairs are Polly's birds—twenty-seven more to make an even two hundred. I like to wrap a job up, have a thing done. But I've got time.

I eat some lunch at noon. The day is one of those that calls you out into it—warm, but not too warm, enough of a breeze from the south. I take my bike, do the loop, nine miles down to the beach. It'll be another nine back around.

It's not until I am flying down the hill past the sanctuary and the Bayside, and the sea rises up and I take the blind hard curve at the Foot of the Lane, faster than I should, and that rank cool smell of the ocean muck and sand hits me so hard I nearly let go and die into it. It's not until the road straightens out again, the power lines staggering alongside, that I see him, Huck, parked at the other end of the Town Beach stretch, just this side of the rope where someone has tacked up a homemade sign that reads PRIVATE, which someone else, likely him, has spray-painted a red X right through.

There's junk in the back of his pickup—parked ass toward the road, the tailgate down—an Adirondack chair, rakes and buckets, a milk crate full of driftwood, some of it carved. He's sitting on the hood of the truck, his back to that heap of junk in the bed, Dutchess the mutt perched next to him. They are facing the sea. He is eating what would appear to be his lunch, and the sky is like an opaque bowl overturned, a globe of sea and sky tucked all-in around him. He's just sitting there, with his dog, his soda, and a sandwich, in the blue home. I slam my brakes, stop so short I almost go over the handlebars. A Jetta flies by me. I let my foot slip off the pedal, touch ground, staring down the road to where he is, knowing then of course that, without knowing, this has been my destination all along.

I don't stay still long enough for him to notice me there. There is no reason, really, for a moment between us. Yet still, biking past him, I take my time, a leisurely pace. I let my eyes turn as I go by. He is like salt wind there, at the corners of my eyes.

My cellphone rings as I am turning back onto Pine Hill Road. I hear it ring, and my heart jumps. I pull over, but it's only Yvette, who also works down at the restaurant, wondering if she could swap a shift with me, if I could take her shift this coming Tuesday. A slow night, she knows, and is sorry to ask. She could take a slow one off my hands in exchange. The sun is hot on the back of my neck. I can feel it there, burning.

Take tonight for me, I say.

You sure? It'll be busy tonight.

No, take it, I say, there's something I've got to do.

Back at home, I check the messages. No blinking light. No calls. I shower and drag a load of clean laundry upstairs. As I am turning a pair of jeans right-side in, my eyes fall on the library book left on the night table. I pick it up, and flip through until I find a passage I came across early on. My mother had marked it off at one point in her life, written lines in the margin, silvery pencil—

And I saw in the turning so clearly a child's
Forgotten mornings when he walked with his mother

Through the parables
Of sun light

> *Who is he then—that boy—I glimpsed you there,*
> *in his eyes full of nothing,*

I feel a shudder move through me—like I have found her—touched that changeless intangible essence that is her. I wish I could know what this book was to her, I wish I could ask, why she wrote what she wrote, what she was seeing, feeling, what she hid, grieved, hoped, what she knew. For a moment, I want to go back, read every scrabbled note she made into the margins of this book, like all those fragments will come together, reveal a story, make sense. Like loose ends aren't what we live on—*I glimpsed you there*—like there is a sense to be made.

In the kitchen, I use an ordinary knife and take a square from the page. I cut it in such a way that I keep the passage she marked out and her margin note as well. I spread it flat on the table. Her pencil markings have grown lighter with the years, less distinct, but still I regret what I've done—this cutting, my handiwork—

I begin to fold the paper square, the typed words of the text, and the other words in her handwriting, appearing, disappearing, reappearing again.

I wasn't here when Ada died. It was Christmastime, last winter. I was still in California. I'd been planning to come back for the holidays, but I had work, and there was no cheap flight. It didn't seem worth it.

It was Alex who told me about Ada, when I called home one day and he picked up. She hadn't been well, he said, caught some cold, it got into her lungs, she went fast. He told me like it was just another older person gone by, some scrap of obit news he'd read. But he knew it wasn't. He told me then about our mother and the game. He was reluctant, didn't want to tell me that part, but he did. I hung up the phone and let the implications swim around through me for a day or so before I booked a ticket home.

My mother doesn't talk about her Fridays. Just gets up in the morning, drinks her coffee, packs her lunch, and off they go. She's never said outright it's Ada she goes there to meet. But I know. I remember coming on her in the unused room upstairs. I remember how tenderly she folded those small clothes, Samuel's clothes, folding, refolding, with such intention, such exquisite care. She wasn't crazy, I'm starting to see. She was a woman in love.

It's after five in the evening when my parents pull into the driveway. While my mother is in the kitchen, starting on supper, my father walks out to get the mail. I take the Scrabble game from the shelf where she has set it. I bring it into the dining room, unfold the board, set out two racks. In the box-lid, I turn all the letters facedown. I sit at the table, the folded bird I made for her from the page of the book set at her place.

Once, when I was young, a swallow got trapped in the house. My mother was with me and that little bird flying everywhere through these same downstairs rooms—striking ceiling corners, it dove toward a window, hit the glass, and dropped with a thud to the floor, stunned. It sputtered up again, wobbly. My mother came up behind it and trapped it in her hands. She carried it to the door. "You want to hold it, sweetheart," she asked, "before we let it go?" I reached for it. "Be gentle. Don't squeeze." She slipped the shaking thing into my hands and cupped her hands around mine.

It's not a thing you ever quite forget—a heart's shudder—the silky iridescence of those wings.

The phone rings. In the kitchen I hear my mother answer it. I hear her say his name. I wait. When she comes in to find me, she sees the board laid out. She looks at me, then smiles.

"Come on," I say, taking the phone from her hands. I nod to the empty chair. "Let's play."

Acknowledgments

For unwavering faith in my work, I am grateful to my editor and mentor, Kate Medina, and to my agent, Kim Witherspoon. Also to Frankie Jones, Vincent La Scala, Lindsey Schwoeri, William Callahan, and Kim Wiley. Every gratitude to Millicent Bennett.

ABOUT THE AUTHOR

Dawn Tripp graduated from Harvard and lives in Massachusetts with her husband and sons. She is the author of the novels *Moon Tide* and *The Season of Open Water*, which won the Massachusetts Book Award for Fiction.

www.dawntripp.com

ABOUT THE TYPE

The text of this book was set in Janson, a typeface designed in about 1690 by Nicholas Kis, a Hungarian living in Amsterdam, and for many years mistakenly attributed to the Dutch printer Anton Janson. In 1919 the matrices became the property of the Stempel Foundry in Frankfurt. It is an old-style book face of excellent clarity and sharpness. Janson serifs are concave and splayed; the contrast between thick and thin strokes is marked.